P9-CMT-152

# FOUL PLAY
## AT FOUR

# FOUL PLAY AT FOUR

❧

ANN PURSER

BERKLEY PRIME CRIME, NEW YORK

**THE BERKLEY PUBLISHING GROUP**
**Published by the Penguin Group**
**Penguin Group (USA) Inc.**
**375 Hudson Street, New York, New York 10014, USA**
Penguin Group (Canada), 90 Eglinton Avenue East, Suite 700, Toronto, Ontario M4P 2Y3, Canada
(a division of Pearson Penguin Canada Inc.)
Penguin Books Ltd., 80 Strand, London WC2R 0RL, England
Penguin Group Ireland, 25 St. Stephen's Green, Dublin 2, Ireland
(a division of Penguin Books Ltd.)
Penguin Group (Australia), 250 Camberwell Road, Camberwell, Victoria 3124, Australia
(a division of Pearson Australia Group Pty. Ltd.)
Penguin Books India Pvt. Ltd., 11 Community Center, Panchsheel Park, New Delhi—110 017, India
Penguin Group (NZ), 67 Apollo Drive, Rosedale, Auckland 0632, New Zealand
(a division of Pearson New Zealand Ltd.)
Penguin Books (South Africa) (Pty.) Ltd., 24 Sturdee Avenue, Rosebank, Johannesburg 2196,
South Africa

Penguin Books Ltd., Registered Offices: 80 Strand, London WC2R 0RL, England

This book is an original publication of The Berkley Publishing Group.

FIRST EDITION: December 2011

Library of Congress Cataloging-in-Publication Data

Purser, Ann.
  Foul play at four / Ann Purser. — 1st ed.
    p. cm.
  ISBN 978-0-425-24359-6 (hardcover)
  1. Meade, Lois (Fictitious character)—Fiction. 2. Cleaning personnel—Fiction. 3. Theft—Fiction. 4. Burglary investigation—Fiction. 5. Gentry—England—Fiction. 6. Country life—England—Fiction. 7. England—Fiction. I. Title.
  PR6066.U758F68 2011
  823'.914—dc22                                       2011029413

PRINTED IN THE UNITED STATES OF AMERICA

10  9  8  7  6  5  4  3  2  1

# ACKNOWLEDGMENTS

Thanks for invaluable help from Bruce Tolmie-Thomson and Will Kerton, both of Knight Frank, global property agents and consultants.

And to Edwina, justice of the peace and good friend.

# Foul Play
## at Four

# ONE

಄

"FOR HEAVEN'S SAKE, MOTHER, SLOW DOWN!"
Lois Meade and her daughter, Josie, were returning home in New Brooms' van, Lois cheerfully breaking the speed limit and accompanying a Beatles track at the top of her voice. As they sped round familiar corners, almost on two wheels, Josie stood hard on an imaginary brake and made a mammoth effort to quiet her urge to open the door and jump. If you can't beat 'em, join 'em, Dad would say. "'We all live in a yellow submarine!'" she bellowed, only a fraction out of tune.

"Hey, shut up a minute, Josie!" Lois said suddenly, leaning forward and braking sharply. "Look! Isn't that Mrs. T-J's car? Looks like she's gone off the road. Come on, let's take a look. Quickly!"

They hurried over to the big car, and saw that it had come to rest at an angle, its front wheels in the ditch.

"Oh no, she's still in it! Look, Mum, she's slumped over the wheel."

Lois already had her mobile in hand and dialled for an ambulance and the police. When she had finished, she said that they should probably try to open the driver's-side door and see what there was to be done. To their relief, the door opened easily, and as they leaned in, Mrs. Tollervey-Jones stirred and groaned. Then she pulled herself away from the steering wheel and looked around in a daze.

"Mrs. Meade! What on earth have you done? Why am I in the ditch? For goodness' sake, woman, help me out."

Not much wrong with her, then, thought Lois, and between them, she and Josie helped the heavy old woman out of her car.

"Take it easy, now. You may have damaged something. Stop moving the minute you feel any pain," said Josie anxiously.

In no time at all, an ambulance arrived, accompanied by a wailing police car driven by Sergeant Matthew Vickers, who not entirely coincidentally was the fiancé of Josie Meade and nephew of the legendary Detective Chief Inspector Hunter Cowgill.

"Matthew! Thank goodness it's you," Josie said, whilst Lois greeted the paramedics and led them to where Mrs. Tollervey-Jones was perching on the edge of the sloping car seat, frowning and protesting that all this was totally unnecessary, and that all she needed was Thornbull's tractor to pull her car out of the ditch.

The paramedics answered her soothingly and said that she should come with them to the hospital, just as a precaution. "We need to check you over, madam," the fresh-faced youngster said.

"Absolute nonsense," she replied. "I have no time to waste this . . ." Her voice faded away, and the two paramedics caught her expertly as she keeled over in a faint.

\*     \*     \*

FARNDEN HALL WAS A PLEASANT MANSION IN THE HEART OF England, and had been the home of the Tollervey-Joneses for many years. In earlier days, the nearby village of Long Farnden had served the hall and farmland, supplying maidservants, agricultural workers, gardeners, grooms and horsemen, and drivers for carriages and then cars. Money had been plentiful, and the family had taken their life of rural ease for granted.

Along with this, they had had a sense of responsibility for their village and its residents. The Tollervey-Joneses had been patriarchal, looking after the health and welfare of villagers, repairing their cottages, sorting out their problems. Sometimes the solutions were harsh, but on the whole they were considered fair and kindly.

Now it was very different. Investments had dwindled, and the costs of running the estate—even with cuts and reductions—were high. Mrs. Tollervey-Jones lived alone in the echoing mansion, with one part-time gardener, one old mare in the stable, and twice a week the services of New Brooms cleaning team, the successful business run by Lois Meade.

This morning the old lady had received her council tax bill, and her mind had been fixed on the impossibility of paying it when she swerved to avoid a large, loping hare and ran into the ditch. "Didn't want to kill the animal," she said weakly now, her memory returning.

The paramedics nodded consolingly and said that as soon as she had been checked, they would take her home again. Unless there was someone who would come to pick her up from the hospital?

"Like who?" she said crossly, her voice growing stronger. "My son lives in London, and has a family to look after, and an important position to maintain." And important though it may be, she reminded herself, in these difficult times he could not afford to prejudice his job by taking time off to visit his old mother. Or so he said.

"Someone in the village, perhaps? That nice lady with the van seemed very helpful."

"Mrs. Meade? Never a minute to spare, that one." She closed her eyes and sighed, realising just how alone and friendless she felt. Then she opened them again, and said, "But her husband, Derek Meade, might help. Very nice man. On my parish council. Always willing to help. Telephone him."

"We'll see to that later, Mrs. Tollervey-Jones. Now, here we are. Don't move until we say so."

Derek was working in Waltonby, a village four or five miles from Farnden, when he received a call on his mobile. He knew the voice at once, even though it was more mellow than usual, no doubt because its owner was asking a favour.

"Yes, I could manage that, Mrs. Tollervey-Jones," he said. "Just sit quietly in the reception area. I have to make this job safe to leave, and then I'll be with you. Sorry you've had an accident. Don't worry, I'll be there."

Derek was an electrician, and he and his wife, Lois, together with her mother, Mrs. Weedon, known to most village people as Gran, lived in a substantial Victorian house in the main street. Derek and a few friends from the pub had won the lottery jackpot, and he and Lois had been able to install their daughter, Josie, in the village shop when it came up for sale. She had now become a highly respected and experienced shopkeeper, and the village was waiting curiously to see what would happen when she married her policeman.

Lois had been a cleaner working on her own, but her independent and ambitious nature had led her to set up the New Brooms cleaning team of loyal cleaners, including one, Andrew, who also took on interior décor projects. All this worked harmoniously, with Gran more or less running the household, and Lois and Derek financing it.

But not all was harmony, unhappily for Derek. His still desirable and lively Lois had for some years been enjoying assignments which involved working with one Detective Chief Inspector Hunter Cowgill of Tresham CID. Ferretin', Derek called it. He disapproved strongly, especially as, being no fool, he had come to see that Cowgill was unprofessionally fond of Lois. This affection was not reciprocated, so far as Derek could tell, but it was an irritant, like the grit in the oyster, which he felt could at any time turn into a black pearl.

Sometimes Derek wondered if he would feel happier about this ferretin' if Lois was willing to put the whole thing on a professional footing and receive a financial reward. But she refused payment, saying it was a hobby, and she took on only cases that appealed to her or involved the family.

When Derek arrived at the hospital, Mrs. T-J, as she was known far and wide, was standing on the outside steps waiting for him. He helped her into the passenger seat of his van and set off slowly through the back streets of Tresham, taking a shortcut to avoid the town centre.

"Kind of you, Derek. A lot of fuss about nothing. Can I give you something for the petrol?"

Derek shook his head. "No need. I was able to pick up some stuff I needed on my way in. Just you take care of yourself, now. Shall I ask Lois to call? You might need an extra hand for a day or two."

"I might need it," she said, "but I certainly cannot afford

it. No, don't worry. I shall be fine. And I always have the telephone if I need help." If it hasn't been cut off for nonpayment
of the bill, she thought to herself, and said no more until they
drove into the stable yard of the hall and Derek helped her
into the kitchen.

"Sure you'll be all right now?" he said, and when she said
he was to think no more about it, he left, but not without a
feeling of unease.

# Two

L OIS, DEREK AND GRAN WERE SITTING AT THE BIG TABLE IN the kitchen, with Lois's small cairn terrier curled up in front of the Rayburn, idly chatting after a substantial supper prepared by Gran.

"So did she say what was wrong with her? Did she doze off and steer off the road, or did they think it was something like a little stroke, like your father used to have, Lois?"

"I don't know, Mum. Ask Derek. He brought her home."

Derek shook his head. "You know only too well our Mrs. T-J, magistrate and chairman of the bench, is renowned for being a tough old bat in court. If they did suspect that she was past it or even driving without due care and attention, she wasn't going to tell me, was she?"

"Well, she must be a good age," said Gran. "Must be nearly seventy. They have to retire from being a magistrate at seventy. She never stops. Parish council, magistrates court, chairman of the local Conservatives . . ."

"And President of the Women's Institute," added Lois. "Which reminds me, aren't you going to WI tonight? They've got that woman who sings and dances and changes costumes as she goes. A one-woman musical show, she says on her leaflet."

"Lovely Betty," Gran said, peering at the luridly coloured flier. She looked at the clock. "Plenty of time," she said. "I'm not doing teas tonight. You coming, Lois?"

Lois was about to refuse as usual, but then thought it might be a bit of a laugh. She had had a trying day, with Dot Nimmo, the sparkiest member of her cleaning team, registering an angry complaint that one of their clients, a farmer's wife over at Waltonby, had said she hadn't washed the floor properly and made her do it again. Lois had smoothed her down with difficulty, and had promised to have a word with the client. Yes, she thought now, Lovely Betty might be just what she needed.

IT WAS A COLD, WINDY EVENING, AND GRAN AND LOIS WALKED quickly down to the village hall, well wrapped in scarves and gloves.

"Soon be Christmas," Gran said as they approached. "Only ten weeks to go."

Twenty or so women had gathered and were sitting in a semicircle in front of the President's table, where Mrs. T-J sat in earnest conversation with the secretary, Mrs. Pickering from Blackberry Gardens, mother of Floss, one of Lois's cleaners, and a good friend of Gran.

"Here she comes," whispered Lois to her mother. A tall, plump woman, with shining blonde curls and liberally applied makeup, hovered in the doorway, carrying two heavy cases and smiling hopefully. In time-honoured WI fashion, Mrs.

T-J and everyone else ignored her completely, and it was left to Lois to walk over and offer a welcome and a helping hand.

Finally the members were settled in their chairs, the business of the meeting dispensed with in record time, and Lovely Betty was introduced.

"You can have half an hour, Mrs. er . . ." said Mrs. T-J. "We like to have our tea and biscuits then. Most of us like to get home to watch television by nine o'clock."

"Right, then," said Betty, stung into a sharper tone than she'd intended. She usually performed in old folks' homes, and was used to a warmer welcome than this lot offered. She sighed. It was going to be hard work, she guessed, and rightly. The semicircle folded their hands and dared her to amuse them.

After a while, one or two members began to mumble the old songs along with Betty, as she proceeded to change her costume from soldier boy off to the war, to music hall favourite, to Dorothy from *The Wizard of Oz*, and many more.

Lois felt deeply sorry for her, and decided to do something about it. "Come on, you lot," she said. "We can do better than that. Can we have a request, Betty?"

A grateful Betty said of course, if she had the music for it on her sound system. "Right, let's have some suggestions, then," Lois said, ignoring the evil looks directed at her.

Gran helped out immediately. "My favourite was Vera Lynn's song about the White Cliffs of Dover," she said, and Betty smiled widely. "Wonderful," she agreed, and found the accompaniment at once. With a wavy brown wig and soulful expression, Betty became a very creditable Vera, and was relieved to see that most of the ladies remembered the words and were singing lustily.

At the end of the allotted half hour, Mrs. T-J looked at her watch and began a stiff little vote of thanks, and all members

clapped heartily. They were on Betty's side now, and intended
to make up for their President's chilly words.

It was not until tea had been served and Betty had been
positioned on a chair next to Gran that Lois noticed Mrs. T-J
standing by a row of coat pegs used by the daily play group,
holding on with one hand and passing the other across her
eyes, as if to clear her vision. Lois walked over to her, but not
rapidly enough. Just as if an invisible arm had scooped her
legs from under her, Mrs. T-J folded heavily onto the wooden
floor with a loud thud.

This time she did not lose consciousness, and with help
struggled to her feet looking dazed. She quickly regained her
composure and sternly forbade any of the worried women to
telephone for an ambulance.

"Well, one thing's sure," said Lois firmly. "You're not
driving yourself home. Your car will be quite safe round the
back here, and I'll run you home."

"In a van with 'New Brooms' emblazoned on the side?"
said Mrs. T-J, quite restored. "Well, I suppose I must accept
your offer, Mrs. Meade. Perhaps you will organise returning
my car to me tomorrow. I have to go into Tresham." She had
arranged to see her bank manager in the afternoon, and was
not looking forward to the meeting.

Lois gritted her teeth and said she would do her best. Then
she extracted a promise from Mrs. T-J that she would make
an appointment to see her doctor as soon as possible. "After
all, twice in one day is a warning that something might be
wrong," she said.


"I thought you were very brave, Lois," Gran said when
they got home. "She actually listened to you, though, so she

probably knows in her heart of hearts that something is not right."

"So I expect you and me will have to get her car back to her?" Derek said when they told him what had happened. "It's a pity that son of hers don't live closer. She's got nobody else to turn to, really, has she?"

Gran shook her head. "Not like you lot," she said smugly. "I'm always here, a tower of strength and reliability."

Lois and Derek looked at one another. "And we are eternally grateful," they chorused.

# THREE

❧

THE BANK MANAGER WAS NOT SMILING. HE SHOOK MRS. T-J's hand firmly, and indicated a seat. Then he explained in detail the financial position of the Farnden Hall estate, expressed his regret that he couldn't be more optimistic, but said that he was sure she would consult with her son and perhaps they could find ways of increasing revenue. Lots of estate owners diversified these days, and some of them were quite lucrative. Unfortunately, he added, the Farnden Hall position was so serious that small diversifications would not be sufficient.

He looked at the big woman sitting opposite him, and realised that she was pale and not at all her usual confident self. Too many times he had been patronised by her overbearing manner, and he found himself thinking biblically that the mighty were now somewhat fallen.

After agreeing that she would consult her son and think seriously about making the estate pay its way in the future, she prepared to leave. But the manager had not finished with her.

"Just one more thing, Mrs. Tollervey-Jones," he said. "If all else fails, and I am afraid the bank can advance no more loans, you and the family might consider selling part of the estate. You may even think of selling up completely, and retiring in comfort nearer to your family? Many people in your position are doing that kind of thing these days."

"I am not 'many people,'" Mrs. T-J retorted, and slammed out of the room without any further conversation.

By the time she reached home, her heart was fluttering, and she sat down in the warm kitchen, grateful for the reassuring ticking of the old shelf clock and her aged dog's comforting head on her knee.

JOSIE MEADE, STANDING BY HER SHOP DOOR AND WONDERING IF IT was worth ordering fresh flowers for the weekend, saw the big car go by with Mrs. T-J at the wheel. Her mother had told her about yesterday's alarms, and she watched until the car was out of sight. It was certainly going slowly, but then there was a speed limit through the village and the old girl *was* a magistrate. It would look bad if she got done for speeding! This reminded her that she must ask Dad to have a go at Mum about driving too fast.

A small truck pulled up outside the shop, and she could see two men in the cab. The driver began a mobile phone conversation, and the other got out and came towards the shop.

"Afternoon, duckie," he said, and followed Josie inside, where she took up her position behind the counter. She had never seen him before, but smiled her usual friendly welcome, and asked what she could get for him.

"Twenty Marlboro Red, please," he said, and Josie turned to take a packet off the shelf, but found the last had been sold

that morning. Must have been Gran, when she took over
whilst Josie went to the dentist. She apologised and said if he
could wait a couple of minutes, she would fetch more from
the stockroom.

When she returned, the shop was empty, and she saw the
man leaping into the truck cab, which then left at speed. "Oh
no," she groaned, cursing herself for being so careless and
naïve. How often had she been told not to leave a customer
alone in the shop? Then it struck her that he must have made
off with something. Fortunately the post office cubbyhole
was shut today, so no cash from there, then. She looked in the
counter till, and saw that there was very little left, only a few
copper coins. Sod it! She had filled up with notes and silver
first thing, and knew that there had been at least a hundred
pounds all told.

The bell over the shop door jangled, and she looked up to
see her fiancé, Sergeant Matthew Vickers, coming in with a
loving look on his face. It was not returned, and he said,
"Hey, what's up? You look as if you've seen a ghost."

She shook her head mutely, and he snapped immediately
into policeman mode. "Something to do with those characters
in the truck outside? I noticed one of 'em making a hasty exit."

So then Josie was able to tell him what happened. She was
expecting a lecture on foolish carelessness, but Matthew said
nothing until he had finished writing something rapidly in
his notebook.

"Just the number of the truck," he said. "I'm lucky. I've got
a good memory for numbers, but I need to write them down
fast, otherwise they fade. Now, how much did he take?" After
establishing that it was a largish sum, he ran out of the shop
and drove off in pursuit. The lanes leaving Farnden were narrow and twisting, so he stood a good chance of catching them.

After he had gone, Josie sat on the stool behind the counter and tried to compose herself. She needed a consoling word from somebody, and decided that when she had closed up the shop at five thirty, she would go home and fill them in before they heard from the village gossip network. In spite of living in a flat over the shop, she still thought of Mum and Dad's house as home.

THE TRUCK THIEVES WERE BROTHERS. GERALD MOWLEM DROVE, and his young brother, Clive, obediently did the business. They were in a small way, and sometimes Clive thought he would like to try his hand at something more ambitious. "Rob a bank?" Gerald had said caustically when he suggested it, and added that he should remember his name was Clive, not Clyde. And anyway, look what happened to *him* and his Bonnie.

Now they trundled through the lanes back towards Tresham, where they lived in one of the myriad of back streets, looked after by their elderly mother. She was vaguely aware that what they did to bring in the housekeeping money was best not mentioned, but with her own cleaning jobs around town, they managed to make ends meet.

She was beginning to wonder, nevertheless, what they would do when she could no longer get down on her hands and knees to clean and polish floors, and even worse, get up from her knees back into a standing position. She went cleaning to only two houses now, and in each case, the clients were widows of much her own age. One of them had casually dropped into the conversation over coffee break that she expected in a few months' time to be moving to a residential care home. The time had come, she said. And the other was due to move to live with her daughter as soon as the annexe they were building was ready for her.

"Better stop somewhere to get the bread Mum wanted," Gerald said. "Don't suppose you thought to lift a couple of loaves from Farnden?" He grinned, and thumped his brother on the shoulder affectionately.

Clive shook his head. Then they both heard it. Behind them, a police car was approaching with its wailing alarm filling the countryside around.

"Bloody hell!" said Gerald. "Where did he spring from? Didn't see him back there, did you? Anyway, play dumb. We got the stuff into the hiding place, didn't we?"

Clive nodded. "They'll not find it," he assured his brother as Matthew Vickers tapped on the window and produced his identity card.

"Play dumb!" hissed Gerald, and then lowered the window. "Good day, Officer," he said. "Can we help you?"

"I'm sure you can," Matthew said, and saw with satisfaction that another police car was approaching from the opposite direction, trapping the truck. "Get out, please. Both of you."


WHEN JOSIE HAD TOLD HER STORY TO LOIS AND DEREK, AND TO Gran, and been given hot, sweet tea—for shock, insisted Gran—she felt a little better. All were sympathetic, and only Lois said it was a shame Josie hadn't seen that story in the local paper last week, where a village post office had been robbed at gunpoint.

"Gunpoint!" said Josie. "But Matthew went after them, and he was all on his own!"

"He'd call for support. Don't you worry about him. He's well trained to take care of himself. And anyway, your bloke didn't have a gun, did he?" Derek took hold of her hand and squeezed it. "Never mind, me duck," he continued. "It'll be a lesson you won't forget in a hurry. This is quite a week, what with Mrs. T-J conking out all over the place, and then this. Let's hope next week will be more peaceful."

At this point, the telephone rang, and Lois went to answer it in her office at the front of the house. "Yes?" she said abruptly. She wanted to get back to the kitchen and Josie, who was looking distinctly pale and wan.

"Lois, my dear," said Cowgill's voice. "So sorry to hear about Josie. Matthew phoned in to let me know. I don't suppose it's any consolation, but this is not the first robbery of its kind in a small area around Tresham. Nasty one over the other side of town, where a gun was used, but the others have all been petty thefts."

Lois bridled. "It may be petty to you, Cowgill," she said sharply, "but in my Josie's shop the takings are not in thousands. A hundred pounds is a big loss to her. Get your feet on the ground, Inspector. Think small for once."

Cowgill grinned lovingly. His Lois was in good form. He said he would certainly take her advice. Ever since Josie and Matthew, his nephew, had announced their engagement, he had felt able to keep in touch with the Meades on a regular basis, and not necessarily to ask for snooping help from Lois.

"Is this a social call, or do you want something?" said Lois. "Because Josie is here, and needs some lovin' to cheer her up."

As soon as she had said it, she knew it was a mistake, and could not help a muffled laugh when Cowgill said that he knew exactly how she felt. Then his voice changed, and he said that yes, he did want something. And he knew Lois would want to help, after what had just happened.

"We reckon there are a couple of small-time villains operating around here. They're quite smart. Never too greedy, and according to witnesses, they drive a small truck with the name of a builders' business painted on the side. Trouble is, there's no contact address or number, and we've been unable so far to trace them."

"What about the two that have left my Josie in a real state?"

"Plain white truck. No details painted on. There was no trace of stolen cash. But Matthew reckons they lied through their teeth when they gave addresses, et cetera. We'll find out, of course, but I'd appreciate it if you could keep your ears open for reports of any other thefts in your area."

"Yeah, well, I suppose I must. I'll be in touch. Now I must get back to Josie. And if you ask me one more time if she's fixed a date for the wedding, I'll never speak to you again."

Cowgill heard the dialling tone and his face fell. The thought of never speaking to his Lois ever again was unthinkable! He got up from his desk and went down to the operations room to find someone to bawl out.


THE BROTHERS MOWLEM WERE TAKEN TO THE POLICE STATION for more questioning, and now they were told they were lucky. The gun-toting thief who had raided a local post office had just been brought in; otherwise they might well have been detained on suspicion of that one.

Clive kept as quiet as possible, allowing Gerald to answer the questions, but he, too, was ordered to respond, and did his best not to put his foot in it. They were told the cop who had followed them out of Farnden had seen Clive leaving the shop, and had talked to the distressed woman inside. Although the police were still searching the truck, now parked outside the police station, Clive was confident the stash was safe. But it was important to get home as quickly as possible to remove it and conceal it elsewhere.

His imagination ran riot as he sat listening to Gerald's carefully prepared answers. If the cops did find it, they would be sent to jail. Their old mother would be heartbroken, inconsolable, and would probably die before her time. They would be responsible, and the vengeful God she was always quoting would have a dire punishment waiting for them.

When they were finally released with a caution that they would hear further, and—as an aside—not to try skipping the country, Gerald strode out with Clive stumbling along behind him. "Get in, and don't say a bloody word," he said, and Clive nodded dumbly.

When they were almost home, he muttered, "What do we tell Mum?"

"Nothing, of course, you idiot," Gerald said. "She don't need to know nothing about it. Here, give me the cash and I'll deal with it."

"IS THAT YOU?" GLADYS MOWLEM SHOUTED FROM THE KITCHEN.

"Yeah, it's us," Gerald yelled back.

"Got the bread?"

Gerald did not answer, but Clive called out they had forgotten, and he would run down to the corner shop and get a loaf. "Thick or thin sliced?"

"Thin, as usual," said his mother as they appeared in the kitchen. "And none of those fancy things with cabbage seeds all over them. A nice thin-sliced white."

Clive disappeared out of the back door and took the short-cut through the passage that ran between the terraces of small houses put up during the boot-making boom in Victorian times. They were listed now, protected by regulations from being arbitrarily bashed down with bulldozers. Gladys Mowlem had said many times she'd rather have a nice modern bungalow than her pokey, damp-smelling house that had belonged to previous generations of what she referred to scathingly as slaves.

Clive emerged into the road and heaved a sigh of relief. The money was safe, and just to get away from Gerald was a blessing. Although he relied heavily on his older brother, always following his instructions and never arguing, he only really felt like himself when he could be on his own.

"Hallo, Clive! How're you doin'?" The Pakistani family who had bought the corner shop knew everyone in the warren of terraced houses. They had been there for ten years, and were completely accepted by ninety-nine percent of the local people. They reacted stoically to the one percent who tormented them from time to time for being illegal Pakis stealing British houses and jobs.

"Not s'bad," Clive lied. He still felt shaky, and was glad to lean on the counter and have a chat about football for a few minutes.

# FOUR

⁓

JOSIE UNLOCKED THE SHOP DOOR AND SHIVERED. A CHILL WIND
was blowing from the east, down the empty High Street and
past the bus stop, where a group of Tresham comprehensive
schoolchildren was waiting, the older girls looking frighten-
ingly adult, and the boys sneaking speculative looks at them.

Nothing changes, thought Josie as she carried out cellophane-
wrapped flowers for the stand outside the shop. She had kicked
over the traces in her time, but now felt almost too settled and
dull by comparison.

"Morning, Josie!" It was the vicar, smiling broadly at her.
He was a nice, innocent man, popular in the village, and he
and his wife bought all their groceries from Josie, stressing
that the only time they went into a supermarket was when
they couldn't get what they needed at the village shop. He
followed her inside and, after looking closely at her, remarked
that she looked pale. "A nice long walk across the water meadows

with your mother's little dog is what's prescribed this morning," he said.

Josie smiled. "And who will be the shopkeeper, if I do that? Are you offering?"

There was a pause, and Josie wondered if she had offended him. Then he said, "Do you know, Josie, that has given me an idea. All week I walk around the village, hoping to meet people, sometimes visiting the sick, and on Sundays I preach to a congregation of half a dozen, two of whom are usually happily dozing off. But now, if I put in a couple of hours every week behind your counter—you could show me the ropes— just think how many folk I would meet!"

Josie blenched. Oh crumbs, she thought. How do I deal with this one? I can't think of anything more likely to turn my customers away than the sight of a dog collar behind the counter! Not that he wasn't a very nice man, of course. But most of the village would react in the way they did to the occasional pairs of Jehovah's Witnesses, who knocked at their doors and were relentlessly polite, talked about God and were very difficult to get rid of. Most villagers took evasive action, made an excuse and shut the door in their faces.

JOSIE WAS RESCUED BY THE VICAR HIMSELF. "DON'T WORRY, MY dear," he said kindly. "I was only joking, though it isn't actually a bad idea. No, I have plenty to do now they've made me rural dean. Meetings, meetings. You know the kind of thing."

Josie sighed with relief. "And anyway," she said, "you'd not want to be held up at gunpoint whilst thieves raided the till, would you?"

The vicar looked alarmed. "Has this happened to you? When? Is that why you're looking pale this morning? My dear child, why didn't you stop me in my ridiculous wanderings? Just tell me what happened. Unless you'd rather not? I only came in for my chocolate, and I've plenty of time to listen."

Luckily, since Josie wanted to get on with checking stock and in general getting back to a normal day in the shop, the door opened and Floss Cullen, née Pickering, came in and the vicar left with a cheery wave.

"Hi, Josie. Got any of that Greek yoghurt? Ben is fast becoming an addict."

Floss had worked for Lois's New Brooms team for a long time now, and though her family—and sometimes her new husband, Ben—had suggested she might give up cleaning and do something more satisfying for her lively intellect, she refused, saying they had no idea how varied and stimulating the job could be.

Josie pointed out the yoghurt, and asked where Floss was working this morning. "For her up at the hall," she said. "She asks for me, because I like horses."

"Naturally," said Josie. "Why didn't I think of that?"

They laughed, and Floss said now that Mrs. T-J was not up to riding anymore, she had asked her to exercise her gentle old mare once a week. Floss quite enjoyed a slow hack around the estate, and the arrangement suited all three of them.

"I'd better take some of the cereal Mrs. T-J has, please, Josie. She's always running short, and then making a special trip just for a packet of muesli. Old age is a horrible business, isn't it? Thank goodness we're a million years away from that, huh?"


NOT ONLY HAD MRS. TOLLERVEY-JONES RUN OUT OF MUESLI, but she'd also used up the milk, and she realised she had two choices. No, three. She could ring Floss and ask her to bring some on her way up to clean this morning. Or she could drive down to the shop later on today. Or she could go without. She decided on the last, and put the subject of milk to the back of her mind.

She had hardly slept a wink, and now had difficulty concentrating on the problems confronting her. Perhaps if she took a walk in the garden, the fresh air would clear her head. A big decision had to be made, and soon. She was no fool, and knew that opening the park and providing teas in the stables was not the answer. She needed big money, and the only practical solution she could see was to sell something. That nasty little man at the bank was right, of course. It was his job, she supposed.

Not bothering with a coat, she stepped out into the stable yard and headed for the walled kitchen garden. It was the only well-maintained part of the estate, and all thanks to Jack Hickson, who, now that she could no longer employ him full-time, came along in his spare hours and refused payment.

Jack had had a troubled period in his life, but now he was reunited with his wife and family, and had settled down in Farnden. Mrs. T-J was a good enough judge of character to know that she could trust him absolutely. His wife, Paula, was one of the New Brooms team, and he had been taken on again by the County Council Parks Department to work on its municipal flowerbeds.

The kitchen garden was protected from the east wind by high brick walls, and the sun had broken through clouds to brighten the day a little. Mrs. T-J walked slowly round the grassy paths, admiring Jack's neat rows of leeks and purple sprouting, the bean poles ready for planting runner beans, and expertly pruned currant bushes lined up by the end wall, where espalier pears caught the sun in high summer. For a few minutes she was a child again, running agilely round the vegetable beds, chased by her brother bent on punishing her for being a girl.

An old wrought iron seat, slowly tipping itself into the ground at one end, could just about support her now. She sat down and tried to concentrate. The most valuable land would be a large field close to the road just outside the village. Planning permission was not a sure thing, but to raise the amount of money needed, it would have to be a sizeable development. She thought of the disadvantages for herself. There would have to be access roads, noisy building works and an inevitable disturbance of her way of life. And most important, the new estate would be in full view of the main windows of the big house. Finally, and this meant more to her than anything, she would become extremely unpopular in the village. She sighed. "I'm too old for all that," she said to her faithful hound.

She heard the gate click behind her. It was Jack Hickson, and at first he did not see her. She called to him, and he came down to stand beside her. "Morning, ma'am," he said. "I've got a few hours free, so thought I'd give meself a treat and come up here. But I'll go, if I'm in your way?"

She said of course he must stay. "No, no, Jack, I'm very pleased to see you. I'm sitting here trying to solve an insoluble problem."

"Can I help?" he said, looking more closely at her and realising she looked what his mother would have called "a bit peaky."

"Just supposing," she said, "that a new development of houses was proposed and passed the planning application, doubling the size of the village? How do you think that might be received by the parish?"

Jack smiled. "Remember that bloke who tried it? Forgotten his name, but he was going to build us a new village hall, and oh yes, as an afterthought he mentioned a few, forty or so, attractive new executive dwellings destined for the playing field. Remember him? It was turned down flat, wasn't it? And he ended up arrested for fraud and God knows what all."

"Well, it wouldn't be an outsider. It might be me." The minute the words were out, she knew she shouldn't have said them. They would be all around the village . . . Unless . . .

"Jack, can I ask you not to mention to anyone that I had even considered it? Just a flight of fancy, that is all."

"My lips are sealed, ma'am. In fact, I've forgotten what you said already. Now," he added, "you look blue with cold. Can I come up to the kitchen with you and cadge a cup of coffee off Floss? She must be there by now."

# FIVE

❧

ROBERT TOLLERVEY-JONES WALKED SMARTLY DOWN SHEP-herd Road, a long, straight street in North London. The area was rapidly gaining in popularity as one after another the dingy houses were restored and emerged in all their Georgian elegance.

Robert had had a trying day at his chambers in the City, where he worked as a successful barrister and pillar of respectability. He looked forward eagerly to turning into the neat front garden of his comfortable Edwardian house, where his wife, Felicity, would be waiting with a large gin and tonic at the ready. The girls should be up in their rooms doing homework, and with luck he could collapse into a comfortable chair and watch the television news in peace.

His mobile trembled in his pocket, and he fished it out. Blast! It was his mother calling, and he was tempted to leave her to the message answering service. He would call her back later, after he felt more relaxed and ready to face whatever she had to say. She had always been a domineering mother, and he sometimes confessed that he was still a little afraid of her.

He sighed, and answered the call. "Mother? Hello, how are you? Nice to hear from you—"

"Forget the fibs, Robert," Mrs. T-J said sharply. "I'll come to the point. We need to have a conference about the future of the estate. I shall be coming up to London next week, probably Wednesday, so can you make sure you have a free afternoon on that day? We can meet at the flat, say two o'clock? We shall be undisturbed there. Now, must go. Goodbye . . . dear," she added as an afterthought, and was gone.

The family flat was in one of the streets leading off Baker Street, and had been used by many young Tollervey-Joneses in all branches of the family over the years. It was extremely handy, being near the tube station, which had lines going in all directions. Now it was chiefly a bolt hole for Mrs. T-J, when she felt the need for a wider horizon than that afforded by rural life in a small village. The flat was tiny, but adequate, and Robert saw the sense in his mother's decision to meet there.

He kissed Felicity and accepted the glass in her hand. "Thank you, my love," he said. "Had a good day?"

Felicity began an amusing account of her day at the Citizens Advice Bureau, and after a minute or two was aware that Robert was not listening to a word. She said, "And then a lioness came into the back garden and ate up the girls, so we needn't worry about them anymore."

"Jolly good," said Robert, nodding his head wisely.

"Robert! What did I just say?"

"Um, well, about meeting Honora for coffee?"

"Oh dear," Felicity said, and sat down opposite him. "So what's wrong? Trouble at the office, or is it Farnden Mother?"

From his expression, she could see exactly what it was, and leaned back in her chair, waiting for him to tell her.

"She just caught me on the mobile. Conference needed on the future of the estate, she said. Wants me to meet her at the flat on Wednesday afternoon next week. I must say that from the sound of her voice, there are urgent decisions to be taken about the old place."

"Sell it," said Felicity simply.

"Not as easy as that," Robert said, and added that if it was up to him alone, he would suggest the same. "It's a millstone now, I'm afraid. Worth millions to some Arab, with luck, and needing millions to put it in good order. But it is still Mother's home, and I suppose should be considered as a rightful inheritance for the girls?"

"Oh, blow that," said Felicity. "Can you imagine either of them wanting to live in that dump in the Midlands? They would die of boredom. No, you'll have to persuade her to sell. She can always resettle in one of the cottages on the estate. She'll have plenty of money to do it up nicely, and then she can divide her time between country and town, and see more of us. Not too much more!" she added, and leaning over, squeezed Robert's hand.

He returned the squeeze, but reflected that if he'd had a son to inherit and perpetuate the family name, things might have been different.

Mrs. T-J put down the phone and walked into the drawing room. The evening sun was pouring in through the long windows, lighting up the lovely plasterwork ceiling and fine old oak double doors. Family portraits smiled down benignly upon her, and in glass cabinets, displays of exquisite porcelain collected by successive generations shone and twinkled in the sunlight. She supposed she could sell some of those, but however enthusiastic the valuers had been, she knew it would not be enough.

She shook herself. Now that she had talked to Robert and arranged to meet him for a practical discussion on what was to be done, she felt a little better. Not that she had any hopes of her only son working a miracle, but at least she did not feel so alone. Between them, they had to come up with a solution of some sort. Deep down in the pit of her stomach, she felt sick at having to acknowledge that selling was the only possible answer; selling the lot, or selling off building land, which would change the character of the estate and the village forever.

Her attention was taken suddenly by the appearance of a small white truck slowly approaching up the long drive to the house. Who on earth could that be? She had ordered nothing to be delivered. She watched as it swung round towards the stable yard and disappeared.

"Floss!" she called loudly, and then remembered the girl had gone hours ago. She walked quickly through to the kitchen and peered out of the window. A man was jumping out of the truck and approaching the door. She locked it quickly, and retired out of sight by the big cupboards.

His knock was slight, feeble even, and came only once. After that he returned to the truck and climbed in next to the driver. Mrs. T-J moved so that she could see them without being seen herself. They were talking animatedly, and then the driver looked at his watch, and nodded. She could see them laughing, and then the truck reversed, turned around and went back the way it had come.

Obviously they had been lost, she told herself. Came in to

ask the way to somewhere. That must have been it, she decided, and went to put on the kettle. She looked in the fridge, saw that it was empty and decided she was not hungry. She would sit down for a while and listen to the radio, then think again about supper.

In the battered old chair by the Aga, she sat down and closed her eyes. The characters in her favourite soap chattered on, but Mrs. T-J did not hear them. She was fast asleep, and dreaming of miracles.

# Six

### ✺

"So, did Mrs. T-J go to the doctor, Floss?" Lois sat in her office, trying to concentrate on New Brooms, but still worrying about her most irascible client. As Floss had been riding the old mare at the weekend as usual, Lois thought it worth checking, so had lifted the phone and was glad to find her at home.

"Not sure," Floss said. "I didn't like to ask her outright. You know what she is!"

"Of course. Anyway, I'll see you later at the meeting, and we can catch up."

The weekly team meeting was in Lois's office in the Meades' house, in a room that had, in more formal days, served as the morning room for family breakfast. At that time, the family would have had a cook and housemaid to bring kippers and eggs and bacon under covered dishes, all the way from the kitchen and through the swinging green baize door to the front of the house. The green baize door had long gone, and all the Meade meals were eaten in the large, warm kitchen.

As Gran came into the office with a coffee, grumbling about her poor old legs, all this went through Lois's mind, and she said puzzlingly to Floss, still on the phone, "By the way, I expect there's still a green baize door at the hall?"

"What's that got to do with Mrs. T-J going to the doctor?"

"Absolutely nothing. Sorry, Floss. Mind wandering. No, I just rang you about the doctor because she's not right, is she? Keeling over at WI, and driving into the ditch. Not like the Honourable Mrs. Tollervey-Jones at all."

Floss agreed, and said she would check with the old girl about the doctor. "I'll be up at the hall this morning, so I can tell you more at the meeting. We can ask Paula, too. See you later, Mrs. M."

Paula Hickson, wife of Jack, who gardened at the hall, was a fairly recent member of New Brooms' team, and also worked for Mrs. T-J, at first cleaning in tandem with Floss, and now, in addition, cooking one or two meals and leaving them in the hall freezer each week. The Hicksons needed every penny they could raise, having four young boys to clothe and feed, and at the same time trying to save enough for a mortgage to buy the roomy old house they were living in, handily placed opposite the shop.

Lois put down the phone and made a note on her pad to ask the team if they'd heard anything about a suspicious-looking white truck and sinister drivers around the area. Then she finally settled down to arrange the cleaning schedules for the next week.

At twelve noon exactly, there was a knock at Meade House's front door, and Gran was there to open it. She loved to do this and, before Lois could get there in time, had sent packing more than one stranger she considered undesirable.

"Morning, Mrs. M." It was Dot Nimmo, strutting in on her high heels. She was a tough customer, widowed by her dodgy husband's drowning accident. Did he fall or was he pushed? In spite of a life with him spent sailing close to the wind, and more than once on the wrong side of the law, she missed him, and when her only son had been killed in a road crash, she went to pieces. Now she was solidly loyal to New Brooms, and especially to Lois, who had given her a job when nobody else thought her employable.

Then Floss and Paula arrived, followed by Andrew, clutching a briefcase and swatches of fabric for the girls to look at. Sheila Stratford was next, smiling as always, and hoping for a gossip with the others after the meeting, and lastly Hazel, former cleaner and now wife of local farmer John Thornbull and manager of New Brooms' office in Tresham.

"Right, shall we start?" said Lois, smiling round the team settled in a semicircle in front of her. "First of all, any emergency matters we should deal with? Perhaps Mrs. T-J might come under that heading. Floss? Paula?"

"Go on, Paula," Floss said. "You said she'd said something about a doctor."

Paula nodded. "She was jotting down jobs she had to do, and muttered something about an appointment to see the doctor. But she didn't write it down, and if I heard right, she said it would keep until next week. She was sort of talking to herself. She's done a lot of that lately. That's all I know, Mrs. M. But I shall keep an eye on her now, after seeing her at WI. And also that accident she had last week."

"Well, we can't force her, I suppose," Lois said. "Perhaps both of you could watch out for her, and let me know if anything goes wrong. Now, Andrew, cheer us up with your décor plans for young Mrs. Norrington over at Fletching."

Andrew Young had joined New Brooms after the death of his parents, and a period of drifting about, not knowing what to do with himself. Finally he had decided to use his interest and talent in interior design, and had made a useful move in joining Lois's team, where he could infiltrate potential clients' homes. This had worked well for all of them, with Lois taking a cut on his fees, and now he was to tackle the complete refurbishment of a house in the next village. "What's more," he had told the team previously, "there seems to be a bottomless pit of cash there, so whoopee!"

He had found it very useful to have a female input on colours and fabrics, and now produced the swatches and circulated them round the team for approval. This was followed by the routine scheduling of tasks, and then Gran came in with coffee and biscuits, giving them all an opportunity to relax and bring up less important matters.

"Oh, and by the way," Lois said, "I expect you've all heard about Josie's robbery in the shop? Yes? Well, I thought you would have, Farnden being Farnden."

"Have they caught the thieves?" Sheila said. "Sam reckons it was one of them fly-by-night lot who drive round the villages looking for likely pickings. He said they'd done one in Waltonby. A car parked outside the pub was broken into. Window smashed, and a laptop taken. All done in seconds. Sam says they come off the motorway, drive round and do a job, and then back down to London like bats out of hell."

"Must have been a stupid bloke to leave a laptop on his car seat," Andrew said.

"Wasn't a bloke," said Sheila, smiling. "It was that Miss Yates from the council, come to inspect the pub kitchens."

"Oh, *her*!" they chorused, and then Hazel added that, in her opinion, Miss Yates deserved all she got.

"But seriously, team," Lois persisted. "If you do hear of anything more like that, can you let me know? Poor Josie was really knocked sideways, and she's still a bit shaky. I'll make sure those scumbags get caught, if it's the last thing I do."

"On the job again, Mrs. M?" said Dot, looking eager. She was the only one of the team who'd dare to say such a thing, and Lois began to splutter crossly, but then she stopped and burst out laughing.

"Something like that," she said. "Now, if we're all finished, time to get on with our work. Bye, everybody. Oh, and Dot, can you stay behind for a minute or two? Thanks."

After the others had gone, Dot looked nervously at Lois. "Did I do wrong?" she said.

"Don't be daft," Lois said. "No, I might well need your help on this Josie thing."

"You mean my knowing about the criminal underworld of Tresham? If that's not exaggerating," she added, chuckling.

"Exactly," replied Lois. "Ear to the ground, and all that. I'd be grateful, Dot. See what you can come up with, and give me a ring. Anytime."


ANDREW YOUNG DROVE OFF, WAVING A CHEERY GOODBYE TO HIS colleagues, and headed towards Fletching and Mrs. Norrington. She was a nice woman, and he guessed the obvious wealth was newly acquired. Maybe the lottery, he thought. Anyway, she was not too sure what she wanted, and so was an ideal client for him. The girls had unanimously liked a heavy cream brocade for the drawing room curtains, and he had now completed the plans for the entire house.

He drew up outside Fletching Grange, and jumped out of the car, striding towards the door with cheerful enthusiasm. Nobody answered at first, and then he heard slow footsteps approaching. He was shocked as the door opened and Mrs. Norrington peered out at him. Her face was blotched and grubby, her hair untidy, and she looked as if she had slept in her clothes. He could smell alcohol on her breath.

"Oh, Andrew!" she said, and burst into tears.

"What on earth—" he said, and stepped inside, closing the door behind him.

"Burglars," she said. "Bloody burglars. Taken everything. Jewellery, pictures, silver, computers, everything."

"But when?" he said. She sniffed hard, and said it had been sometime last night.

"But the alarm? Didn't that go off?"

She shook her head. "I forgot to set it. Geoffrey will kill me. Do you want a drink?"

# SEVEN

M<small>RS.</small> N<small>ORRINGTON LED THE WAY INTO HER DRAWING ROOM,</small>
which looked as if a party of drunken chimpanzees
had careered about, knocking things off tables and out of
china cabinets, pulling out drawers and scattering the contents on the floor. Even precious books had been dragged off
shelves and tossed about like confetti.

"Have the police been?" Andrew asked immediately.

"Yep. They were good. Made lists, fingerprints and all of
that."

"Is your husband at home?" Andrew was beginning to feel
inadequate. Surely some close member of the family should
be here, propping up this poor woman.

"In Hong Kong," she said flatly. "Goes there a lot, on business. I've phoned him, and he's coming home as soon as poss."

Thank God for that, thought Andrew. "So have you got
someone coming to be with you until he's home? I'm sure
Mrs. Meade could arrange something, if not." He was not at

all sure about that, and was relieved when she said her sister from Birmingham would be arriving around teatime.

"Right, well. I'm dreadfully sorry," he said, and backed away towards the door.

"Don't go, Andrew," she said, and began to cry again. "Couldn't you stay for a bit, and we could go over the décor plans. It would give me something else to think about. And don't worry about the money. Everything's insured."

Feeling very awkward, Andrew suggested he should help her clear up as much as possible, and then they could sit down and look at plans. She nodded, and waved her hands about helplessly. "Where shall we start?" she said.

An hour later, order was more or less restored. Pieces of broken china and glass were safely in the bin, and the books back in their shelves, though not, Andrew suspected, in the right order. They looked to him suspiciously like books by the yard, bound in mock leather and with some of the pages still uncut.

He was sorting out cutlery, and putting it back in place, when he felt something blocking the way at the back of the drawer. He reached in, grasped a cold, heavy piece of metal and brought it out. A gun. He stared at it in horror, and turned around to ask Mrs. Norrington about it.

"Oh, Andrew! Where did you get that?" she screamed. "Goodness, why did you bring that along?" She was retreating away from him rapidly, and stood behind the sofa, looking terrified.

He began to explain, protesting that he had only just found it in the drawer, when he heard the front door open and heavy footsteps approaching. Then a loud voice called out, "Melanie! Where are you?"

She rushed past Andrew and out into the hall, where her

husband stood waiting. He put his arms around her protectively, and glared at Andrew. "I'll get the police back," she said in a muffled voice into his coat. He ignored her, and shouted at Andrew.

"What the hell do you think you're doing? Give me that thing at once. Melanie, pull yourself together. And you," he added, advancing on Andrew, "give me the gun, and kneel down on the floor with your hands behind you."

Norrington had such an air of authority that Andrew obeyed. But his mind was working fast. "For heaven's sake, man," he said irritably. "The police have been already. My name is Andrew Young. Your wife has probably told you about me. I'm doing the interior décor on your house, and when I arrived this morning, I found your wife in a terrible state. We've cleared up a bit, but the whole place was turned upside down. All happened whilst she was asleep. Isn't that right, Mrs. Norrington?"

She hesitated, then nodded. "That's right. Andrew was very helpful."

"The gun was in the back of that drawer," Andrew continued. "I was helping clear up, and found it. Nothing to do with me. Perhaps you have some explanation?"

Norrington looked uncomfortable. "Is this true, Melanie?" he said, pushing her gently back from him, and picking up the gun from the floor.

She nodded. "He found it in the drawer. Took me by surprise. Sorry, Andrew." She turned to her husband, and said she was sure Andrew wouldn't hurt a fly. He had been so helpful. Perhaps he could go now, and the two of them could talk about all they had to do. "Including finding out what a gun was doing in our cutlery drawer," she said, and walked towards the front door. "Goodbye, Andrew, I'll be in touch. Thank you so much."

Andrew got to his feet, and tried not to hurry towards the door. He managed to exit in a dignified fashion, and drove off without looking back.

HE WENT STRAIGHT TO LONG FARNDEN AND PARKED OUTSIDE Meade House. Gran answered the door, and said Lois had gone down to the shop to see Josie. "You all right, boy?" she said, staring at his pale face.

"Fine, thanks. I'll go down to the shop, then."

He left the car parked outside, and walked swiftly down to the shop. Lois was the only person there, apart from Josie, and they were laughing at some private joke. One look at Andrew, and both stopped at once. "Blimey! What have you been up to, Andrew?" said Josie, and Lois silently indicated the high stool by the counter.

"Long story," Andrew said. "Do you think you could rustle up a coffee, Josie? We'll man the store."

"I'll go," said Lois. "Josie's a bit nervous about leaving the shop at the moment."

"She'll be even more nervous when she hears what I've got to tell," he said with a brave attempt at a grin.

MELANIE AND HER HUSBAND, GEOFF, SAT ON OPPOSITE SIDES OF the kitchen table, staring at each other. Melanie was the first to speak.

"Go on, then," she said. "Tell me where it came from, and what it was doing there."

Geoff frowned. "I meant to tell you," he said. "I bought it after we heard about those burglaries. Thought it would make you feel safe when I'm away. Then I forgot all about it. Sorry you had to find out that way."

"So it just slipped your mind, did it? Such a little thing, buying a gun and leaving it around the house? I don't believe a bloody word, Geoff. And where were you? That number you gave me was nowhere near Hong Kong. I may be a stupid blonde, as you're always saying, but I'm not that stupid. Even you couldn't get back from Hong Kong in the time it takes to get here from London! If you're lucky! You're up to your old tricks, aren't you?"

"Don't be ridiculous!" he said, and got up from the table. "Trust you to get us into a fix so soon after we've moved here! You'd better tell your boyfriend a good story as soon as possible. We don't want him going to the law and have them sniffing about."

"He's not my boyfriend, and they've already been sniffing about. It seems to have escaped your eagle eye that the house has been thoroughly done over. I suppose I was wrong to call them in, was I? A revenge visit from a disillusioned colleague, to be expected and not talked about, was that it?"

He looked at her sharply. "So you know who did it?" he said.

"No, but *you* do," she spat at him, and walked out of the house into the carefully manicured garden.

# EIGHT

"WELL, ANDREW," LOIS SAID. "THAT'S THE LAST TIME YOU or any member of my team goes to the Norringtons! My God, I could sue them for something or other, I'm sure!"

"Just wait 'til I tell Matthew!" Josie said.

They were all silent for a minute, and then Lois sighed. "I suppose," she said slowly, "if you think about it, it must have looked very suspicious to that husband. Coming in and finding his wife terrified by a strange man holding a gun. In a way, you couldn't blame him."

Josie answered at once, her voice high and angry. "Yes, you could! The man is obviously a liar anyway. If Mrs. Norrington said he was in Hong Kong, how did he get back in no time at all after she rang him? Come on, Mum! You must see that?"

"Yes, I know," Lois said. "But that could be nothing to do with his attack on Andrew. For all we know, the man was tucked up in bed with his fancy woman in Tresham. But that's not our affair—it's his!" she added, and laughed.

Andrew slid off the high stool. "You're probably right, Mrs. M," he said. "What do you think I should do? Wait until things have simmered down a bit? We might hear a bit more about it, and then make up our minds." He made a rueful face and patted his briefcase. "After all," he said, "it is a really good assignment for me, and I am a bit reluctant to lose it."

"Fine," Josie said crossly. "So the man comes stalking in, having arrived from Hong Kong on wings of song, threatens Andrew as if he was a criminal intruder, without giving him a chance to explain, and then we let him and his floozy of a wife get away with it? And I suppose I am not to mention it to Matthew?"

"He'll know about the burglary," Lois said placatingly. "It sounds like a big job, and the police will be keen to talk to everyone around. Especially you, Andrew, unfortunately. You were the first one, apart from the police, to enter the house after Mrs. Norrington found the wreckage, weren't you? O' course, if they ask questions about her husband and his speedy return, you'll have to tell the truth. Better leave it like that at the moment."

"And I suppose now you'll go home and get straight on to your friendly neighbourhood Inspector Cowgill," said Josie bitterly. "It's Matthew who goes out investigating, you know."

Lois diplomatically said nothing. This problem had cropped up several times lately. Lois had been associated with Inspector Cowgill for several years, and they had a good working relationship. On her side, she loved the whole process of piecing together snippets of information and arriving, with luck, at a successful conclusion. But she had her own strategies, and knew when to tell the police. Cowgill had no option but to respect this, and apart from wishing their relationship could be otherwise, he took pleasure in her company and made use of her talents.

Josie was her mother's daughter. She was a strong character and an ambitious supporter of her fiancé, and had begun to resent her mother's assumption that Cowgill must come first.

Andrew neatly smoothed over the awkwardness. "I shall give Mrs. Norrington a call," he said. "I'll tell her I understand her husband's reaction, and say that I intend to do no more about it *for the moment*. That should get the message over. Their private life is their concern, as you say, Mrs. M. But I'll make it clear that I should hate anything like that to happen again. Then I'll concentrate on the décor job, and refuse politely to discuss anything else. I'd be quite glad if we three could keep it to ourselves for now. How would that do?"

"Perfect," said Lois. "Good lad. Happy, Josie?" Josie shrugged, and made no comment.

"Oh, and by the way, Andrew, you could just keep your eyes and ears open whilst you're there. No harm in that," added Lois.

DOT NIMMO HAD NOT FORGOTTEN WHAT MRS. M HAD ASKED her to do. She lived in Tresham, where, many years ago, she and her sister, Evelyn, had married the Nimmo brothers within a year of each other. Dot's husband, Handy—short for Handel—had been the undisputed boss of the Tresham gang of what some referred to as the local mafia. This was true, in that their network was quite widespread and had strict rules about gang loyalty and a policy of you-scratch-my-back-and-I'll-scratch-yours, but it was more like a Masonic lodge than a ruthless killing machine.

"If one of us is in trouble, it's our duty to help him out of it," Handy explained to Dot when they were first married. She had accepted this, but could not help questioning gang loyalty when her much-loved husband was found floating facedown in a deep gravel pit up the road from the village of Long Farnden.

"*And* he were a good swimmer," she said acidly to the police when they carried out a perfunctory enquiry. To her sister she confided that, as far as the fuzz were concerned, one less Nimmo was a bonus.

Dot remained in the house where she had lived since her marriage, and rebuilt her life. By coincidence, the house was in Sebastopol Street, where Lois had set up the Tresham office of New Brooms, and Dot had passed by a dozen times before deciding to go in and offer her services. Now, after making a success of the job in her own eccentric way, she considered she knew what loyalty really meant.

After a scratch meal of an out-of-date sausage roll and an apple, she dialled her cousin's number and left a message that she wanted to talk to him. "Pronto," she added. She hadn't much respect for him and considered he was a softy, without any of the Nimmo guile or determination. But he had connections, and might well know of a couple of regular thieves operating in his area. He might even be interested in curbing their activities on his patch.

Following another line of thought, she put on her best coat and tidied up her blonde hair under a scarlet beret, and left the house. She had remembered an old friend, Gladys, the wife of one of the gang, who had been very helpful to her in the early months of her marriage. She lived not far away, and Dot found the door ajar.

"Gladys? Are you there? It's Dot. I've brought half a packet of delicious sausage rolls for y'tea. Can I come in?"

A voice from the back kitchen yelled that of course she could come in. Wasn't she in already, anyway?

Dot walked through, and found Gladys sitting at the table, checking her football pool results. "Me luck's out," she said without looking up. "The boys keep tellin' me to give it up. Put y'money on a horse, they say. Stands a better chance, especially if I take their tips! Huh, in that case, I say to them, why aren't you two rich, instead of scrapin' around to keep us afloat?"

"Still at it, are they?" Dot said sympathetically. She waited, and Gladys looked up at her suspiciously.

"Who wants to know?" she said.

Dot shrugged. "Nobody I know," she said. "Just polite conversation."

"Oh, yeah," said Gladys. "That'll be the day, when Dot Nimmo has a polite conversation!" She cackled loudly, and then stopped, cocking her head on one side. "Is that them?" she asked.

Dot heard the front door slam shut, and wished she had left a couple of minutes ago. Still, she had every right to visit an old friend.

"Well!" said Gerald to Clive as they came into the kitchen. "Look who's here! Still workin' for the snout, are ya, Dot?" he said insolently. "Time you found yerself another husband. What do you think, Clive?"

"Too right," he said obediently. "Some big bloke to protect you, Dottie Nimmo. From nasty men like us." They laughed and jeered as Dot pushed past them and made for a quick exit.

No matter, she thought to herself, as she walked away. Sticks and stones, an' all that. An' I got me answer, didn't I?

# NINE

~

ROBERT TOLLERVEY-JONES SAT AT HIS DESK IN THE CITY OF London, staring at a page of one of his latest cases, and thought about Farnden Hall. His mother had decided to come up to town and had more or less ordered him to be at their flat at two o'clock sharp today. It was Tuesday, and he was sure she had originally said Wednesday, and had arranged his diary accordingly, but no, she insisted she had said Tuesday, and anyway, it was the only day she could possibly manage. He rearranged his appointments accordingly, and now awaited his first client of the morning.

His thoughts strayed again. Farnden Hall. It had been his childhood home, and it was a happy childhood. He had run wild round the estate, ridden his pony at local gymkhanas, played cricket with the village people on the bumpy pitch at the back of the village hall and spent his pocket money in the village shop. His father had been indulgent with his son, often countermanding rules laid down by his mother, and writing subversive letters to him at his boarding school. When his father died in a hunting accident, he had been heartbroken. And then, of course, his mother had become sole dictator.

"Mr. Tollervey-Jones?" His secretary of many years had put her head round his door and for one moment thought he had dozed off. "Mrs. Fitzpatrick is here."

The morning passed smoothly after that, and after his last client had gone, Robert reached in his drawer for the packet of sandwiches prepared for him by Felicity. He would take them to the small patch of garden outside the office and sit in the sun. Then hail a taxi, he decided, to meet his mother. She had not offered to give him lunch. More a case of "see me in my study at two o'clock, Tollervey-Jones, and don't be late," he thought.

When he pressed the bell on the door phone, his mother's voice was strangely subdued. Not her usual strident self at all, he thought, and frowned. He arrived at the second floor and found her waiting with the door open and a worried look on her face.

"Come in, Robert," she said, and he noticed that she limped a little as she crossed the room to sit down. He took a chair opposite her, and asked how she was.

"You're looking a tiny bit pale, Mother," he said. He expected this to be greeted with a volley of reasons why she was, in fact, in the pink of health. But instead, she passed her hand across her eyes, and said she had not been sleeping too well lately.

"Goodness, that's not like you," he said. "Have you seen the doctor?"

"Doctor?" she said, sounding more like herself. "Why should I see a doctor? Two or three good nights' sleep is all I need, and don't dare to suggest pills! You know what I think about *pills*, Robert!"

Better start again, he thought. "So what is on your mind about the estate, Mother?"

"Crisis, that's what," she said firmly. "We are in a state of crisis. Money is owed to the bank, there are debts to be paid and I bear all this on my own shoulders without complaint. But now I need to consult you, because you are the heir and will inherit."

Not that old thing, thought Robert. Am I to get the usual lecture? But his mother carried on in no uncertain terms.

"I do not see your taking over as an event likely to happen in the near future, but we must be prepared. Also," she added with some chagrin, "that stupid little man at the bank seems to think we are no longer safe enough for further loans. In spite of my protestations, he considers we must do something, and soon, to raise funds to settle debts."

"Oh, dear," Robert said. "I am afraid this is a familiar story from many of my estate-owning clients. So we must put on our thinking caps. Have you any ideas?"

"Not mine, but suggestions from the bank manager do not appeal. He proposed selling, either the whole estate and moving to a small property in the village, or a parcel of land for building houses." She then expanded on her considered rejection of both these proposals, whilst Robert listened and noted that her hands, clenched in her lap, seemed to have acquired a tremor.

She listed concisely the reasons why she could not possibly sell off land for building, and his thoughts began to wander. He could see over her shoulder the view from the window, which was of an extraordinary building with oddly shaped, curving framed windows, and a spiral fire escape unusually decorated for its purpose. He knew from past enquiries in their shop that it was the Rudolf Steiner building, and its interesting interior and exterior had been designed in the nineteen twenties to be in accordance with the German philosopher's theories of universality. Peace, at-oneness, and all that. Just at this moment, thought Robert, it seems quite a nice idea.

"Robert! Are you listening to me?"

"Of course I am, Mother. You just said that you are too old to move from your ancestral home."

"I said nothing of the sort," she exploded. "You must realise that I am very busy, and have come all the way into town to talk to you. The least you can do is have the courtesy to listen!"

He saw her colour rising as she continued hotly in this vein, and then, to his horror, she stopped in midsentence and keeled over the arm of her chair.

He rushed to her side and put his arm around her, gently lifting her into an upright position and propping her up with spare cushions. What does one do now? he thought, and was about to ring for an ambulance when she heaved a great sigh and blinked rapidly.

"What on earth are you doing?" she said, taking the cushions and throwing them over to the empty sofa.

"I am going to suggest that you have a rest, and then I shall call a taxi and insist you come with me to Shepherd Road, where we can talk more calmly and decide what I shall do next."

He was relieved, though somewhat surprised, when she agreed without demur. As he helped her to her feet, however, she corrected his last words, saying that the decision would ultimately be hers.

\*          \*          \*

FELICITY HAD JUST COME HOME FROM HER SHIFT AT THE CITIZENS Advice Bureau, and had put her feet up on a stool ready to relax and watch her favourite antiques auction show on television. The work was consistently gloomy, with worried citizens bringing in their troubles for advice and, hopefully, solutions. After a morning at the Bureau, she often felt emotionally drained, and about once a month decided to give it up, but then didn't.

The telephone rang, and she sighed. She looked at her watch. It was probably Robert, desperate to tell her what his mother had said and enlisting her help in dealing with it.

"Hello? Ah, Robert, how did it go? She's still with you? Did you say lying down? What on earth has happened?"

Robert gave her a brief account of his mother's collapse, and ended by saying he was bringing her home so that they could get a doctor to take a look at her before allowing her to go back alone to Farnden. Felicity's heart sank, but she was a good soul and rose to the challenge.

"Right," she said briskly. "I'll make up the bed in the spare room. The surgery will be open, and I'll ring the doctor. Will she be able to get down there for him to take a look at her? Oh, good. They don't seem to like making visits to the sick these days."

Robert said that in his experience, visiting the sick was now the province of the church, but even their new swinging vicar was seldom seen about on pastoral duties. She laughed, and said she would see him in an hour or so.

The spare room on the second floor had a pleasant view over the garden, and they had recently installed a small en suite shower room. The only problem, Felicity thought as she shook out clean sheets, would be the stairs. But it sounded as if Farnden Mother had rallied pretty well. "Fingers crossed, then," Felicity said to their black-and-white cat, who had followed her upstairs.

Back in Farnden, Lois was behind the counter in the shop, filling in whilst her daughter had gone on a mysterious errand to Tresham. Josie was not usually close about her comings and goings, but this time she had muttered something about an important appointment before shooting off at speed away from the village.

"Surely it's not . . . well, you know, Derek," Lois said as Derek came into the shop.

"Up the spout?" said Derek.

"Yeah, well, it does happen," said Lois defensively. "Best-laid plans, an' all that."

"Wouldn't be the end of the world. It'd just mean they'd have to name the day a bit sooner, maybe. Anyway, it might be nothing like that. Could be anything. I expect you'll get it out of her soon enough."

"That sounds a bit nasty," said Lois.

Their conversation was interrupted by the telephone, and Lois put her hand over the mouthpiece and said, "It's her up at the hall." Derek made for the door, but Lois shook her head violently. "Wait," she whispered.

"Another of those funny turns," she said after the call ended. "She's staying in London for a day or two, and wants you to go up and check on locks and things at the hall. She had planned to be back today, she said."

"Not looking good, is it," Derek said. "At least her Robert will insist on her seeing a doctor. Perhaps a good thing it happened when it did. Was it serious this time?"

"Dunno. You know what she's like. Makes light of aches and pains. Do you remember when she had that terrible flu and insisted on carrying on?"

"Thereby infecting the whole parish council," Derek said. "Of course I remember! Anyway, might as well go up there now, on the way to Fletching. It'll make me a bit late back, but can't let the old thing down."

Halfway there, his van was passed by a scruffy white truck, which, to his surprise, turned into the drive up to the hall. Scruffy white truck? That rang bells, and he instinctively slowed down and stopped before turning in himself. He had seen two men in the cab, and decided it would be best not to let them see him following. Whatever they were up to, he planned to take them by surprise and so slowed to a halt for a few minutes. It did not occur to him that it would be one against two.

# TEN

Once they were well out of sight, Derek started off up the long drive to the hall. He guessed they had gone round the back to the stable yard. He had given them time to find nobody at home and turn around to return down the drive. They hadn't reappeared, so he planned to leave his van down a little lane a hundred yards or so from the turn to the stables. He would walk the rest of the way, and see for himself exactly what they were doing. If it was petty thieving, they would be as quick as possible. Grab what they could and be up and away in minutes.

He felt in his pocket for the pencil and notebook he always carried for work. The one thing he could definitely do was write down the truck's registration number. He parked the van, and began to walk through the trees that bordered the drive as it turned round the side of the house.

Still in the protection of the spinney, he could see the truck, parked close to the back door, and hear its engine still running. The men were nowhere in sight, and he supposed they were already inside the house. On Mrs. T-J's recent form, it was quite likely she had forgotten to lock it.

He jotted down the number of the truck, then edged round the side of house and approached the back door. If he could frighten them by knocking innocently and enquiring for Mrs. T-J, he might stall their thieving. Might even stop them breaking some of her priceless porcelain. With any luck, they'd scarper like frit rabbits.

He knocked. The engine juddered on, and then coughed. Then even that was silent, and Derek felt a sudden frisson of fear. For the first time it struck him that what he was doing was not sensible. Ah well, he could retreat without any damage. But at that moment the kitchen door opened, and a big bloke growled at him that the missus was in Tresham and they were doing some plumbing work in the house.

He was about to shut the door in Derek's face, when another voice came from behind him. "We'd better clear out, Gerald. It's risky—"

Derek frowned. "Perhaps you'd better clear out," he said. "Before I ring the police."

He turned to go back to his van, but the big man lifted up the jemmy he was carrying and brought it down hard. Derek crumpled at the knees and saw nothing more.

"You stupid bugger!" Clive shouted at his brother.

"Get in the truck. *Now!*"

"Don't run 'im over," Clive said anxiously as they backed away from Derek's prone figure. In minutes, the truck was flying down the drive and out into the road.

"Where *is* he, then?" Lois was back home now, and outside the kitchen window the light was beginning to fade.

"He said he'd be a bit late, didn't he? Because of having to go up to the hall?" said Gran soothingly. In truth, she was also beginning to worry. It was not like Derek to fail to let them know if he was unexpectedly delayed. "Why don't you ring his mobile if you're fretting?" she asked.

"Oh, you know, he doesn't like me checking up on him," Lois said. "Not since that time when . . ." Her voice tailed off, and she walked out of the house to look up and down the High Street for signs of his van.

An hour passed, and there were still no messages, nor a sign of Derek. "Well, here goes," Lois said, dialling his number. "Nothing! It's completely dead," she said. "For goodness' sake, Mum, what can have happened to him?"

"Calm down, Lois. Where was he going after checking on the hall?"

"Fletching, to do some rewiring at that house restoration. There's nobody living there yet, so I can't ring him there."

"The hall, then. Could he have locked himself in by mistake? She's got the whole place bolted and barred."

"So why hasn't he rung me?"

"Mobile out of money?" said Gran.

Lois was silent for a few minutes, then looked at the shelf clock and said, "Right. That's it. I'm off to the hall to see if I can find him. I'll keep in touch," she added. "Whatever."


IT WAS DARK NOW, AND LOIS DROVE CAREFULLY ALONG THE UNLIT road that led to the hall. The gates were still open, and that was odd. Mrs. T-J could well have left them open on her way out, but Derek would certainly have shut and locked them when he left.

There were no lights in the house, and Lois's heart sank

when she saw Derek's vehicle parked by the drive. She drove on into the stable yard and heard the old mare whinnying loudly in her stall. Probably hungry, Lois thought, though Mrs. T-J had repeatedly told Derek not to forget to feed the horse.

Then she saw him. Her van lights picked up a dark hump on the ground outside the back door. The hump was not moving, and had not moved as she drove in with her lights on full beam.

"Dear God, no, no, not Derek!" Lois yelled, and almost fell out of the van door.

# ELEVEN

❧

"HOW MANY TIMES DO I HAVE TO TELL YOU!" YELLED GLADYS. "Don't bang that door! It'll fall off its hinges for two pins."

Gerald and Clive had come indoors in a rush, jostling each other to get in first. "Oh, shut it, Mother," said Clive. "Got the kettle on?"

"Sodding tea?" snapped Gerald. "I need something stronger than tea. Where's yer whiskey, Mother?"

"I ain't got no whiskey, as you very well know," said Gladys.

"Wha's this, then?" said Gerald, opening a high cupboard door and pulling out a half bottle of Famous Grouse. "My God, woman, you've bin having a go at this lately! Or did your precious Dot Nimmo help you out with it?"

"She wasn't here long enough before you come home and frightened her away."

"Frightened her away? Dot Nimmo's never been frightened of nobody. You wanna watch her, Mother. She's working for Cowgill on the quiet. Not s'quiet now, mind you. We all know to keep out of her way."

"Old Cowgill?" said Gladys. "He must be about retiring age now surely."

"Not that old. And he's got a nephew coming up the ranks to take his place."

"That young nephew, Vickers is his name, is engaged to the Meade woman's daughter who runs the village shop in Farnden," Gladys said. "Dot told me. They're all pleased apparently."

Clive and Gerald looked at one another in alarm. "*Farnden* shop, did you say?" Gerald growled.

His mother nodded, and Clive groaned. "Bloody hell," he said.

AFTER THEY HAD EATEN FISH AND CHIPS FRESH FROM THE SHOP, Gerald told Clive to switch on the telly. "News time on ITV," he said. "We want the local news."

"Why?" said Gladys suspiciously.

"Him that asks no questions gets told no lies," said Gerald. "Turn it up, Clive. Can't hear a word when Mum's talking."

They watched through to the end of the news bulletin, and then settled down to their favourite cops-and-robbers serial. "There weren't nothing about it," Clive said.

"Don't count yer chickens," Gerald cautioned. "Bit early yet. Anyway, I didn't hit him that hard." That wasn't how it looked to Clive, but he said nothing. Gladys, however, had just come into the room after washing up, and heard the last sentence.

"Hit who?" she said. Her absent husband was spending some time as a guest of Her Majesty as a result of grievous bodily harm, and she was well aware that Gerald was exactly like him. Not Clive. He was more like her. Anything for a quiet life. And as a result, Gerald pushed his brother around and used him without scruple to do the dirty jobs.

"It were just an ole dog what had a go at us," Gerald said. "One of them pit bull terriers. Illegal, they are."

"And so are you two idiots," Gladys said with some feeling. "Don't blame me if you end up sleepin' in the next cell to your stupid father. None of you care what'll happen to me," she continued, sitting down heavily and wiping her eyes on the corner of her apron.

"I've had enough of this," said Gerald. "I'm off down the pub—you coming, Clive?"

Clive shook his head. He looked unhappily at his mother. "I'll stay here," he said. "Keep an eye on the telly."

DOUGLAS, LOIS'S ELDEST SON, THANKED GOD FOR MOBILE PHONES as he sped through the dark lanes on his way to the hall. His mother had contacted him at home in Tresham, and when she had calmed down, he gathered she was in the stable yard behind Farnden Hall, watching over his father, who had been attacked and was still lying on the ground, just coming round from being dead. Or that's what Douglas thought his mother had said. Anyway, he was nearly there now, and could take charge.

After establishing that his father was not dead, but certainly very groggy, he said to Lois that they should send for an ambulance. "He'll need checking over, Mum," he said.

His father tried to raise himself off the ground. "No ambulance," he said thickly. "Get me home, boy. The women'll look after me."

Between them, Douglas and Lois helped him into Douglas's big car, and they set off in convoy for the village. When they half carried him into the kitchen, Gran took one look and rushed towards the phone.

"No, Gran, wait!" said Douglas. "He says he'll be all right. Doesn't want an ambulance. What d'you think, Mum?"

Lois looked at Derek. He was pale, and seemed to have laid a large egg at the back of his head. He winked at her, and she sighed. "Looks as if he'll live," she said. "Best put on the kettle, Mum."

"Hot sweet tea," said Gran, and took no notice when Douglas said that was for shock, not for a bash on the head.

Eventually, they all settled down in the warm kitchen, with Derek downing strong painkillers for an almighty headache. They considered what had happened.

"They were already in the house," Derek said. "When I knocked, I thought nobody was around. But their scruffy old truck was still there, and the engine had been running. When the door opened, I only had time to see one of 'em. Big bloke, with black hair and eyebrows that more or less met in the middle. Lowbrow wasn't in it! Then I heard this scared-sounding voice saying they'd better scarper."

"And then you turned your back on them and gave 'em the perfect opportunity to bash you into Kingdom come!"

"We don't all have the same expertise as you, Lois, when in tricky situations. I just said if they didn't beat it right away, I was calling the police. It was the best I could think of. Got the registration number of the truck, though."

He fumbled in one pocket, and then another. "Here it is," he said, and handed it to Lois. She tore out the page and handed the book back. "This'll be useful. Well done, love.

Now, if you've had enough of being the man of the hour, I reckon bed would be the best place for you."

Douglas stood up. "And I suppose I'm not to mention it to anybody, Mum? And certainly not to Matthew Vickers or Josie?"

"Not for the present, Dougie, if you don't mind. This attack on Dad has probably got something to do with other theft jobs going on round the county. I'll get on to Cowgill tomorrow, I promise. And thanks for coming over so quickly."

"He's me dad, isn't he?" said Douglas, and patted him on the shoulder. "Night, everybody," he added, and left.

"So what's going on, Lois?" Derek said.

"At the moment, it looks like a load of burglaries, probably done by the same pair of villains who did the shop, but not the one with the gun, who's been arrested. He was more in the big time, apparently. Only interested in money, and lots of it. Or big hauls of valuables, like my client over at Fletching, where Andrew's doing a big interior design job. I need to report to Cowgill tomorrow, then we'll know more."

"Except that you always say he don't mind taking information, but isn't s'good at giving it out," Gran said. "If you ask me, as Ivy Beasley used to say, I'd get on to him right now. Sooner the better. Them criminals could be a long way away by morning."

"Not in that vehicle!" said Derek. "No, let's leave it to Lois. Deal with it in the morning." He began to stand up, and Lois rushed to his side.

"Steady now, boy," she said. "One step at a time."

# TWELVE

*✣*

COWGILL WAS AT HIS DESK EARLY NEXT MORNING. HE HAD taken a day off yesterday to play in a golf tournament at his club, and there was, as always, a pile of papers waiting for him.

"Morning, Chris," he said as his assistant poked her head round his door.

"Did you win?" she said. He looked up at her, and after a pause, she said, "Ah, I see. Well, never mind. Better luck next time."

"Come in," Cowgill said sternly. "Just one thing I have to say to you."

"Sir?"

"Don't take up golf. Ever. That's an order."

"Right, sir."

"Now, let's get down to work."

Five minutes later, the phone rang, and Cowgill answered. "Lois! How are you, my dear?"

Chris got up. Coffee break, and an unspoken order to take her time about it. She signalled to her boss that she would be back, and closed the door behind her.

"I'm all right," said Lois, "but Derek isn't. He's been beaten up and has a lump on the back of his head the size of a goose egg. That's why I'm calling. And don't ask me if he's been to the hospital, because he wouldn't go. I've looked up concussion, and he hasn't got it, and apparently an egg is a good thing."

She gave Cowgill brief details of what had happened, and said it looked very likely that the burglars had been the same pair that took money from Josie's shop. Derek had taken a note of the truck number, she said, and read it out.

"I'll get it checked. Probably best if I come over and have a word with Derek," Cowgill suggested, scenting an opportunity of seeing Lois. "Is around two this afternoon convenient? Good. And don't worry," he added. "We can pull those two in anytime we need to. They're known to us. Following in their father's footsteps unfortunately."


"WHERE DO YOU THINK YOU TWO ARE GOING?" SAID GLADYS. Gerald and Clive were coming down the stairs, carrying large bags stuffed to the gills and spilling out a sock where the zips would not close.

"Off for a few days, Mum," Clive said. "Time we had a break, Gerald thinks. Just taking off and following our noses. We'll let you know where we are. Probably the west country. Maybe see Auntie May in Bristol. Maybe not."

"Not definite," said Gerald. "But we'll be in touch."

"You goin' in that old truck?" Gladys said, frowning. There

was something funny going on here, but she was too well trained to ask for details.

Gerald shook his head. "Nah. It'd never get there. We'll swop it with something better from Arthur over on the Churchill estate. He'll see us right. So if anybody wants to know, Mother, you don't know where we've gone, or how. You know the drill."

Gladys sighed. She knew only too well, and she also knew that it was never any good. The cops always caught up in the end. And look where it had landed her no-good husband! She heard the front door bang as her sons departed, and turned to look up at the top cupboard. They'd left her a drop, surely. She fetched the steps to climb up and find the bottle. She stood on tiptoe and then lost her balance. Her foot slipped off the top step, and she lurched sideways, clutched in vain at the cupboard door and fell heavily onto the kitchen floor.

"D'YOU THINK SHE'LL BE ALL RIGHT ON HER OWN?" CLIVE SAT IN the passenger seat of a well-used Ford, which Arthur had said would take them anywhere they wanted to go. Just fill her up, and off she goes, he had assured them. He'd taken the old truck from them, promising to reduce it to a flattened cube by tomorrow. "Them breakers know their job," he had assured Gerald. "It ain't worth nothing anyway," he had added slyly, holding out an open palm, on which Gerald placed a bundle of twenty-pound notes.

"You've not seen us, then," Clive had said anxiously as Arthur gave them the Ford key.

Arthur had shaken his head wisely. "Never 'eard of you," he said, and winked at Gerald. "Good luck, mate," he had added, and waved cheerily as they drove off.

Now Gerald turned and looked at his brother. "Is who all right?" he said.

"Mum, of course."

"She'll be fine. Nobody like our mum for looking after number one. Dad always used to say she was the trickiest of all of us. Now, for God's sake, be quiet for a bit. I got some thinking to do."

It was warm in the car, and Gerald slotted in some loud music, saying he could only think when he'd got music to shut the world out. For a while, Clive watched the country-side slip by, until it became a blur and his eyelids drooped. Gerald glanced at him. Poor devil, he thought to himself. Not really bright enough for this job, but I have to look after him. After all, I only got one brother. Then a thought struck him. Maybe he'd looked after him too well over the years, not let him stand on his own feet enough. Maybe if things got too hot, he'd be better ditching Clive and see if he'd manage better on his own. It was a thought anyway.

Gerald had a rough idea of where he would find a sympa-thetic bed for the night, and turned off the old northbound Great North Road—no chance they'd go west!—onto a small side road that ended up in a farm high up on moorland that stretched for miles and miles with no other sign of habitation. It was getting dark now, and his headlights picked up a bad-ger crossing the lane. He stepped on the accelerator and felt the bump as he hit it. Great! He began to whistle, and Clive stirred in his sleep.

There were no lights in the farmhouse, and Gerald drove round to the back of a large barn, where cattle shifted and snuffled in the straw. He switched off the engine and looked at his watch. Harry should be home shortly. Market day in town, and the old boy always went for a drink with his mates before coming home. It'd be a surprise for him! And a nice one, Gerald hoped, feeling in his pocket for the bottle of whiskey he had remembered to get at the corner shop before they left.

# Thirteen

❧

Cowgill and his assistant Chris knocked at Lois's door at two o'clock exactly, and Gran shot out of her kitchen to answer it as usual.

"Inspector, please come in. Lois was going to speak to you today. She didn't tell me to expect you in person," she said conversationally. Now that Josie was engaged to Cowgill's nephew Matthew, Gran felt entitled to a warmer relationship with Lois's senior cop.

"Ah, there you are," said Lois, coming out of her office and indicating to Cowgill that he should go into the sitting room, where Derek was resting and watching racing on the telly. Gran was about to follow, but a look from Lois caused her to hover in the hall. Chris sat on a chair by the window, and took out her notebook.

"Afternoon, Derek," Cowgill said. He knew that he was not Derek Meade's favourite person, and quite understood why. But his conscience was clear. In all the time he had worked with Lois, he had never overstepped the mark of proper behaviour for a policeman. Affectionate banter, yes, and a genuine concern when Lois had got herself into dangerous situations, certainly. The fact that he had lusted after her—still did, if he was honest—and had loving feelings for her that he had never felt for anyone else, was neither here nor there as far as it concerned Derek. Cowgill occasionally wondered what he would do if Lois finally agreed that there could be something more between them. Back out probably! Anyway, it was not likely to happen.

"Morning, Inspector," Derek grunted. "This won't take long, I hope?"

"No, no," said Cowgill soothingly. "Just a few questions for you, and then we'll see if Lois remembers seeing anything unusual in the stable yard. Now, when exactly did you suspect that something was wrong?"

Derek gave him a good, factual account of what happened up to the time he was knocked unconscious, and then Lois took over, saying the most unusual thing she found in the stable yard was her husband lying on the ground, out for the count.

"So you only saw one of them, Derek?" Cowgill checked.

"Yep, the other was just a scared-sounding voice in the background. I reckon they hadn't had time to get going on the job they come for."

"I expect you'll check with Mrs. T-J about missing or broken items?" Lois said. "I wouldn't like any suspicion to fall on my girls."

"Who do you send cleaning up there?" Cowgill asked.

"Paula Hickson and Floss Cullen. They both get on well with the old duck, and that's not an easy thing, believe me. You know she's not well?"

"I heard she'd been excused duties on the bench for a while," Cowgill said. "Still in London, then. I presume that's why Derek went up there? To check everywhere was locked up safely?"

"Not safely enough," Derek said. "Even I can work that out." He shut his eyes and frowned for a moment, and Lois immediately said that if Cowgill had finished asking his questions, it was time to leave Derek in peace.

"We had an emergency this morning at the station, needing all hands," Cowgill said, rising to his feet, "but one of my officers will be going round this afternoon to chat with the Mowlem brothers. Not like them to be violent, but there's always a first time, especially with a father like theirs. I'll keep in touch. Take care, Derek."

"Lois will do that," Derek said bluntly.

AFTER A QUICK SANDWICH, MATTHEW VICKERS FOUND HIMSELF negotiating the back streets of Tresham, in search of the two dodgy characters he'd followed from Farnden. He strongly disagreed with the decision to let them go with a caution. If he'd had more time, he reckoned he would have found where they'd stashed the cash in their truck. But these days, with so much gang warfare and serious weaponry on the streets, the theft of the till takings from a village shop received only cursory attention from the police.

Well, it was his Josie's shop, and if he had to work in off-duty hours, he intended to find out if his suspicions were true, and if not, who *had* put the frighteners on a defenceless girl, his girl.

He checked the address held at the station, and pulled up a couple of hundred yards away. This was an area of town where the appearance of a police car was guaranteed to send an alarm signal round the neighbourhood. If he had parked outside their house, the Mowlem brothers could be out of sight before he'd got out of the car.

He knocked at number eleven, and after a long pause, he heard slow footsteps approaching. The door opened a fraction, and a woman's face looked out. She had a bandage round one eye, and hobbled with the help of a stick. Good God! And his uncle had said the brothers were not violent!

"Mrs. Mowlem?" He showed his identity card and asked her if she would answer a few questions. He suggested it would be better if he let him in, as she clearly needed to sit down. "What happened to you?" he enquired with no hope of a truthful answer. As he expected, she said she had fallen from a stepladder whilst trying to reach a high cupboard. How many times had he heard that one? But he said no more about it, and helped her into a chair.

"Now, I wonder if your sons are about?" he said. "I need a word with them. An emergency, and they might be able to help."

"What kind of an emergency?" said Gladys suspiciously. She was used to dodging police questions, but immediately thought something might have happened to the boys.

"An accident up at Farnden Hall. We know your sons were in the vicinity a day or so previously, and wondered if they could help us."

"Not here," Gladys said blankly.

"Where are they working, Mrs. Mowlem?" Matthew had little hope of a straight answer, but watched her face closely. That is, he watched half her face. There was a lot of bandage, and one eye was completely covered.

He was sure she stiffened before saying that they had gone

off on a big job down in the west country. Could be away for weeks. And no, she didn't have an address. They said they'd be in touch. She laughed hollowly. "Not that that means much," she said.

"Mobile number?" Matthew asked, hope now more or less extinguished.

"Not working," Gladys said. "Never is. Either out of money or battery. Useless things, if you ask me."

After Matthew had gone, Gladys wondered whether she had done wrong to mention the west country destination. But no. She reasoned that if they'd said west, they almost certainly meant east, south or north. No, she had done the right thing.

MATTHEW WALKED BACK DOWN THE STREET, LOOKING ALL ROUND for sight of the old truck. They had the registration number, but he would recognise it without. If he could have a quiet search . . .

He approached his car, and stopped twenty feet away. All the tyres had been slashed, the windows cracked, and when he got closer, he could see a big dent in the roof. Sod it! His uncle had warned him it was a rough area, but it had seemed quiet enough when he parked. How long had he been with Mrs. Mowlem? It couldn't have been more than a quarter of an hour. Twenty minutes at the most. He looked up and down the street, but there was nobody in sight. With a sigh, he dialled the station, half dreading what the lads in the ops room would say. As it was, he came under fire more than most, just because he was Cowgill's nephew. Now they would have a field day.

After he had made the call, he walked around, aware of

twitching curtains and eyes at every window. On an impulse, he dialled Josie at the shop.

"Matthew? Where are you? Is something wrong?"

If he needed proof that she was the girl for him, here it was. Before he had said a word, she knew he was in trouble. "Just wanted to say I love you," he said, and signed off as he saw a breakdown van approaching.

# FOURTEEN

☙

In the guest room in Robert's house in Shepherd Road, Mrs. Tollervey-Jones opened her eyes and squinted at the sunlight streaming in. She never drew her curtains at night, saying that by so doing she would miss the best part of the day. She looked at her watch. Half past seven, and shouts from her grandchildren reached her from the kitchen below.

She sighed. She had dutifully submitted to an examination by her son's doctor, and he had pronounced that she should have a few days' complete rest, and then could go home and make sure she saw her own doctor for further tests. He would write, so that the Tresham surgery would be expecting her. Time to go home, she decided. She would have a word with Robert as soon as possible. Meanwhile, she had to admit that her bed was very comfortable. She turned over so that the sun was not in her eyes, and dozed off.

A knock at the door heralded a grandchild. "Bye, Grannie!

We're just off to school. See you later!" She smiled. Farnden Hall was going to seem quiet after this. Blessedly quiet maybe, but she was surprised at her own misgivings about returning to a huge, empty and silent house. But she knew she must go, possibly tomorrow. Felicity was a dear girl, but mothers-in-law and daughters-in-law trod a narrow path, full of hazards. One comment too many about child rearing could cause a very chilly response.

Another knock at the door, and in came Robert, smart in his city suit and clutching a bulging briefcase, ready for the day. "How are you this morning, Mother?" he said.

"Much better, thank you," Mrs. Tollervey-Jones said. "In fact," she continued, "if you could make the arrangements, I shall be fine to return to Farnden tomorrow. I intend to make some telephone calls to enlist the help of Mrs. Meade and her team."

Robert sat on the edge of her bed. "Are you sure about this?" he asked. "You know you are very welcome to stay here for as long as you like." He knew that she knew and Felicity knew that this was not entirely true, but it was necessary to say it.

"Very kind, my dear," she said. "And I promise I shall be extremely sensible and do exactly as the doctor recommends. And now off you go. Have a nice day, as the Americans say."

Robert went slowly downstairs and put his head round the kitchen door. "She says she's going tomorrow," he said. Felicity could not suppress a smile. "Oh, good. I mean, good that she's feeling well enough. I shall do all I can to help her. I'll warn the bureau that I can't be in tomorrow. Do you think it would be a good idea if I drove her down to Farnden? Then I could see her safely settled in."

"Brilliant!" said Robert. "You're an angel." He blew her a kiss, and left for the city.

AT ABOUT THIS TIME, DEREK AND LOIS DROVE UP TO FARNDEN Hall and parked in the stable yard, not far from where Derek had been felled to the ground. He had reluctantly agreed to see the doctor before deciding to go back to work, and had been given advice on looking out for indications of concussion and advised to take the rest of the week off. "Go for a nice walk with Lois," the doctor had said. He had been looking after the Meade family for years, and knew they seldom missed a day's work, and almost never took a holiday.

"A walk?" said Lois. "Where? And what for?" On hearing what the doctor had recommended for Derek, she reluctantly agreed, and then suggested they walk round Farnden Hall park. "The trees are lovely at the moment," she said innocently.

"You don't fool me, Lois Meade," Derek said. "A walk round Farnden park means a spot of ferretin' on the side. Well, why not?" he added, saying he would dearly like to see those two thugs brought before the beak.

"Talking of beaks, have you heard when Mrs. T-J is coming back?"

"You're more likely to have heard than me," Derek answered. "She'll ring us, I daresay." He walked over to the kitchen door and tried it. "Still locked, I'm glad to say. No signs of breaking and entering. Perhaps they were frightened off by Derek Meade's reputation for being a hard man, dangerous if crossed, let alone knocked on the head."

"Yeah, an' pigs might fly," said Lois. "More likely heard of

New Brooms' sideline, and I don't mean Andrew's interior décor business."

They walked out of the stable yard, through the high wall into the kitchen garden.

"Sssh!" Derek said, grabbing Lois's arm and standing quite still. He pointed to the corner of the garden, where a figure in a dark jacket was bent over, his head down, clearly unaware of their presence.

Lois gently removed his hand, and began to walk forward. "Jack?" she called, smiling at Derek's horrified expression. "Lovely morning! Just the weather for a spot of gardening."

Jack Hickson straightened up and waved a hand. "Morning, Mrs. Meade. And is that Derek? Don't often see you two out together! Nothing wrong with Paula, or the kids, is there?" he added, suddenly anxious.

Lois assured him that all was fine. Paula would be up in the house soon, and she and Derek were just checking that there'd been no break-ins or vandalism. "Amazing how quickly news of an empty house, especially one with valuables in it, gets round the criminal fraternity," Derek said.

"And are you feeling better?" Jack continued. "Heard you'd had an accident up here."

Derek sighed. How *did* news travel so fast in villages? Of course, he knew the answer. The shop, the pub, the nursery school and, most important, the gossips network. "Yep, thanks," he said. "Nothing serious anyway. Better get back, Lois."

"We'll leave you to it, then, Jack," Lois said, sensing they were on dangerous ground. Then she remembered that Jack was once more part of a team of municipal gardeners in Tresham, and might well have heard of two brothers working the area for quick opportunities.

She turned back, and added, "You know Josie had cash

taken from the shop? They ain't got no further finding the couple of villains who took it. I suppose you haven't heard about a couple of brothers who've scarpered, have you?"

Jack leaned on his spade in time-honoured gardener's fashion, and considered. "Don't remember anything. But if I hear anything useful, I'll let you know."

Lois's mobile ringing interrupted the conversation, and she answered it, mouthing "Mrs. T-J!" at Derek.

"How are you, Mrs. Tollervey-Jones? Oh, that's good. How can I help you? We're keeping an eye on the house for you. Paula's coming up later, and Derek and I are here checking locks an' that. Sorry, when did you say? The signal's rubbish round here. Tomorrow? Oh, no, that's no trouble. We'll check everything, do some shopping for you and make sure all's ready. Your daughter-in-law? Oh, that will be very nice. We'll make up a bed in the blue bedroom, shall we? Fine. Anything else you think of, just give me a ring. What time do you think you'll be arriving? About midday? Fine. Paula can be here to make sure everything is tickety-boo."

Derek and Jack looked at each other. "Going to be back by herself, is she?" Jack said.

"No, her daughter-in-law will stay for a day or two," Lois said.

"And then she'll be alone again," Derek said. "It's not right."

Jack nodded. "She needs a companion, or some such."

"Or sell up and move to a smaller house with neighbours." Derek looked worried. He was remembering how easy it must have been for the brothers to get into the house. An old lady, even one so authoritative as Mrs. T-J, wouldn't stand a chance.

"Well, one thing at a time," said Lois. "Maybe her son's talked some sense into her while she's been there. Anyway, I must get back and make all the arrangements. Come on, Derek. You can come shopping with me and carry the groceries."

"No fear," said Derek. "I'm safer going back to work."

Jack laughed. "See you, mate," he said.

# FIFTEEN

⌘

THE NORRINGTONS' DRAWING ROOM HAD BEEN RESTORED, more or less, to its former elegance, and Melanie and Geoff stood at the long windows looking out at the autumn garden.

"I'll never feel the same about this house," Melanie said. "It's like it was smirched."

"It was what?"

"Smirched—you know, dirtied up, too dirty to be cleaned."

"Besmirched, I think you mean," Geoff said loftily. "And anyway, that's all rubbish. It's just the same house. A few things missing, maybe, but all replaceable. Next thing you'll be saying you want to move."

"I do," Melanie said. "I'll never feel comfortable again in this place."

Geoff hit his forehead with the flat of his hand, and swore. "Oh no! So we've got to go through all that searching, all over again?"

Melanie turned to look at him. "Yes," she said. "And if you won't, I will. You can even stay here if you want. I've got that money from Mum and Dad. That'll buy me something round here. A little cottage for one."

"Melanie, darling!" Geoff suddenly realised that she meant it. Surely she must know that in spite of his little peccadillos, she always came first? He could not imagine life without Melanie. He turned the full force of his charm on her, took her in his arms and explained exactly why he was perfectly prepared to do anything she wished. Her happiness was all he cared about. They would start looking at once, to see what was on the market.

"So you'd better get hold of your décor chap and cancel the order," he said. "You can say that we'll certainly use him in the future, when we find the right house."

Melanie softened. "All right, then," she said. "But no backing out. And you can take me along on some of your trips abroad. Other men do, so why not you? Now, I'll go and ring Andrew straightaway. We shall have to pay him for what he's done so far. But that's only fair, and he's a nice chap."

ANDREW WAS FAR FROM PLEASED. HE HAD BEEN SENT BY LOIS TO help Felicity Tollervey-Jones and Paula sort out cupboards and stores up at the hall. Lois herself would come along later to see how they were getting on. Yesterday's return to Farnden had gone smoothly, and Mrs. Tollervey-Jones had been pathetically pleased to see her old mare in the stable. Loud whinnying had greeted her, and she had remembered to put a couple of Polo Mints in her pocket.

Felicity and Paula had liked each other at once. They had

compared notes about children and schools, and although they were worlds apart, the job of managing Mrs. T-J soon brought the two together. Now that Andrew had arrived to help them with heavy lifting, they were having a major sort-out in the kitchen and outhouses, making piles of old tins and boxes. Andrew had just come across half a roomful of old newspapers, neatly tied into bundles, dating back to the nineteen sixties, when his mobile rang. It was Melanie Norrington, and Felicity watched as his face fell.

"Of course. I quite understand," he said. "Yes, I'll let you have an invoice. Shame, really. I had really looked forward to getting it right for you. But I quite understand," he repeated.

Paula, who knew all about the commission, realised at once what had happened. "Has she cancelled?" she said.

"'Fraid so." He explained why, shrugged and suggested they get on.

"Are they looking for another house, then?" Felicity asked. "Presumably they'll want to stay around here?"

"Yep, she said they'd be looking straightaway," Andrew said. He heaved a pile of newspapers out into the yard, and walked away into the kitchen garden.

"Poor Andrew," said Paula. "He'll be back in a few minutes. Probably gone away to have a good curse."

"What kind of people are they?" Felicity asked. "Mon-eyed, I suppose, if they'd commissioned Andrew to do a complete décor design?"

Paula shook her head. "I only know that Mrs. Norrington had told Andrew that money was no object. So I suppose they've got plenty. I think her husband's in business of some sort. Goes abroad a lot."

"How interesting," said Felicity, the beginnings of a plan

forming in her mind. "I must see if Robert has heard of them. Norrington, did you say?"

By the end of the afternoon, the three had done a great deal of work and had managed to keep Mrs. Tollervey-Jones from interfering, and when Lois turned up, she suggested they all sit round the kitchen table and have a cup of tea before Paula and Andrew went home. Mrs. T-J was resting in her room. With much sympathising with Andrew, Lois took over the teapot, and began to pour, when Felicity turned to see her mother-in-law at the door.

"Ah, there you are," she said. "I thought I heard happy voices. Andrew, please draw up a chair for me. And, Felicity, find me a cup, please. Now I want to have a talk with you all, and I want some honest answers."

"Wouldn't you like to—" Felicity began.

"No, I wouldn't, thank you. I shall be better in here. It's warm and wonderfully tidy and clean, after all your efforts. As for all that!" She waved her hand towards the piles of stuff in the yard. "It looks as if I'm moving house."

Nobody spoke for moment, and then Felicity asked what exactly they were to discuss.

"My future," said Mrs. T-J. "I have three alternatives, and although I shall, of course, discuss them with Robert"—here she smiled at Felicity, who nodded gently—"I would very much like to know what you young folk think is the best solution. After all my years on the bench, I have a healthy respect for the views of young people, and find they are often able to see more clearly than those of us encumbered by experiences of the past."

Lois could not believe what she was hearing. Mrs. T-J asking for advice! A new Mrs. T-J? She must have had a really scary attack in London, poor old soul. And how nice that she thought of those present as young people!

When Felicity, too, had recovered from her surprise at this development, she wondered what her mother-in-law was about to reveal. She suspected the financial situation of the estate would not be mentioned. It was not done to talk about money.

As Mrs. T-J began to explain her situation, it was clear that Felicity was right. The three alternatives were all to do with her advancing years, possible ill health and her approaching retirement from the magistrates court, giving her much more free time to develop her other interests. "Including my grand-children," she said with another smile for Felicity. "We have the flat in London, which I intend to keep, and though I mean to have Farnden village as my anchor, I do not need eight bed-rooms, and all that goes with them."

"So," said Andrew, warming to the possibility of new com-missions. Conversion into flats? Restoring one of the estate cottages as a dower house? "How exactly do you plan to pro-ceed, Mrs. T-J?"

"First alternative," she replied, her voice getting stronger, "I divide the house into several apartments, reserving one for myself. Or two, I carry on in the house as I am, but broaden-ing my interests by diversifying into sundry attractions and opening up to the public. And three, selling up the entire estate, and moving into a smaller house in the village, where I shall not be isolated and vulnerable."

"And free to come and go as you fancy," said Felicity firmly. "With Mrs. Meade to keep an eye on a village house while you are away. Perfect!"

Lois stared at her. This was the first time she had met

Felicity, and immediately warmed to her. She seemed pleasantly straightforward and genuinely concerned about Mrs. Tollervey-Jones. But how would her mother-in-law react to this positive piece of advice? She waited for a very firm put-down, but it did not come. On the contrary, Mrs. T-J nodded and said sadly that she thought her daughter-in-law would say that, and perhaps she was right. "But what about you other three? What do you think?"

"I like the idea of opening up to the public," Paula said, thinking of how much fun her children would have in the park.

"You could combine conversion into flats, retaining one for yourself, with the second plan, opening up to the public and having things like a children's zoo, and perhaps an adventure playground?" Andrew's suggestion was not entirely altruistic, as he could envisage months of décor work on interior design in half a dozen new flats.

"Sorry, but I don't agree," said Lois firmly. "I see that as too much work for you, Mrs. Tollervey-Jones, and you'd see all and sundry messing up your estate every time you looked out of the window. Am I right? No, I reckon you should go for the third option. Sell up to some rich bloke who would enjoy living here and make the most of it. You could find a nice house in the village, with a decent garden to give you privacy, but with neighbours around. People you have known for years. And New Brooms would look after the house when you wanted to go up to see your family. Andrew here could make the village house look like a palace!" she added, with a consoling glance at Andrew.

"Well, that's certainly a comprehensive plan!" Mrs. T-J said. "A completely fresh view of the situation. Thank you, Mrs. Meade, and your team. It has all been most helpful. I feel now that after conferring with Robert, I shall be able to make my decision very soon."

"Phew!" said Andrew after she had made her way back to the drawing room. "That was unexpected."

"And really, really useful," Felicity said.

# Sixteen

〜

Dot Nimmo usually carried a tray of breakfast for an extra hour in bed on Sunday mornings. She had a small television on a table at the end of her bed, and as she said frequently to her sister, Evelyn, "I feel like Lady Muck, sitting there with my tray brought in by the butler. Except," she added, "I ain't got no butler. I could really do with a young and handsome butler now and then!" This would usually be followed by a fruity cackle, which never failed to shock her prim sister.

But this morning, she knew that she would have to catch her no-good cousin before he went off to the golf course, and after downing a cup of strong tea and a stale toasted teacake, she dialled his number.

"Whatcha want at this ungodly hour, our Dot?" He was richer than most gentlemen, but had not acquired a gentlemanly polish along with his wealth.

"Two brothers," said Dot, coming straight to the point, "name of Mowlem. Odd job men. Jobs of all sorts tackled, including petty theft and a bit o' knocking about if needed. What d'you know about them?"

"Enough," said her cousin. "Couple o' useless gits. Father inside for a stretch. They got no idea how to make a good livin' at it. Steer clear o' them, Dot. That's my advice. Must go now—"

"Hang on a minute. They've disappeared, so their mum says. She don't know where they've gone. At least, that's what she told the cops who came asking. But they don't believe 'er, and no more do I. Got any ideas where they might have holed up?"

"Why d'you want to know? Feeding info to your boss, are yer? Well, it so happens that I ain't got no idea, but if I had, I wouldn't tell you so's you could pass it on to Mrs. Nosey. They may be useless gits, but we all got to hang together in this business. Cheero, Dot. Nice speaking to yer."

"What a berk!" Dot said to the moth-eaten parrot in the corner. It looked at her with its rheumy eyes, and did not answer.

"Well, that means another visit to our Gladys," Dot said. "An' then I'll pop over and see Mrs. M. She'll be at home of a Sunday morning. I can 'ave a word with Derek, too. I like that Derek. He's a good bloke."

The parrot still did not answer, so Dot got herself ready and set off for the rough quarter of town where the Mowlems had lived for years.

LOIS WAS CLEARING THE FRONT GARDEN, CUTTING DOWN DEAD flowers, pruning shrubs and brushing up leaves. She planned to have a satisfying bonfire later on. She didn't hold with homemade compost. "Nasty mouldy stuff," she told Derek, who tried to tell her she wasn't making it properly. "Well, why should I bother, when I can get nice clean bags of it from the garden centre?" Derek gave up.

Now she stood up to straighten her back, and saw Dot Nimmo's car drawing up outside the gate. What was Dot doing here? She did not encourage staff to contact her at the weekend, unless it was really necessary, and as far as she knew, there were no problems with Dot's clients.

"Got a minute, Mrs. M?" Dot shouted from the pavement.

"Is it urgent?" Lois said.

"Not life and death, no. But I think you'd like to know."

"All right, then. But Gran will have lunch on the table shortly, and she doesn't take kindly to interruptions."

"As I know, only too well," said Dot, opening the gate and marching in. Of all the members of the team, only Dot could talk to Lois like this, ever since Dot had nearly been killed when, in a villainous attempt to prevent her revealing what she had discovered on one of Lois's cases, she was knocked down in a deliberate hit-and-run. Then Lois had seen the frail and vulnerable side of Dot, as she lay unconscious in the hospital bed, making such a small hillock under the blanket.

"Come on into the office, then," she said. "We've got half an hour or so."

As always with Dot, it was very useful information. Josie had passed on Matthew Vickers's car-trashing experience after talking to Mrs. Mowlem, and so Lois knew that the brothers had disappeared. "Did you get out of Gladys where they've really gone?" she asked.

"Not down to the west country, that's for sure," Dot said. "But it was something she let slip that gave me a clue."

"Let's have it then. Don't spin it out, Dot. Remember Gran."

"Well, she were telling me about some old geezer who'd been after her for years. Blimey, he must've been desperate! Childhood sweethearts, she said, boastin' about it. You don't expect me to believe that, I said. Anyway, when old Mowlem got put inside, the old geezer—Harry, he were called—come down to Tresham and said she'd got no excuse now. She could get divorced and wed him. *And* then she said what was very interesting . . ."

"Dot!"

"I'm gettin' there! She said Harry wanted her to go back with her to his farm in Yorkshire. But she wouldn't go. Said she didn't fancy living on a windswept moor, miles away from Tesco's an' any other livin' soul. So she sent him packing."

"And?"

"And her sons, she happened to mention, had always been very fond of old Harry. So there you are!" she concluded triumphantly. "Worth a trip up to Yorkshire, d'you reckon? If you're interested, I could find out exactly where the farm is, no problem. And without lettin' on we're goin'."

"Dot," Lois said, "you're a marvel. Let me think about it, and then I'll decide who'd be best to go. D'you want a bite to eat with us? Gran'll be pleased to see you, I know."

"Oh no, thanks very much all the same, Mrs. M. I never mix business with pleasure. I'll be getting along now. See you tomorrer at the meeting. Bye."

# SEVENTEEN

❧

IN THE BLUE BEDROOM AT FARNDEN HALL, FELICITY WAS TRAPPED in a nightmare, struggling to escape from a raging fire in the great hall, and could see herself standing at the top of the stairs. Below, her mother-in-law pranced in and out of the flames, laughing and waving a fiery brand around her head, shouting, "This is the answer! Now we'll get the insurance money!"

She awoke in a panic, leapt out of bed and rushed out onto the landing. All quiet, no flames and no choking clouds of smoke. Oh Lord, what an idiot, she told herself. She had been ready to rush downstairs and drag Mrs. Tollervey-Jones out of the flames and upstairs to temporary safety, but now she walked slowly back into her bedroom and drew the curtains back from the window. Her heart was still thumping, and she looked out at a hazy dawn, where there was nothing more dangerous than a fox crossing the terrace on its way to the chicken run.

That nice Paula had put a tea tray with a kettle on the table by the window, and she switched on to make herself a cup of tea. Too late to go back to sleep now, and anyway, she had to admit she was reluctant to restart the nightmare. She shivered, and reached for the wrap hanging on the back of the door. Put there by considerate Paula, no doubt. Paula and Andrew had both been in that extraordinary conference and were in favour of Mrs. T-J staying on and developing tourism in the park. Paula probably knew the old girl well, and sensed how big a wrench it would be for her to sell up. But it was the only practical option, bearing in mind the pressure coming from the bank.

Setting up children's farms and adventure playgrounds cost money. Even resurrecting the pheasant shoot—a suggestion made by Mrs. Meade's husband—would take time and yet more money. But on the positive side, all these suggestions for diversifying could help to sell the estate.

Felicity planned to go back to London later on in the day. Robert and the children would be missing her, and she could report on how well New Brooms would continue to look after his mother. She was still not altogether sure how he felt about the estate. They could have a sensible talk about yesterday's brainstorming session in the kitchen, and then wait for her mother-in-law's decision.

MRS. TOLLERVEY-JONES, SOUND ASLEEP IN HER OWN BEDROOM, was rudely awoken by the same pigeons that had lulled Felicity to sleep. She yawned and rubbed her eyes. All these years I've listened to those wretched, useless pigeons and still cannot sleep through their morning racket! She remembered a colleague on the bench telling her to get some of the new plastic strips with long spikes specially designed to prevent pigeons from landing on windowsills. She also remembered telling her colleague that she had at least forty windows, and how much was that going to cost?

In any case, their favourite perch was the parapet on the roof. And if truth be told, she thought, if I got rid of them, the unaccustomed silence would probably wake me just the same. Just one more problem. She sighed. More and more reasons to sell the estate were stacking up in her mind. She looked around her room. Would she miss those gloomy prints of that smug-looking sphinx and strings of camels crossing the Sahara? No. Or the fly-blown photographs of Niagara Falls and Salt Lake City, taken God knows how many years ago by adventuring Tollervey-Joneses? That one in a bowler hat looked as if he was about to jump into the foaming falls. Wasn't he renowned for populating his village with babies who looked exactly like him? No, she wouldn't miss any of it. It could be a new start. She would divest herself of everything except what she chose to live with in her declining years.

She looked at her bedside clock. Would Robert be up already? He should be, with those noisy children to get off to school. She lifted the telephone and dialled the London number.

"Robert? Have I woken you? Ah, I thought so. I can hear their dulcet tones! Listen, my son. I have come to a decision, and unless you can think of any reason—very serious reason— why I should not do so, I have decided to sell the estate. There will be a great deal of work to be done, but I leave that to you and your contacts. Robert? Are you still there? Yes, well, sooner the better. I think Felicity is coming back today, so do take notice of her advice, my dear. Very sensible girl, that one. What? Oh yes, all right. Hello, both of you! You want a pony? Take Grannie's advice, and have a guinea pig instead. Goodbye!"

Robert shooed the children into the kitchen to have their

breakfast, and postponed thinking about his mother's call until after he had taken them to school. But one thing stuck in his mind. Her voice had sounded strong and cheerful.

By the time Felicity arrived home in the late afternoon, Robert had already achieved a considerable amount towards putting Farnden Hall estate on the market. He had contacted an old school friend who was the senior partner in the most prestigious property agents in town, and set up an interview with him for tomorrow.

He had jotted down a list of clients who had made large profits in the past year, and had happened to mention they were planning to retire to the country. A surprising number nursed this ambition! One of them, he knew, coveted an estate in the Midlands that included a highly rated horse-racing course. Perhaps he could interest him in the idea of creating his own on the Farnden estate?

# EIGHTEEN

ॐ

THINGS WERE NOT GOING WELL AT HILLTOP FARM. HARRY had come home, tired and depressed by the poor prices fetched by his sheep at market, and found Gerald and Clive sitting in his big kitchen, warming their stockinged feet by his Rayburn turned up to full heat, and eating doorstop sandwiches they had made with the last of his home-cured ham.

"What the bloody hell do you think you two are doing here?" he had said. It was true he was very fond of Gladys, but for her two layabout sons he felt nothing but contempt. "*And*," he had continued, "how did you get in? No, don't answer that. Breaking and entering is what you're good at, isn't it? About all you *are* damn well good at!"

Now, six days later, they were still there. They had blackmailed him into allowing them to stay, saying that if he wouldn't cooperate, they would scupper for good his chances with their mother. They had even assured him that if he was friendly, they could persuade Gladys to see what an eligible bloke he was. "Harry and Gladys!" Gerald had said, laughing. "Got a kind of ring about it, ain't it, Clive?"

"And I believed him," muttered Harry to himself. He was out with his sheep on the empty moorland, with his faithful sheepdog, Jess, working instinctively as usual. She don't really need me, Harry thought as he watched her rounding up a ewe determined to run in the opposite direction.

Harry had taken to working out of the house as much as possible. Any suggestions he had made that the two might do some jobs around the farm had been received with mocking laughter. Then, last night, after he had said that it was time for them to leave, he had added that if they wouldn't go, he'd be forced to get the police.

An ominous silence had greeted this, and then Gerald had stood up and come very close to Harry. "I don't think so," he had hissed, and Harry saw a wicked-looking knife flash in his hand. Then he felt the point of it on his chest, and in terror he had raised his hands in surrender.

"All right!" he'd choked, "no need for that. Just let me know when you're ready to go."

Dark thoughts filled his head as he trudged back towards the farmhouse. He had to find a way out of this. He walked into the kitchen and found his two unwelcome guests playing cards and drinking his whiskey. When they ignored him completely, he made his way slowly upstairs.

In the silence of his room, he sat and thought for a long while, until finally he got into bed, hoping that sleep would come. Ten minutes later, he heard footsteps on the stairs, and shot across the room to lock his door. Just before midnight, still awake, he had a flash of inspiration. Many years ago, he had been a keen member of the local branch of the National Farmers Union, and had a good relationship with his neighbouring farmer, John Wilson. He had lost touch, but knew that John had remarried and had two strapping sons, both of whom were farming with him.

By "neighbouring," local people meant a good twenty miles away, down a narrow road that each winter was cut off by deep snow. But it was not winter yet, and tomorrow, Harry had thought, as he finally drifted off into sleep, I shall slip off without them two knowing, and pay a long overdue visit.

"You must be mad," Derek said as Lois announced at breakfast next morning that she was thinking of taking two or three days off and persuading Josie to go up to Yorkshire with her.

"Why *Yorkshire*?" said Gran. "What's wrong with Bognor?"

"Bugger Bognor," said Lois in the immortal last words of King George V of the United Kingdom.

"Well, really, Lois," Gran said. "There's no need to be offensive."

"But Gran's right," Derek said. "Why Yorkshire?"

"Because I've never been there," Lois said. "And nor, I'm pretty sure, has Josie. There's marvellous scenery and very nice people, and amazing ponies running wild, and plenty of things to see. York's got the Minster and the Railway Museum . . ."

"Hey, wait a minute!" Derek said. "You sound like a guidebook! What on earth would you want with the Railway Museum? Or wild ponies, for that matter?"

Lois flushed. "Are you saying we shouldn't go?" she said, and Derek recognised the warning signs of a challenge.

"Of course not. Go where you want. There don't seem much of a reason for Yorkshire, that's all. Have you asked Josie?"

"Not yet. But she could do with a break, after the thieving. She keeps up a brave face, but I know she was really shaken. And now there's the Norringtons been done over. Those thugs could come back here. Apparently a shop over the other side of Tresham was done twice in two weeks. Makes her nervous, I know."

"All right, you win," Derek said.

"So shall I manage the shop while you're away?" asked Gran hopefully.

"You can help Floss. She did well last time. Seemed to enjoy it. So I'll ask her again."

"When are you going?" Derek would not admit it, but he would not be comfortable until Lois was safely back. He did not wholly believe her reasons for going, suspecting that Cowgill would be behind it somewhere.

"Oh, I should think next week sometime. Dot Nimmo is looking up a good bed-and-breakfast place she knows up there. Maybe next Friday? Then we could come back on the Monday after the weekend. That should be long enough."

"Long enough for what?" snapped Derek.

"For a restful break, of course! Blimey, would I take Josie with me if I was heading for a dirty weekend? Honestly, Derek!"


"What, you again?" said Gladys Mowlem as she opened the door and saw Dot Nimmo standing on the step. "Haven't seen you for years, and then you keep turning up like a bad penny. To what do I owe the honour this time?" Gladys was beginning to suspect that Dot had an ulterior motive for her repeat visits. She was almost sure it had something to do with her boys. Well, she could keep Dot Nimmo at bay.

"I brought you this arnica cream stuff. Does wonders for bruises, so my sister Evelyn says. I reckon that tumble you took were really bad. Here, are you going to ask me in? I can tell you how to use the stuff."

Gladys held the door open wider, and reluctantly admitted Dot. It was kind of her to think of it, and she could certainly use something to take the soreness out of her bruises. "Come in the kitchen. I've just made a pot o' tea. Nice and strong. D'you want a cup?"

Dot bravely drank the tea, which, as she said later to Lois, was so strong the spoon could stand up on its own. She made it last, and steered the conversation skilfully back to Gladys's suitor in Yorkshire.

"You know you told me about that Harry of yours," she said. "That's been nigglin' away in my brain—what's left of it. I'm sure I knew 'im from way back. Was he ever a pal of my Handy?" Handel Nimmo, Dot's late husband, had had many friends, not all of them law-abiding citizens.

"Very likely. He knew all that lot at Tresham Technical. They were all in the same class, and were always in trouble. Harry's parents, Higgins they were called, won a lot o' money, and bought a farm up in Yorkshire. His dad's lifelong dream, Harry said. He were very unhappy himself. Had to leave all his school friends. They kept in touch, some of 'em."

"I suppose it was very different for Harry, up there in Yorkshire?"

"Different! I'll say it were different! Right in the middle of nowhere. High up on them moors, and the nearest town God knows how many miles away. Poor kid. It weren't fair."

"I went visitin' a place called Pickering once," said Dot casually. "I think that was Yorkshire. Gateway to the moors, they called it. Like going back a hundred years!"

"That was it! What a coincidence! Pickering—that were the name. I remember that because there's some people in Long Farnden of that name. Pickering, that was it. Not that poor little Harry saw much of the place. Stuck on the farm most of the time. Still, he settled, and now he wants me to settle with 'im! Not a chance, I said, last time he come down."

"You might like it, Gladys. Rich farmer, brand-new four-by-four for his lovely bride? A man to warm your bed. That's what I miss most," she said nostalgically.

"Electric blanket's just as good," Gladys said with a cackle. "Now, Dot Nimmo, you must have jobs to do. Thanks for bringing this stuff. I just rub it in, do I?"

She showed Dot to the door, and then returned to the kitchen, satisfied that she had let nothing slip that would harm the boys.

Dot parked up the road from the Mowlems' house and took out her mobile. "Mrs. M? We're getting close. Nearest town is Pickering, and Harry's name is Higgins. All we got to do now is look in the right phone book. D'you want me to do that? Oh, right, you do it on the computer, then. Let me know how you get on. I told Gladys I'd been to Pickering, and that was true. We stayed in a very clean bed-and-breakfast, I remember. I'll find out if it's still there." Dot was reluctant to be left out of the case, and cheered up when Lois said that would be very helpful. Soon as possible, she said.

# NINETEEN

❧

"OH, YES, AND I FORGOT TO TELL YOU, MUM RANG AND ASKED if I'd like to go up to Pickering in Yorkshire for two or three days. She thinks I need a break."

Josie and Matthew were sitting in his car outside the shop. They had seen a scary film in Tresham, the story of smash-and-grab thieves who left a trail of grief and disaster around the Southern states of America. Now she was putting off the moment when she had to go into the empty shop and her flat above.

"Why Yorkshire?" Matthew asked. He had been told by his chief inspector uncle to take seriously everything Lois Meade said. "She never wastes words," he had advised. "Except when she talks to that daft dog," Matthew had replied.

Josie shrugged. "You know our mum. Always up to something. But what she *said* was that Dot Nimmo recommended a nice bed-and-breakfast place, and that Pickering—

that's where it is—is a good jumping-off place for touring the moors."

"So are you going?"

"I don't think so. I don't feel happy about leaving the shop at the moment. You know, after the burglary and everything . . ."

"Mm. I think you're probably right," Matthew said, giving her a hug. "It's a bit soon. You'll just be fretting in case the thieves return. We've not caught up with those Mowlems yet." He thought for a moment, and then frowned. "Yorkshire, you said?"

"Yep. Pickering. Gateway to the moors."

"Right. Thanks. Now," he added, releasing her, "is coffee still on offer? We need to make a plan."

"A plan? What for? I'll just tell Mum I don't want to go with her. She'll go on her own quite happily."

"Even though the point of going was to give you a break?"

"Oh, yes. There'll be some other motive. Always is. Like when we went to the horse fair in Appleby. Come to think of it, that was pretty disastrous. I wouldn't want to repeat that!"

"Come on, then," Matthew said firmly. "Let's go in, and you can tell your mother in the morning. I'll hold your hand."

"So no early duty?"

Matthew nodded. "Oh, yes. Night duty. Guarding a vulnerable shopkeeper. Come on, in we go."

MATTHEW LEFT FOR WORK EARLY NEXT MORNING, AND JOSIE picked up the phone to speak to Lois. The sooner she let her know, the better. If her mother decided to go on her own, then there was certain to be an ulterior motive.

Me, too, Josie reflected. I have a secondary reason, but for not going. Lois's speedy driving was getting worrying. Perhaps we're all more aware of speeding. One of Josie's customers had been offered a speed awareness course, instead of points on her licence. She had been really shocked at how little she knew about regulations and warning signs. With Mum, Josie thought wryly, a couple of hours' driving at a smart seventy miles an hour, regardless of speed limits, traffic signs and built-up areas, the law must soon catch up with her, and Josie felt she would rather not be there. It might even be Matthew who had to follow her with all sirens blazing!

"Mum? Sorry I haven't got back to you sooner. Busy in the shop, and then a film with Matthew."

"I saw his car go by first thing," said Lois chattily. "Good film?"

"Scary. Anyway, it's the Pickering trip. I'm afraid the answer's no. I just don't feel like leaving the shop at the moment, and if those thugs did come back, it would be awful for Floss, and maybe even Gran. Thanks anyway for thinking of it. Matthew says he'll take me for a weekend to the coast later on."

"Bognor?" said Lois, disappointment in her voice.

"I dunno," replied Josie. "Why? Is it a nice place?"

"Never mind," said Lois. "Now, I must get on. Got to go over to see the Norringtons this morning. Finalise a few things with Andrew."

Josie began to fill shelves in the shop. She could hardly bear to pile up cigarettes. Every time she bought new supplies, they reminded her of that horrible man. Maybe she would stop selling cigarettes and lighter fuel and roll-your-own papers. It'd be a kindness to her smoking customers, wouldn't it? On the other hand, it wouldn't stop them smoking. They'd just go elsewhere, and probably not come into her shop at all. The door opened and Derek appeared. "Morning, love," he said.

"Hi, Dad! What are you doing here so early?"

"Just come to tell you not to worry about saying no to going to Yorkshire on this mad trip of your mother's. It'll be all right. She says she needs the break and will go on her own. So I'm going, too."

"You? Blimey! What did Mum say to that?"

"She doesn't know yet. But I'm sure she'll be delighted." He grinned, blew Josie a kiss and left the shop.

Good old dad, Josie thought. He'll probably drive, and that'll be one more week she'll stay out of the nick.

ANDREW SAT BESIDE LOIS IN HER VAN, AND HELD ON TIGHT TO his seat. Wow! Next time he would offer her a lift in *his* car. They drew into the curving drive leading to the Norringtons' house, and parked by the side gate.

"We're a bit early," Lois said. "Better wait for a minute or two. Have you got the papers ready?" Andrew had wanted to forget about the whole thing, but Lois insisted that he should charge for the work he had already done, planning the décor. She had said she would like to come with him, partly to give moral support, and partly to ask a few tactful questions about the burglary. She was angry all over again about the theft in Josie's shop. Now the poor girl would not leave it, in case they should come back. She would catch those two scumbags if it was the last thing she did!

She looked at her watch. Just on ten o'clock. "Come on, then, Andrew. Let's go and sort them out."

Geoff Norrington answered the door. He had stayed at

home, saying that Melanie should leave the talking to him. He intended to pay them as little as possible, he said. After all, in his line of business, they tendered for jobs all the time, and didn't expect to be compensated if they didn't get the contract. Melanie protested that they hadn't put this job out for tender, but had given the commission to Andrew straightaway. There was nothing wrong with his designs, and it wasn't his fault that she could not bear to live in the house for longer than necessary.

Lois looked at Geoff, smartly turned out in his city suit and old school tie. Which old school? she wondered. And what about those shoes!

"Good morning, Mr. Norrington. I hope we're not late," she said, smiling confidently.

"Come in," said Geoff bluntly. "I haven't got long. But this shouldn't take long, should it? How much do you want?"

They were still standing in the hall, and Lois began to wonder whether there would be any chance of having a discussion leading naturally to the subject of the burglary. She was rescued by a shout from Melanie in the kitchen.

"Come on in, Andrew! And Mrs. Meade, too. Coffee's ready. Have you got time for a cup, Geoff?"

He returned reluctantly to the drawing room, leaving Lois and Andrew to follow behind. "Sit down, then," he said, making it sound more like an order than an invitation. "Got your invoice?" he continued, holding out his hand.

"Oh, Geoff! Coffee first, then business," Melanie said, coming in with a tray of coffee. "Now then, black or white, Mrs. Meade?"

Lois looked around the room. It was only the second time she had seen it, although Andrew had shown her his plans. It was a lovely room, with long windows looking out into the garden. Not a weed in sight.

"You must be sorry to leave, Mrs. Norrington," she said. "Such a lovely house." It was then that she noticed the newspaper spread out on the long coffee table. It was open at property pages. "So have you found somewhere else to go that would suit you better?"

Melanie looked at Geoff. "Well, yes and no," she said, picking up the High Life section of the *Tresham Advertiser*. "Look, have you seen this? Just what we're looking for!"

"Not what I'm looking for," grunted Geoff. "Melanie's joking, of course."

Lois took the newspaper section and looked at the ads for country properties. "Oh my!" she said. "That was quick!" She handed it to Andrew.

"Goodness!" he said. "This is going to rock the village!" He began to read the advertisement aloud: "Long Farnden Hall and estate. Mrs. Tollervey-Jones has instructed Lord & Francis to act on her behalf in the sale of, et cetera, et cetera, et cetera."

# TWENTY

❧

HALF AN HOUR LATER, DISCUSSION IN THE NORRINGTONS' drawing room had turned to desirable residences, and one house in particular. Both Lois and Andrew had known that the sale of Farnden Hall was in the cards, but Lois was astonished by the speed with which Mrs. Tollervey-Jones had made up her mind and set the sale in motion.

"I expect it will be in all the posh mags," Melanie was saying. "I asked Geoff to bring some home, but he only grunted that the partics wouldn't be in until next month. I reckon that if we show our interest straightaway, we stand a chance of getting a good deal."

"Perhaps it is a tiny bit beyond your price range? And won't you want to view it thoroughly, get some expert advice?" said Andrew delicately. He was calculating rapidly just how many rooms at the hall would need the attentions of an interior decorator.

"To tell you the truth, Andrew," Melanie said, "I have absolutely no idea what our price range would be. Geoff is like an old tortoise as far as money is concerned. Keeps everything under his shell! All I do know is that if my husband sets his heart on something, he always gets it."

Lois thought to herself that it was clearly Melanie's heart that was set on it, but she contented herself with supporting Andrew and offering New Brooms' help in any way possible. "And of course," she added, "if you should take over the estate, we have years of experience working there, and could be very useful to you at reasonable rates. After all, you're almost old customers yourselves!"

As she and Andrew drove back to Farnden, Lois cautioned against too much optimism. "I can't think that Geoff Norrington would have that much lolly," she said. "It'll go for millions. Surely they would be living somewhere grander already, if he had?"

"You can't tell, Mrs. M. They could have just won millions on the lottery. It happens!"


AT LUNCH, LOIS BROKE THE NEWS TO GRAN AND DEREK, and although they and many people in the village were expecting it, they felt some shock at seeing it in black and white in the newspaper. It had been a brief early announcement from estate agents Lord & Francis, saying that this highly desirable property would be on the market, and giving details where further information could be obtained.

"This will keep the gossips going for months," Derek said. "Josie should see an upturn in trade. Everybody goes into the shop for the latest local news. Oh, and by the way," he added, "talking of Josie, as she can't come with you to Yorkshire, I've decided to have a miniholiday with you instead. Can't remember the last time we went away together!"

There was a noticeably muted reaction from Lois at this item of news. But Gran went overboard in encouraging the plan. "Everything will be fine here with me," she said. "And you won't have to make no arrangements for the shop. What a good idea, Derek! Don't you agree, Lois?"

"Well, yes. But Derek, aren't you in the middle of that job over in Fletching? You can't leave those people without the electric. Aren't they expecting to move in next week?"

"Nearly finished," he replied happily. "Now, when shall we go? Today's Thursday, so how about Saturday and come back Tuesday? We could start early, and then have Sunday and Monday full days, then leave after breakfast Tuesday? What d'you say?"

"Um, right. Okay. I'll have to get Hazel to take the Monday meeting. Are you sure you want to come, though, Derek?"

"Quite sure. So off you go and book a double room at that bed-and-breakfast place Dot was recommending."

Lois hadn't seen him so masterful in years. What had triggered off this new Derek? Suspicion, she decided. He thinks I'm going up there with Hunter Cowgill. She had a sudden vision of herself and the tall, elegant figure of Cowgill marching beside her across the moors, stopping at remote inns by the wayside . . .

"Lois! Are you listening?" Gran was standing over her, offering her second helpings of rice pudding. "Do you want it or not?"

"No thanks, Mum. That'll be great, Derek," she added firmly. "And we'll take Jeems. She'd love it, speeding across the moors. That's what her ancestors were used for. They hunted otters out of their hiding places in stone cairns."

"Fancy that!" Gran said. "You see, Lois. Derek is really interested in nature an' that these days. You can borrow your dad's binocliers to see the birds. He was very proud of those."

"Yes, well, maybe. It might rain all the time we're there. Even Derek with his great love of nature won't want to trudge about in wet clothes. There's plenty of undercover things to do, though." And so there would be, with luck. Undercover work was what she was about, and now she had to decide how to use Derek without him knowing.

LOIS PLANNED AN AFTERNOON IN HER STUDY, DECIDING WHAT SHE wanted to find out in Pickering. She could do a lot on the computer, but with limited time and Derek in tow, it was not going to be easy. She had to find Harry Higgins and—with luck— the Mowlem brothers. Then she could report back to Cowgill with something definite for the police to follow up. She was well aware that there could be dangers in this plan. She would be looking for a remote farm on the moors, with two thugs and an elderly farmer, and no neighbours to call on. She began to think Derek's presence would be a considerable bonus.

The telephone rang ten minutes after Lois had settled down in front of her computer. It was Dot Nimmo, and she had a suggestion to make.

"I bin thinking, Mrs. M. You and me have worked together in the past on some of your ferretin' cases. Do you reckon it might be a good idea if I came to Pickering with you? I can remember quite a lot about it, and two heads are better'n one. I know you were thinking of taking your Josie, but she's had a nasty shock, and you could easily run into trouble up there. You know I married into the criminal fraternity an' I know their ways."

This was a long speech for Dot Nimmo, and Lois considered it seriously. She could see the sense in Dot's suggestion, and said she'd think about it and ring her back this evening.

WHEN DEREK RETURNED TO HIS JOB IN FLETCHING, HE WAS DISmayed to come across a problem that he had not anticipated. The new owners of the house were not yet moved in, and he came and went as he wished. They had given him a key, and this arrangement suited him very well. Much better than having irritating housewives offering him cups of tea every five minutes.

Now he sat back on his heels and realised that the wiring upstairs would need complete renewing. He had been hoping that it was just one bedroom, but now knew that it would not be a good job and could be trouble later on. He could not risk his reputation, and so faced the fact that he could not be finished in time to go with Lois on Saturday. Perhaps she could postpone her trip to Yorkshire? There did not seem to be any urgency, as far as he could see.

He looked at his watch. Lois would need to know today. She was probably already booking the bed-and-breakfast accommodation and planning trips around Pickering. He should ring her right now, but perhaps half an hour wouldn't make much difference. If he could think of another solution, he could avoid a tussle with her which he knew he would lose. This latest development would give Lois the perfect excuse to go on her own.

# Twenty-One

## ❧

"BUT I'VE ARRANGED EVERYTHING!" LOIS SAID. DEREK HAD suddenly appeared in the middle of the afternoon and told her that they would have to postpone the Pickering trip. She was just about to phone Dot and tell her that it wouldn't be possible this time, but that it had been a really good idea, when Derek himself had turned up.

"There's nothing that can't be unarranged, surely," he said now. "If you let the landlady know at once, it'll be okay, especially if we book another date. And you'll be able to be at the Monday meeting as usual. Doesn't seem too difficult to me."

"Well, it does to me. I have a busy schedule, as you know, and I'd already sorted out all of that. And anyway, Dot Nimmo phoned earlier and offered to come with me. I know she's been a bit low lately, so she can come instead."

"Dot *Nimmo?*" Derek knew that this particular member of the New Brooms team was unpredictable and apt to make her own irregular decisions. In fact, he often thought Lois should consider replacing her. She had some very dodgy connections. "Are you sure about that, Lois?"

She looked at his worried face, and felt a moment's pang of guilt. But only a moment. She thought of Josie and the two thieves, and said firmly that she was quite sure. Dot could be good company, and she knew the area. "You know I'd rather it was you, but we can have a weekend at Bognor later, maybe."

Derek knew when he was beaten. It would be useless to argue, so he reluctantly agreed and said he felt much the same as George V about Bognor, and he would think about somewhere different for a minibreak very soon.

"Dot, is that you?" Lois couldn't be sure. The voice sounded as if was coming from underwater. "Where are you?"

"In the bath," Dot said, spluttering. "Sorry, I nearly dropped me mobile. Sorry about that. Made up y'mind, have you?"

"Yes. Derek was coming with me, but he's got a problem on a job he's doing. So if you're still keen, I'll fix it up. We have to go on Saturday, back Tuesday. That should give us plenty of time to look around. But we have to keep our heads down, too. Just a couple of women friends having a few days' break. So no loud voice in cafés an' that."

"As if I would!" said Dot. "I'm really looking forward to it. An' don't you worry about the expenses. Handy made sure I'd always have reserves."

"I wasn't worrying. So listen, Dot." Lois outlined her plan of action once they arrived in Pickering, and Dot managed to keep quiet and not interrupt. She offered to drive, but Lois said no, they'd go in the van. But then Dot pointed out that if they went in a van emblazoned with the words "We sweep cleaner," they would not exactly be keeping their heads down. "We might as well take an ad in the local paper announcin' our arrival!" So Lois reluctantly agreed.

LITTLE DID DOT KNOW HOW RIGHT SHE WAS. GERALD AND CLIVE Mowlam drove into Pickering most days, sussing out likely-looking premises where a lightning visit in the middle of the night might not be noticed. They already had a small cache of interesting articles stashed away at the back of one of Harry's barns. It was the one where he brought in the old bull for the winter, and the boys reckoned nobody was going to bypass this great animal to look in boxes at the back of the pen. No intruder would know that old Buster was past caring about anything other than a regular supply of grub. Harry knew, of course, but that didn't matter.

They had changed their appearance in small ways. Gerald looked for all the world like a pirate, with his black hair and an infant black beard, and Clive had let his hair grow long, sometimes anchoring it in an elderly hippy–type ponytail. But they were canny enough to maintain a careful lookout whenever in the town. They could spot a plainclothes police-man a mile away, and a sighting of the familiar New Brooms van would have sent them scurrying for cover.

This evening, Harry had once more asked them when they were thinking of leaving. His visit to John Wilson, his neigh-bour, had had to be postponed, as the poor chap was in hospi-tal, having had a serious spinal operation. He would not be home for some time. So Harry had tried to settle down with the idea that he had two unpleasant lodgers whom he would avoid as much as possible. He even opened up the front parlour—only ever used for special occasions, and smelling of damp and mothballs—and lit a fire there every evening. He did not encourage company, and picked up a secondhand television set off the market. It was old, black-and-white, and did not tempt Gerald and Clive to join him.

But as Harry tramped back across the moor, Jess by his side, resentment had risen again, and he decided to try a bit of pressure. Now entering the kitchen, he said, "I've had a call from my cousin Jack. He wants to come and stay for a bit. Keen on hiking. He'd have a couple of friends with him. They're all in the Yorkshire constabulary, and taking a holiday before the winter sets in."

Gerald and Clive stared at him. Then Gerald began to laugh. Soon Clive joined in, until Gerald stopped abruptly and got up from his chair. He came close to Harry, and pointed his finger at the spot where the knife had threatened. "Nice try, Harry boy," he said. "Now you go and watch *Blue Peter*, and give us a bit o' peace. We've had a busy day."

"Right," said Harry quickly. "I'll let them know. But I can't stop them calling if they're walking by. You'll just have to be prepared to risk it."

Gerald pointed to an empty chair. "Sit down, Harry, and listen," he said. "If any members of the Yorkshire constabulary find their way here, and call in to see you, you will never utter a word again. We'll make sure of that. Oh no, we shan't kill you—yet—but there'll be a nasty accident. Farm accidents are common. Bits of machinery flying off and cutting through legs and arms—and throats. Months in hospital, probably. But don't worry, Harry boy, we'll look after the farm for yer. And Jess here will help, I'm sure. If not, we'll have to get a replacement, won't we, Clive? Sheepdogs are vital on these moorland farms."

Harry fled from the room, closely followed by Jess, and shut himself in the parlour, locking the door behind him. He was trembling violently, and then something Gerald had said struck him forcefully. There was still a way out. "And it will all depend on you, Jessie love," he said, fondling her ears.

# TWENTY-TWO

ᘐ

ROBERT TOLLERVEY-JONES HAD DISCUSSED WITH FELICITY late into the night the sale of Farnden Hall. Now, still at home after taking the children to school, he called the office and told them he would be in by midday.

To Felicity, he said, "I should ring Mother this morning, don't you think? That's what we agreed, didn't we? To be honest, darling, it was so late I can't remember all of it!"

"I can," said Felicity. "You are going to suggest you take over all the preliminary contacts with two or three major estate agents, stressing the need for speed, and then present their reports and proposals to Mother for her to decide who shall handle the sale."

Robert grimaced. "She won't wear it, you know. She'll want to be in on everything, right from the beginning."

"Well, it's worth a try," Felicity said, handing him the phone.

*　　*　　*

MRS. TOLLERVEY-JONES HAD ALSO BEEN AWAKE UNTIL THE SMALL hours. This was the biggest decision of her life, and she was well aware that had she been twenty years younger, it would have been a great deal easier. When she did finally fall asleep, she dreamed that generations of Tollervey-Joneses arose from the dead and dragged her screaming to the duck pond to drown her for a witch.

She had awoken fighting her way out from under the duvet, and been relieved to hear the despised pigeons cooing the advent of daylight.

Now she picked up the phone, and was grateful for the sound of her son's voice. She was not, however, so amiably disposed towards him when he made his proposal. "Good gracious, no, Robert! I must be in charge at every step. As for choosing an agent for the sale, that is no problem. Your late Aunt Katherine married a Francis from Lord & Francis. Very old and reputable agents, with branches everywhere. Very used to dealing with sales of country estates. I have already been in touch. Extremely nice young man. Knowledgeable and from a good family. I explained everything, and he is coming here tomorrow. Eleven o'clock. Can you be here?"

Back on form, thought Robert. "Hey, Mother, hold on!" he said. "Wouldn't it be wiser to ask a couple of other agents to submit competitive reports? That is the usual way."

"I am not the usual client. I want this whole business to be completed as soon as possible. Do try to be here tomorrow. I am perfectly capable of managing, as you know, but . . ." She hesitated, and Robert said quickly that of course he would be there.

"Perhaps I'll come down this evening, when we can have a preliminary chat," he suggested.

"Not necessary, dear," she said. "I have everything at my fingertips. Goodbye now. Oh, and love to Felicity and the children. Goodbye."

Felicity looked at his face, and could not help smiling. "So?" she said.

"She's got everything at her fingertips," he said glumly. "I'm to be in Farnden at eleven o'clock tomorrow for a meeting with Lord & Francis. Aunt Katherine married a Francis, apparently."

Felicity raised her eyebrows. "Then of course that is settled," she said. "One fewer decision to make. Thank your lucky stars she's still extremely sharp."

"I suggested going down tonight. But she pooh-poohed that idea."

"Just as well, Robert! It's the school's choral concert this evening. You can't have forgotten? All that singing around the house for weeks?"

"What? You mean *Jeeesus Christ, Soooper Star?*" Robert broke into song, but Felicity was not impressed.

"Yes, and we have to be there, come hell or high water. Now, shouldn't you be going?"


"Is that Mrs. Meade?"

"Good morning, Mrs. Tollervey-Jones. Are you feeling better?"

"I am perfectly well, thank you. Now, I need some help here tomorrow. I have a very important meeting at eleven o'clock, and I shall need someone to be in the kitchen and so on for the rest of the day. Estate agents are coming down for preliminaries, and no doubt they'll be expecting lunch and sundry other refreshments during the day. It would be perfect if Paula and Floss could help out. I am prepared to pay a little more for weekend rates."

"No need," said Lois. "We shall be delighted to help an old and valued customer."

"There will be two of them. And of course, my son Robert will be here."

"Oh, that's good," said Lois sympathetically. She might have saved her breath, since Mrs. T-J replied that she expected him to return by an early train. "With the girls helping in the house, we shall be more than capable," she said, making it clear that Robert was only a minor figure in this whole enterprise.

Poor Robert, thought Lois. A bit like Prince Charles. Always the bridesmaid, never the bride. Never to be master of Farnden Hall. Still, from what she had seen of his wife, Felicity, they were a thoroughly urban family, happily settled in London and likely to remain there.

By the time she had called Paula and Floss, and shuffled the rota to accommodate Mrs. Tollervey-Jones, it was lunchtime, and she followed the appetising smell of cottage pie through to the kitchen.

"Any help needed?" she said. Gran replied that the offer was a bit late. Everything was ready and waiting for Derek to come home.

"But he took sandwiches. Needed every hour of the day to finish the job by Monday, he said."

Gran shrugged. "I told him it would be on the table at one, and left it at that. We shall see."

"But I made him delicious ham and pickle sandwiches!"

"We shall see," Gran repeated.

On the dot of one, Derek appeared. "Hi, girls," he said as he came into the kitchen. Lois greeted him with a stony face.

"I shall be going into Tresham this afternoon," she said. "I need new walking boots for going to Pickering, and then I'll call in to see Hazel in the office. She says we have a couple of new clients to see."

"Ah," said Derek. "I've just remembered. That Norrington chap, where Andrew was going to do some decorating and stuff. He must have recognised my van, and came looking for me. He asked me to give you a message. Said he might have a large contract for you in due course, and wants to come and discuss it with you."

"Why didn't he ring?"

"Saving money, I suppose."

"If it's Farnden Hall he's talking about, he should be able to afford a phone call. Anyway, I'll give him a ring. Thanks, Derek. More cottage pie?"

FOR THE REST OF THE DAY, MRS. TOLLERVEY-JONES WENT through all the papers her husband had kept so methodically in his study. She had had no reason to disturb them since his death, apart from extracting his will, which had been meticulously prepared by solicitors many years ago. It had been unusually straightforward in many ways. The estate had been left to her in its entirety, with provisos for Robert and other members of the family, and restrictions on what could be done with the tenanted farms in the event that the estate should be sold. It had plainly been in Mr. Tollervey-Jones's mind that this was a very unlikely eventuality. He had a son, and it did not occur to him that in due course he would not want to carry on running the estate.

She set out all the relevant files on the large desk, which was, on Mrs. Tollervey-Jones's instructions, regularly dusted and polished by New Brooms. Since Paula had started work at the hall, a small vase of flowers had appeared each week on the desk. Mrs. Tollervey-Jones had said nothing, but smiled. Her late husband had suffered terribly from allergies of all kinds, and could not bear the scent of flowers anywhere near him.

John Thornbull, husband of Hazel, who managed the Tresham New Brooms office, held the tenancy of one of the two farms, and retired workers from the estate occupied three small cottages. Details of their secure tenancies were carefully detailed, and all seemed to be in order for the arrival of Lord & Francis tomorrow morning. There was even a yellowing, ragged old map showing the boundaries of the estate, and as far as Mrs. T-J could see, nothing much had changed for generations.

"LUCKY FOR YOU, LOIS, THAT PAULA AND FLOSS CAN DO TOMORrow," Derek said when he came home for tea. "No chance of you filling in, like you usually do." He was still sore over Lois's determination to go off tomorrow with Dot Nimmo to Pickering. "I should have thought it would be just up your street," he added acidly, "eavesdropping on such an important meeting. Who knows what you might have picked up?"

"Not a lot on who were the two thugs who beat you up!" Lois was stung. Derek was not usually so nasty. Now he pounced.

"Ah, so *that's* why you're off to Yorkshire, is it? Might have known it wasn't just a treat for Dot Nimmo. I didn't approve before, Lois, and I don't approve even more now. Those high moors are dangerous places! Supposing the car breaks down and you're miles from anywhere."

"And it begins to snow, an' a great black dog comes howling through the blizzard, showing its huge teeth and baying for blood. Oh, come on, Derek. They didn't have mobile phones in Sherlock Holmes's day, but I'll make sure Dot's and mine are charged up."

Gran was grinning. "I should give up, if I were you, Derek," she said.

"You're not me, an' I'm her husband and head of the family, and if I thought it would do any good at all, I'd forbid them to go."

# Twenty-Three

⤜

D OT DREW UP OUTSIDE LOIS'S HOUSE, HOOTING LOUDLY AND waving madly, at eight o'clock sharp.

"The silly woman'll wake the neighbourhood," Derek said, taking Lois's bag from her to carry out to the car. He put it in the boot, slammed the door shut and stood glowering at them from the pavement.

"Morning, Dot! Punctual as ever!" Lois said, smiling broadly to make up for Derek's sour expression.

"And 've got me a Satnav," Dot said proudly. "But you'll have to programme it, or whatever you do. I can't say I shall trust it, so there's a map book in the back there, just in case."

Lois turned to give Derek a hug and a kiss, but he was halfway up the drive to the house. "Bye!" she yelled. "I'll give you a call when we get there." He waved dismissively without turning round, and Dot glanced at Lois. "All right to go, then, Mrs. M?" she said.

"The truth is that Derek is not too happy about our going

off into the unknown. But he'll come round. He always does, bless him," said Lois.

"I saw old Hunter Cowgill yesterday," said Dot, as if the two things were unconnected. "He stopped me in the street and said I should move my car off the double yellow line if I didn't want yet more points on my licence. He's a nice man, deep underneath! Asked after you, of course," she added slyly.

Lois changed the subject. "Now then, you know the way to Tresham, so I'll get busy setting the Satnav. Do you want a man's voice or woman's?"

"Man's, of course. Nice to have a man in my car again. Not that my Handy knew the way to anywhere! No sense of direction, that man."

"You must miss him, Dot," Lois said, suddenly aware of a change in their relationship. With Dot at the wheel, about to share a few days with her, they could no longer be boss and team cleaner. "And then you lost your son in that dreadful accident. Not a good time for you, one way and another."

"In a funny way, and I wouldn't say this to nobody else, Mrs. M, I miss my Handy more than our son, Haydn. He was slow, as you know, and somehow always in trouble. Handy used to say he weren't quite slow enough. Backward, we used to call it. People thought he was cleverer than he was, an' that was half the trouble."

"Right!" said Lois briskly, sensing that Dot's spirits were sinking. "We're ready to go now. Ready to receive instructions?" She touched the small screen, and a ribbon of road began to disappear as they went along. Then the voice said, "At the next roundabout, take the third exit," and Dot's face was a study.

"Cor! Does he hear me if I answer?"

"No, but you can answer anyway. I have conversations with my Prudence."

"Okay then. Message received, um, um, Beethoven!"

"Well, go on then, take the third exit," said Lois, chuckling as they approached the roundabout.

"So I'd better be off to work, Gran," Derek said, pulling out yesterday's sandwiches from his bag, and then putting them back in again. "These'll be fine for me today," he said as Gran took a loaf from the bread tin ready to start cutting. "I hope that Dot Nimmo will remember to take a break now and then. Nothing worse than losing concentration at the wheel."

"Lois will see she does," Gran said comfortingly. "Now don't you worry, Derek. They're a tough pair. And Lois has inherited my good common sense, thank heavens. Her father had none at all, you know? I spent all my time squashing his rash ideas! O' course, he said Lois took after him, but I didn't agree. Not then anyway," she added darkly.

"Great," said Derek, thinking nobody knew better than Gran how to put their foot in it.

Lois and Dot chatted easily as they drove steadily up the A1 north. "I like this road better than the M1 motorway," Dot said. "It's got more things to look at. And lots of history," she said. "Highwaymen, holding up coaches and demanding yer money or yer life!"

They approached the now much-modernised Ram Jam Inn, and Dot said she remembered her dad taking her fishing nearby when she was about six. "We went with me Uncle Charlie," she said. "It rained cats and dogs all day, and we just sat there on the riverbank. Never caught a single fish!"

"Not all day?"

"Nope. They packed up around teatime, and took me to the Ram Jam. They were really nice there. Dried me off, and we 'ad scones and jam and cream, and a huge pot of scaldin' hot tea. Funny how things come back to yer, ain't it? It didn't look nothing like this, o' course," she added as they parked. "Still, they might do us a toasted teacake an' a cup of coffee."

Settled by a wood fire, they tucked in. Leaning back in her chair, Dot said they'd made a good start, anyway. "Mrs. M?" She could see Lois frowning and staring across the room. "You seen somebody?"

Lois shrugged. "Dunno," she said. "That bloke over by the window, on his own. I reckon I've seen him before somewhere."

"Not me," said Dot. "Complete stranger. Maybe he's on the telly? Could be you seen him in something?"

"Maybe," Lois said. She looked closely at Dot. "You didn't happen to tell Cowgill about our little trip, did you?"

"Me? O' course not, Mrs. M," Dot said, crossing her fingers out of sight under the table. "I'm not that daft."

Beethoven took them safely on towards Pickering, and found Ourome, the bed-and-breakfast where they were to stay. Dot drove in and admired the immaculate little house on the outskirts of Pickering. "Looks clean anyway," she said. "Oh, look, there's Mrs. Silverman in the garden. Leastways, I guess that's her. Yoo-hoo! It's us, here at last!" she called, and Lois wondered whether Dot was capable of keeping her head down, whatever the circumstances.

# Twenty-Four

❧

Thomas Truelove and Adam Goldman, rising stars in Lord & Francis, arrived in Farnden village well before the time of their appointment with Mrs. Tollervey-Jones, and stopped outside the shop. Adam went in to buy a newspaper and a couple of bars of dark chocolate for Thomas. "Addicted to it," he had said to Adam. "See if they've got Green and Black's."

"I suppose you haven't got Green and Black's?" Adam said to Josie, not meaning to sound patronising, but doing so nevertheless.

Josie replied huffily that she always kept a good stock, as the vicar could not write his sermon without it. She wondered what these two young men in their discreetly luxurious Jaguar were doing in Farnden, but her attention was taken by a troupe of infants brought into the shop by their teacher to buy coloured pencils and improve their money-handling skills. As their eyes were permanently fixed on sweets and they did not care a fig for coloured pencils, Josie often wondered whether the lesson stuck.

"Well done, Adam. Have a square?" Thomas said, breaking into the chocolate. "Might as well sit here and go through what we know already."

"One thing I have to confess," Adam said, colouring in embarrassment. "I've discovered my family has a distant connection with the Tollerveys way back. I suppose I should declare an interest?"

Thomas laughed. "Up to you. William Drew could take over, if you prefer. It may be best. I'm afraid there's no possibility of you being in line for the estate! All looks pretty straightforward otherwise, as far as I can see. Did you remember to bring the post?"

Adam leafed through obvious junk mail, opened one or two letters relating to other properties and then examined an unfamiliar envelope. "It's postmarked Tresham," he said, at once curious. "I wonder who it's from?"

"One way to find out. Open it."

Adam extracted the letter and frowned. "Don't know the name. Somebody called Norrington. He wants to make an appointment regarding the sale of Farnden Hall. Looking urgently for a property of this kind, he says. Suggests next week, early in the week."

"Really? The name's not familiar. Better see what we can find out about him when we get back."

"We should be moving on," Adam said, looking at his watch. They were exactly on time, the clock in the little family chapel behind the trees striking eleven as they drove through the gates. "Right, here we are," said Thomas. "I'll go slowly up the drive, so's we can get the feel of the place. Wants it sold quickly, did the old girl say? Good time of the year for the photographs. Just look at the colour of those beeches! Wonderful. Shouldn't take long to move this one, Adam. If not to Mr. Norrington, there are plenty of other likely buyers on our list."

ROBERT HAD ARRIVED EARLIER, THINKING HIS MOTHER MIGHT need some support. They sat now in the drawing room, staring out at the approaching car. "It's not too late to change your mind, Mother," he said, seeing her hands gripped tightly in her lap.

"You should know by now, my son," she said with a slight quaver in her voice, "that once I have made up my mind, I never change it. Robert, they're coming to the front. Just go and tell them to park around the back, in the stable yard."

"Tradesmen's entrance, Mother?" Robert said, grinning.

"Just go," said Mrs. T-J magisterially.

Robert disappeared, and Paula put her head around the door. "Will you ring for coffee when you're ready?" she said. "Me and Floss have got it all ready." She felt important this morning, as if at the hub of a major change in Farnden society. Speculation in the village was rife, and a number of locals were dreading that the old house would be bought by new money, wealthy foreigners or pop stars who would hold wild parties.

"It'll be the end of the feudal system in this village, I reckon," Floss said to Paula when she returned to the kitchen. "It is amazing how it's lingered on, isn't it? Most people look up to the old duck as a kind of matriarch up at the big house. Mind you, Paula, she encourages that. But nobody can say she hasn't done a huge amount for the village in her time. They'll miss her on the magistrates bench when she retires."

Floss laid out coffeepot, cups and saucers, brown sugar lumps and cream.

"No biscuits?" said Paula.

Floss shook her head. "Not the done thing," she said.

"What about the parish council? She's practically glued to the chairman's chair. Been there for years, hasn't she?"

"Not sure about that. There's probably an age limit for staying on. They'll be a pretty hopeless lot without her, I should say. There's something about these old families," Floss said. She was fond of Mrs. T-J. They had a love of horses in common, and Floss never found it difficult to talk frankly to her.

"What? You mean they were bred to govern?" said Paula, laughing. "I don't know what my Jack would say about that. He's a longtime socialist, you know."

"Well, he's happy enough to work for Mrs. T-J in the garden. Been really helpful to her, so she says. I suppose his job will be at risk, once the sale gets going."

Paula frowned. "Don't say that! He's had a hard time, and he loves coming up here. And most of the time he don't take anything for the hours he puts in. Says it's peaceful and full of echoes of grander years. Did you know they used to have peaches and apricots in the greenhouse and prepare trugs full of vegetables to take into the kitchen for the cook? Mrs. Tollervey-Jones told him that years ago the gardener's boy would bring in a bunch of herbs neatly tied with string alongside the veg. Must have been a lovely way of life. If you were rich," she added.

The drawing room bell over the kitchen door rang. "Time for coffee," Floss said. "Do you want to take it in?"

"Wouldn't mind," said Paula. "I can tell Jack how the other half lives," she added, smiling at Floss.

In the drawing room, the preliminary introductions had been made, and Robert stood by the door to help Paula with the coffee tray. She put it down on the table and had no idea whether she should stay and pour out, or leave it for Mrs. Tollervey-Jones. Kindly Robert had noticed her dilemma. "Won't you pour for us?" he said. This saved Paula having to say, "Shall I be Mother?"—which was what they always said at home.

"And I'm sure we can manage some biscuits, Paula," said Mrs. T-J.

IN THEIR MUCH LESS HISTORIC DRAWING ROOM IN FLETCHING, the Norringtons were poring over back numbers of *The Field* magazine, comparing large houses, with or without estates, to get some idea of comparative prices.

"We can *never* afford this kind of money!" Melanie said. "I don't know why we are looking."

"Do you want to go for Farnden Hall or not?" said Geoff.

"It'd be my dream house," she replied. "But it *is* a dream, isn't it?"

He looked at her over the top of his glasses. "I want it, Melanie. And as you know, I always get what I want." Except for children, if we don't count one or two illegitimate ones, he added to himself with a grin.

"I've done all the calculations, and I reckon we could do it. I'd have to develop the estate, of course. Turn it into a money-making enterprise. But that could be a real challenge for both of us. Wouldn't you like to be lady of the manor? I must say I can see you happily taking it on."

"But would we be accepted?" she said hesitantly. "You know, by the people working on the estate already? And the village people? They're a snobby lot, so I've heard. Would we be really happy living such a different life?"

"It'd be what we make of it. I'm not looking to be another huntin', shootin' and fishin' squire."

"But those things could earn us money," Melanie said, suddenly full of enthusiasm. "We could get the pheasant shoot going again, let out fishing permits for the lake, have the first meet of the hunt here, so's you could get to know some good business connections. Oh, Geoff, is it really possible?"

"I've asked for an appointment with the agents next week, so we shall see."

"I expect it'll be months before things can be settled," Melanie said.

"Not if what I've heard is right. The old dear has run out of money apparently. Needs to sell as quickly as possible. The agents will pull out all the stops. It's amazing what they can do when there's a few million at stake. We might even get it at a good price. Leave all that side of things to me, sweetie. Now, I must be off. I need to get a haircut in town. Can't go to Lord & Francis looking like a spiv!"

# TWENTY-FIVE

～

Lois and Dot had unpacked their small cases, downed strong hot cups of tea with Mrs. Silverman and then announced their intention of walking into town to have a good look around. "We've got a couple of hours before everything shuts up," Dot said.

"Where should we go first, Mrs. Silverman?"

"There's a nice museum, and the church is very interesting," she said. "Or you could just wander where the fancy takes you. Plenty of lovely old houses and public buildings. You could go on the steam railway tomorrow. We're a very historic town, you know. Here," she added, going to a table in the corner of the lounge, "here's a few leaflets to help you choose. You're not here for long, so you'll not want to waste your time."

Dot and Lois glanced through the leaflets. Dot said she'd like to see round the shops, and Lois said perhaps they could have a quick look in the church first. She was aware that this was supposed to be a treat for Dot, but wherever she went, she loved to look at the church and its surrounding grave-yard, feeling closer to the people and their lives and deaths than in a carefully planned museum. She was also aware that few people shared her enthusiasm.

"The church?" said Dot unbelievingly. "What d'you want to see that for? One church is much like another, Mrs. M. No, you come along with me, and we'll explore. I expect we'll be going up to them moors tomorrow?" She winked at Lois, who said they'd have to see what the weather was like.

"Anyway," she said, shepherding Dot towards the front door, "let's get going. We'll pop in somewhere for a snack. Can we have a key, Mrs. Silverman?"

Mrs. Silverman's expression hardened. "I expect my guests to be back reasonably early in the evening," she said. "I shall be in. You only have to ring the bell. But if you insist . . ." She looked at Dot, dressed to kill, and Lois, very attractive but more sober in appearance, and began to wonder what was the real reason for their visit. After all, they seemed an oddly assorted pair . . .

"A key would be very useful, thank you," Lois said firmly. "Then we shall not have to disturb you."

"Very well," said Mrs. Silverman, opening a drawer in the hall desk and fishing out a key. "Breakfast is from eight to nine o'clock. Enjoy your visit," she added grudgingly, and turned to retire to her kitchen.

"Oh, one more thing," said Lois. "My mobile number's on this card, if you need to get hold of us whilst we're out." She handed her a "New Brooms—We Sweep Cleaner" card and, ignoring Mrs. Silverman's raised eyebrows, left with Dot and set off towards the town centre.

"She's a bit of a misery, ain't she?" Dot said.

"Probably a widow, earning her keep and missing her husband." She realised too late what she had said, and watched Dot's face fall.

"Yeah, well," Dot said slowly. "It ain't much fun, being widowed. Depends on what your late beloved was like. My Handy was a good husband, in his way. But he was always involved in dodgy deals, and I never knew when he'd be phoning me up from the cop shop, asking me to take in his pyjamas."

Lois laughed. Then she stopped suddenly, just as they reached the flight of steps leading up to the looming church. "Don't look round, Dot. Pretend to be taking a stone out of your shoe."

"Why—"

"Just do it," hissed Lois. She stood apparently nonchalantly whilst Dot fiddled with her shoe. Turning in a full circle, she said quietly, "You can stand up now. Have a quick look over there by the café. That bloke. Him in the baseball cap and dark glasses."

Dot obediently looked, and then turned back to Lois. "We seen 'im before," she said. "Walk on, and we'll see if he follows."

Lois walked slowly up the steps and into the churchyard. She stopped at the foot of another flight of steps into the church, and looked round at Dot, who was following reluctantly, glancing back every now and then. "I don't like creepy churches, Mrs. M," she said when she reached Lois. "An' that bloke has crossed the road to our side. He's stopped at the bottom of the steps, fiddlin' with his cap."

"Could be a complete stranger," said Lois. "Or more likely, one of Cowgill's men keeping an eye on us. I wouldn't put it past Derek to tell him where we'd gone. Come on, you're safe with me."

The door stood open, and at once they realised there was a service in progress. Lois took Dot's arm and led her to sit in a pew at the back of the church. To her surprise, Dot immediately fell to her knees and covered her face in an attitude of prayer. Blimey, Lois said to herself, never thought Dot was a churchgoer. Lois herself had, when a small girl, been taken by her grandmother to services once or twice, but was not at all confident that she would know when to stand up or sit down. But no matter. Dot would lead the way.

"How long are we going to stay?" Dot asked in a stage whisper, which caused several heads to turn around disapprovingly.

"We'll see," Lois murmured, and opened the prayer book handed to her by the verger.

"Evening prayer," whispered Dot. "Page sixty-six, Nunc Dimittis. 'Now lettest thou thy servant depart in peace,'" she sang in a surprisingly sweet voice.

Lois did her best, but her attention was elsewhere. She was waiting for footsteps at the back of the church. They would be clearly audible on the tiled floor. Sure enough, as they reached "and to be the glory of thy people Israel," there were the sounds of someone walking on tiptoe behind them. She turned round quickly and saw the shadowy figure of a man who crept in and then seemed to vanish into the dark side aisle.

"Was that him?" Dot was standing straight, her eyes fixed on the altar and saying mostly the right words, but here and there they differed from the Apostles' Creed. "'Maker of heaven and earth,' where has he gone?" she continued. Lois gave up trying to shut her up, but answered in like manner as softly as possible. She established that she wished to stay to the end of the service, when they could hang about until the man emerged from wherever he was hiding. She intended to accost him.

"'. . . the forgiveness of sins,' and won't that be dangerous?" sang Dot.

"'. . . and the life everlasting,' and no, it won't. 'Amen,'" answered Lois.

The service came to an end, and the vicar reminded the congregation that tea and coffee were being served at the back of the church. "I do hope you will all stay," he said. "We have one or two new faces, and we would love to welcome them to Pickering and to our church."

"There you are, then," said Dot. "We have to stay, I suppose. Eyes peeled now, Mrs. M. Can't see any sign of him yet."

Lois and Dot tried hard to monitor the comings and goings of the congregation, but were surrounded by well-meaning welcoming members of the church. By the time most had gone, they realised sadly that he could easily have slipped out without their noticing. But why should he do that, if his mission was to follow them? No, he must still be skulking in a side chapel. Lois excused herself from a conversation about cairn terriers with the dog-loving vicar, and walked swiftly up to the chancel, where she had seen an elaborately carved door. If that led to a useful hiding place, she intended to investigate. She pushed open the door quietly, and peered in.

He was there, seemingly absorbed by two recumbent stone effigies, a knight in armour, and his lady, a little larger than life-size, lying close together with their hands folded in prayer. Lois crept in, followed by Dot, meaning to take the man by surprise, and saw that the small room was a chapel, with pews and an altar. An enormous wooden clock with no hands and a dark face hung on the wall in one corner.

"Excuse me," Lois said loudly.

The man turned, and Lois saw that he had a pale face, a pony-tail protruding from under the baseball cap and an unlikely-looking moustache. He also looked terrified. "Wotcha want?" he said in a hoarse voice.

"Um . . ." For a moment Lois was stuck for something to say. Of course he was not a cop. No cop would be so scared-looking, not with the might of the law behind him.

Dot was quick to answer. "What d'you think you're doing, following us around? We saw you outside. And don't say you weren't, 'cos I know from long experience when 'm being fol-lowed."

The man made to push past them and escape, seemingly too scared to argue.

"And don't I know you?" Dot continued. "I've seen you before, nothing surer. Where do you come—" But before she could finish her question, he had pushed past them and left the church at a quick trot. There were still parishioners lin-gering in the porch, and one of them tried to stand in his way, thinking he had been after the church silver or the collection plate. But the man was as slippery as an eel, and ran off down the street, disappearing round a corner.

Lois and Dot were still standing in the lady chapel, and Dot took Lois's arm. "Are you all right, Mrs. M?"

"Of course I am," Lois said. "But thanks, Dot. Anyway, who did you think it was? Had you seen him before, like you said?"

"Oh yes, I know who he was," Dot replied. "At least, I'm almost a hundred percent sure, though he's tried to disguise himself. I tell you what, though, I never saw such a messy mustache!" Her face more serious now, she said that they were definitely on the right track and if that hadn't been

Clive Mowlem, she'd eat her hat. Then she began to laugh, and Lois, much encouraged, relaxed and joined in.

The vicar appeared, and said it was such a treat to hear laughter in the church, and he was sure our Lord would approve. "Not to mention that splendid knight of old," he added. "Quite a lad, according to all reports. Now, let me give you a few tips on how to find the best that Pickering has to offer. And do please come in again! Lots more to see in our church, including another knight in chain mail, with his legs crossed, apparently a sign that he was a Crusader. We've had lots of other suggestions, of course, and not all of them devout!"

# TWENTY-SIX

❧

"HOW MUCH LONGER ARE WE GOIN' TO STAY ON THIS BLOODY godforsaken moor? I bet the sun is shining in Pickering." Clive Mowlem looked out of the dusty window at the rain driving across the gloomy landscape. He had just reported to Gerald that he'd seen the two women in Pickering, first at a distance and then close up after he had followed them into the church.

"One of 'em, the little one, was that nosy Dot Nimmo, friend of Mum. I'm sure it was her."

"And who was the other one? Queen Elizabeth the Second?"

"You can laugh, Gerald, but you'll laugh on the other side of yer face when the cops come knocking on the door. I tell you it *was* Dot Nimmo! An' she half recognised me, I reckon!"

"All right, if you say so. Keep yer hair on, brother. But why should the Nimmo woman be in Pickering, sodding miles from home? An' anyway, if it was her, and even supposing she is looking for us, she'll never find us up here on the moor. No, Clive, I got plans, and no Nimmo woman is goin' to scupper them."

There was complete silence for a minute or so, and Clive resumed his post at the window. Then from the outbuildings came the sound of the bull, bellowing angrily. "Poor bloody animal needs a bit of the other," Clive said sadly. "All that stonking great tackle and nothin' to do with it."

Gerald laughed nastily. "Thinking of the ole bull, or your own self, Clivey boy? Just have patience. When we do the really big job, we'll be out of here afore you can say knife, an' off to Tenerife. Topless girls on every beach. Change our identity and live happily ever after."

"What about Mum?" Clive said. "Is she coming, too?"

"Good God no. She'd never keep her mouth shut. Give or take a couple of hours and the whole of the Canary Islands would know what we'd done and where to find us."

"Anyway," said Clive sceptically, "what big job? All we done so far is a few bits of old statues from people's gardens and the small change from an honesty box in the church. That wouldn't get us nowhere!"

"I got a plan," Gerald said in a hushed voice. Harry was in his room, and sometimes he turned off his television so that he could overhear the conversation in the kitchen.

"What plan?"

"It's not finished yet. I'll tell you when I got it properly sorted. But believe me, it'll make headlines in the paper."

"What, the *Pickering Beacon*?"

"Ha ha. Very funny. And yes, it'll be in the local paper, but probably the nationals as well."

"Well, go on, what is this master crime?" Clive had heard it all before. The big one that was going to make their millions never happened, and when Gerald had come down off his high place, he sank into a deep depression and then God help all his friends and relations.

"You remember Ronnie Biggs?" Gerald said.

Clive nodded. "One of the great train robbers, wasn't he? Don't tell me you're planning to rob a train? That'll be difficult round here. There ain't no trains to Pickering."

"Think, Clive, think. Haven't you seen all the posters and signs to the steam railway that goes from Pickering to Whitby? Well . . ."

"Well what?"

Gerald tapped the side of his nose. "All will be revealed," he said. "But first I have to go for a ride on Pickering's finest tourist attraction."

"Can't I come, too?"

Gerald shook his head. "No, no chance. Two of us'd be suspicious. Two blokes going on a jaunt together. Well, need I say more?"

Clive said nothing for a few minutes. What on earth was Gerald planning? What could possibly be gained from a trainful of families on holiday? He looked across at his brother, who was sitting in Harry's favourite armchair, with his feet propped up against the fireplace. Had he finally lost his marbles? He was often scared by Gerald's mercurial moods, especially when he was at the top of the scale. But none of his plans had ever sounded as ridiculous as this one. Was he planning to dress up as a highwayman and hold up the train with a couple of pistols from a museum? He sighed. He had no alternative but to go along with the plan, but he wished he could make the trip, too, just in case Gerald went too far.

"When are you going, then?" he asked, but Gerald again shook his head. "That'd be telling," he said in a mock-mysterious voice.

\*     \*     \*

HARRY COULD HEAR THE BROTHERS TALKING IN THE NEXT ROOM, but could not decipher the words. He had noticed recently that his hearing was not as acute as when he could hear the slightest sound out on the moor. In the end, he gave up and turned up his television. He planned a long trek with Jess tomorrow, and was content to have his thoughts diverted by a new comedy show.

# TWENTY-SEVEN

❧

Lois and Dot walked along Eastgate into the centre of Pickering town. They had had a leisurely breakfast, so substantial that Lois said they'd not need anything else to eat all day. Mrs. Silverman had given them a timetable for the North York Moors Railway, and sung its praises for a marvellous way of seeing the countryside in comfort.

"Might be just the job, Mrs. M," Dot had said. "We could watch the woods and moors go by, and who knows, we might catch sight of those two thugs on the way. I'd know that old lorry anywhere. Gladys was moaning about it and wishing they'd get a decent car she could use."

Lois looked away from a window of fishing tackle, complete with life-size heron. She tried hard to dispel the thought that Derek would love this place, with its winding streets and mysterious passages between shops, inviting the curious.

"I don't reckon they'll still have the lorry," she said. "They're much too fly for that. No, they'll have dumped it and be using a vehicle bought from one of their dodgy associates. You know the form, Dot, used twenties and no questions asked. Still, we might very well pick up some information on the way about a couple of strangers seen loafing about suspiciously." She privately doubted this, but was determined to take a train journey that they could enjoy and describe to Derek when they got home. It would be a real tourist thing to do.

"We'll get the eleven o'clock easily," Dot said, marching along purposefully. "Should we get sandwiches for a picnic? Or rely on local catering?" Dot gave the impression that nothing north of Watford could be relied on. But Lois had read the leaflet, and said they would go as far as Grosmont, about an hour's journey, and find a place to eat before returning in the afternoon.

"We can get into conversation with people in a café and see if anybody's seen a couple of scruffs loitering about. We can say they're our long-lost relatives."

"We could say they've come into money from a will, and we're helping to find them. That should smoke them out!"

Dot was pleased with herself for this refinement of their plan, and Lois hadn't the heart to discourage her. Besides, knowing Dot's easy way of buttonholing strangers and discovering anything she might want to know, on consideration she thought this might be a productive idea.

They arrived at the station, now lovingly restored over several years into the heartwarming kind of station Dot used to know in her youth. Her eyes were everywhere as Lois bought the tickets. "Look, Mrs. M! See that big ad for Virol? 'Schoolchildren need it.' Do you remember Virol? My mum used to give it to us by the spoonful! Used to swear by it, she did . . ."

Lois's eyes were also everywhere, but she looked swiftly along the lines of people filling the platform. It was the tail end of the holiday season, and many young families had taken this Sunday to have an outing in the autumn sun. There were tables and chairs outside the refreshment room, and her heart lurched as she saw two men, one tall and heavily built, and the other small and weasely. But then they were joined by cheery blonde wives and several small children. Not our Mowlems, then, she told herself. But she continued to check down the platforms on both sides of the lines.

"Let's walk up to the end of the platform and watch the train approaching," she said to Dot, who was peering longingly into a shop full of railway memorabilia and other eminently buyable souvenirs. "We shall get a good view of the whole station from there."

"How's about going up onto the footbridge over the tracks?" Dot said. "We'll get an even better look from there."

"You go up there, and I'll go to the end of the platform. Then we can get together and find a seat."

Dot disappeared and then, above the heads of the crowds, reappeared, athletically mounting the steps of the bridge. She waved gaily to Lois, who walked slowly towards the end of the platform. She passed the end of a wall and the beginning of a wooden fence, and leaned over to look down. Some distance below, a fast-running shallow stream glinted through leaves, and a sudden thought occurred to her. If you were wanting to escape unseen, you could easily leap the fence and splash across to freedom.

Her attention was taken by a mellow whistle from the approaching train, and she watched it appear, marvelling at the drama of the big locomotive belching out smoke and steam. Just think, she told an invisible Derek, every journey in the old days must have felt like an adventure.

"Mrs. M! Over here!" Dot yelled. Lois made her way through

groups of tourists and joined Dot at the door of a coach. "I thought you'd want a corridor one," Dot said breathlessly. "Come on, here's an empty compartment. We can have a window seat each. Keep our eyes open!"

The wood-panelled compartment soon filled up, and in minutes Dot was deep in conversation with a middle-aged woman, clearly the grandmother of the family party. "So you live round here, d'you? I expect you know what's going on in Pickering, then!"

"Not so easy when the tourists are in town," the woman said. "But off-season is different. There's still families in Pickering who've lived here for generations, and we have what we call an information network."

"Or gossip shop, more likely," her husband said. "Can't get away with much in Pickering."

Lois could see exactly what Dot was up to, and decided to join in. "Do you get much crime with all these strangers around? Burglaries an' that?" she asked.

"Not bad, considering," the woman answered. "We've had one or two thefts from gardens lately. Statues and birdbaths, that kind of thing. Stupid really. Nobody's going to be fool enough to leave anything worth money in their gardens. All of it was that reproduction stuff made out of concrete or some such."

"Any clues as to who did the thieving?" Dot asked casually.

The woman shook her head. "The police can't be bothered with such trivial stuff. But my husband—him sitting next to me here—reckons he saw a susupicious-looking couple of men carrying one of them concrete nymphs with no clothes on. You saw them, didn't you, Jim?"

Jim, grateful for being allowed to speak, smiled seraphically and said yes, he saw the men carrying the nymph upside down and watched as they put her in the boot of a car. "Scarpered quickly when they saw me," he said. "Shot off up the road to the moor."

"Well," said the woman disapprovingly, "if that's the only woman they can get, I wish them joy of it!"

Dot looked meaningly at Lois, and they joined in the hearty laugh from all in the compartment, and then the train drew slowly to a halt in Levisham station.

"'Our 1912-style station,'" Dot read out from a leaflet, "'accessible by one solitary hill road and surrounded by the magnificent North York Moors.'" She looked out of the window and saw an old railway coach adapted for camping holidays. A woman came out of it and draped some washing over the steps up to the door. Dot lowered her voice, and said to Lois that this would be just the ticket for the Mowlem men for a hideaway. "Who would ever track them down to this place?" she said.

"Probably the police, if they were looking for them. And maybe us, if we catch sight of them. But it'd be like looking for the proverbial needle in a haystack, I daresay. They'd have worked out an escape route through those woods where nobody could follow."

Dot was not discouraged. "You can never tell, Mrs. M. I don't always believe in coincidence. Sometimes I think we get a helping hand, 'specially if it's in a good cause. Just keep your eyes peeled. You look left an' I'll look right. They'll be disguised, but any two fellers together, one big and one small and shifty-looking, could be them. Might be doin' a bit of bag snatching in stations, or shopliftin' from souvenir shops. Just keeping their hand in."

Lois smiled at Dot's stage whisper, which was perfectly audible to all. The woman from the information network leaned forward conspiratorially. "You looking for somebody, you two?" she asked. "You're not—" She stopped and shook her head.

"Not what?" said Dot.

"Um, er, you're not plainclothes policewomen?" The woman's voice had become a hiss, and now everybody in the compartment was listening. Lois could see that Dot was preparing herself for a speech, and so she stepped in at once.

"Good gracious me, no!" she said. "No, we were talking about people we used to know. They had two sons and moved up to a farm in this part of the world. But I don't think it was this station they told us about. No," she continued, turning to Dot, "it began with a *G*, didn't it."

"Grosmont," said the woman. "We're getting off there, so you'll know when you're there. Hope you find them! We know most people in Grosmont, but I don't remember any newcomers, d'you, Jim?"

Jim agreed that no people of that description had moved in lately. "But if you don't mind my saying so, them two I saw thieving could've been the ones you're looking for. I should try somewhere on the moors. Only be careful. Easy to get lost, if it's a farmhouse you're looking for."

"Thanks," said Lois. "We'll have a drive round."

She and Dot continued to stare out of the window as they puffed through deep ravines, woods in dappled sunshine, and fast-flowing streams, and stopped at picturesque small stations, Newton Dale Halt, Goathland. Then it was Grosmont, and they got up to alight.

"I need the loo, Mrs. M," Dot said, making a beeline for green-tiled toilets, sparkling clean and smelling of disinfectant. Lois said she would wait outside. "Like a camel, me," she said, not entirely accurately. "I can go for hours."

Lois wandered along the platform towards the level crossing, where the gates were shut against cars, in order to let the
train travel on its way to Whitby on the coast. A small crowd
of people had gathered to watch the train go by, and as she
watched a small girl crying because her ball had gone between
the train lines, her eye was caught by a small, thin figure wearing a railwayman's hat, sweeping up ice cream wrappers and
empty cans from the platform. From under his hat she could
see, as he turned away from her, a skimpy ponytail sticking
out. There was something furtive about the way he did not
look up from his job as the train passed by, huffing and puffing and blowing its whistle to the cheers of the watchers.

Dot's voice called from behind her, and she turned. "Here,
Dot! Quick!"

"What's up, Mrs. M?"

"That railway chap there, sweeping up—isn't he the one
we saw in the church?"

Dot looked towards the figure, who, for a moment, raised
his head and seemed to search them out. As soon as his eyes
fixed on them, he shoved his brush into his little cart full of
rubbish, and made off rapidly round the back of a shed.

"It was that Clive! I'd swear it was him! Come on, Mrs. M,
let's follow him."

Lois put a restraining hand on Dot's arm. "Hey, not so fast,
Dot. He'll be out of sight now anyway. He recognised us, didn't
he? You anyway. No, now we know where he's working—did
you see the hat?—we can find out more. Come on, we'll go and
get something to eat and have a look around, then come back
here and sniff out somebody who knows him. He'll be miles
away by now. We need to know where they're living, and it's
probably that farm of the man your friend Gladys knew."

Dot stopped, disappointed at Lois's instructions. "Well,

okay, Mrs. M. But what are you going to do when an' if we find out where they are and what they're up to?"

"Send a message to our mutual friend," Lois said.

"What? Hunter Cowgill, superman detective of Tresham cops?"

"That's right," answered Lois. "No point in a couple of weak and feeble women having a go at them. It's a police job, an' I shall convince 'em that two thugs who can knock my Derek unconscious deserve a little attention."

# TWENTY-EIGHT

❧

CLIVE ARRIVED BACK AT THE FARM, PUFFING AND PANTING like the steam train he had just seen chuffing away along the valley.

"What the hell's the matter with you?" Gerald said. He was sitting in the kitchen with his feet up, reading the sports pages of the Sunday paper.

Clive sank down onto a hard kitchen chair, and with elbows on the table, he put his head in his hands and groaned.

"Are you ill, boy?" Gerald said in some alarm.

Clive shook his head. "Worse than that," he said. "They're onto us."

Gerald, with exaggerated patience, put down his paper and said, "*Who* is onto us? And what for? We ain't done nothing wrong. Well, nothing worth worrying about anyway."

"What about that bloke we knocked cold at the back of the stately home in Farnden? I wouldn't call that nothing. And it's his wife and old Dot Nimmo who's onto us. I saw them this afternoon. Y'know our new plan, thieving stuff from the station platforms. Well, I found a railwayman's hat lying on a chair, put it on and took one of them litter carts we picked up in the market. Very convincing, I looked, though I do say it as shouldn't."

"If you don't get to the point, you'll not be saying anything anymore! Where did you see the two women? An' did they see you?"

"I was pickin' up litter on the platform. The train just come in, and they must've got off it. Next thing, I saw them comin' towards me, and the Meade woman pointin' in my direction! I scarpered as quick as lightnin', and got the cart and meself in the car and drove away like a bat out o' hell."

Silence fell. Clive looked imploringly at Gerald, hoping for reassurance that all was not as bad as he thought. Gerald was weighing up everything Clive had said, and decided that, all things considered, the two women had not necessarily seen Clive.

"They could've been pointing at anything," he said. "Were you near the ladies' toilet?"

Clive thought. "Well, yeah. It was up that end of the platform. Oh well, maybe they didn't see it was me," he added with a sigh of relief. "Come to think of it, it weren't likely, what with me ponytail and the railwayman's hat, an' all the tourists milling about. But still, I reckon we should be very careful. If they're around and about, even if they're just tourists, we don't want them recognising either of us."

After a long pause, Gerald said, "There is one other thing we could do. We could face up to them, ask them what they're doin'—nicely, y'know—and pretend not to know who the Meade woman is. Perfectly natural for us to say hello to one of Mum's friends, innit? Then, in the nicest possible way, we could put the frighteners on them."

Clive looked doubtful, "D'you reckon that's a good idea? We've always kept our heads down, ain't we? O' course, you're the boss, so I'll go along with whatever you say."

Gerald rose slowly to his feet. "Right, boy," he said, "this is what we'll do. And when we've dealt with them, we'll put our minds to work on what to do about our genial host, Harry himself."

LOIS AND DOT ARRIVED BACK IN PICKERING, RELAXED AND PLEASED with their journey. Not only had it been a delightful trip, with the scenery and plenty of people to talk to, but they had discovered that the new employee of the North York Moors Railway was not, in fact, an employee at all. None of the station staff at Grosmont had seen him before, but in response to Lois's enquiries, they very helpfully said they would keep their eyes open for him.

"That's where your cap went, Tom," one of them had said to his colleague. "That'll teach you to be more careful!"

"Could've been one of these railway nutters," answered the hatless Tom. "They'll do anything to belong to the North York."

Now Dot and Lois sauntered back through the town, and decided to stop at a café and have tea before they returned to Mrs. Silverman and Ourome.

"What shall we do tomorrow, Mrs. M?" Dot sat back in her chair and gazed out of the café window. The sun lit up the pale honey-coloured stone of the buildings, and the crowds walking by in their brightly coloured summer clothes, regardless of the chilly wind of early autumn, gave her a pleasant feeling of ease and tranquillity.

Lois's next words dissipated this somewhat, but Dot, as usual, was ready for anything.

"I think we should go for a long walk on the moors tomorrow," said Lois firmly. "It's obvious that if that mystery railwayman *was* Clive, then the Mowlems are staying up there with the romantic Harry. We've got the address, and if we pop into the tourist office, I'm sure they'll give us directions. There's bound to be parking places, where you can get out and see the view. We'll leave our car and walk. Should be nice weather, according to the forecast. Have you brought good shoes, Dot?"

"O' course I have," said Dot. "Didn't I go and buy some of them walking boots? An' two pairs of thick socks, the man in the shop said I should have. God knows when I'll ever need them again, but we're here on a mission, ain't we, Mrs. M, and the large amount of money I shelled out on boots will be worth it."

"Hint taken," said Lois with a smile. "Give me the bill, and I'll let you have the money as expenses."

Dot did not argue, quite convinced that she was entitled to the payment. Although they were in Pickering partly as tourists, she reckoned her value as Assistant Agent Watson to Mrs. M's Holmes was considerable.

"So, tomorrow's Monday, and then we'll be going back on Tuesday. That means if we want to clinch our job up here, it'll have to be tomorrow. Better get an early night, Mrs. M. You never know what tomorrow will bring."

BACK IN LONG FARNDEN, THINGS WERE GOING SMOOTHLY. BUT however smoothly they went, Derek was not happy. The more he thought about the expedition to Yorkshire, the more sure he was that Lois was up to something that had nothing to do with tourism. And Dot Nimmo was not exactly somebody who would be likely to squash any harebrained scheme that Lois had in mind. No, Dot Nimmo was fly and, before her husband drowned, had been used to living what Derek would consider a dangerous life.

He had been gardening all Sunday and now it was evening, and he sat in front of his favourite programme on the television but could not concentrate. Gran came in with two cups of coffee, sat herself down and handed one to Derek.

"Here, drink this. You look like you've lost sixpence and found a penny. I suppose it's Lois, is it? Well, no good worrying, Derek. She'll not change. I blame her father. He spoilt her rotten, you know. Only child, and the apple of his eye. No wonder she's wayward and stubborn."

Derek turned to look at her. He was not having this kind of talk about his Lois. "Oh, I wouldn't say that, Gran," he said. "She's been a very good mother, wife and businesswoman. Not many can say that. No, it's just that I'm always uneasy when she's off on her own. My fault, I know."

"I wouldn't call a trip north with Dot Nimmo being on her own!" Gran was stung at his defence of Lois, and continued to accuse anyone named Nimmo of being shifty and untrustworthy. "In the extreme, I should add," she said sharply.

"You're probably right, me duck," he said kindly. "Anyway, they'll be back on Tuesday, and not much can happen to them in one more day."

"Don't tempt fate!" said Gran. "A lot can happen in twenty-four hours."

NEXT MORNING, WHEN DOT PULLED BACK THE CURTAINS IN HER bedroom, a dismal sight met her eyes. Sheets of rain blew across Mrs. Silverman's garden, rattling the windowpane and almost obscuring the view beyond the wooden fence. Dot's heart sank. Would Mrs. M insist on going for their long walk over the moors in this downpour? Well, if she did, it would be the end of them. Dot had visions of lonely, rainswept moorland stretching for miles in every direction, and the pair of them up to their knees in mud.

She showered and dressed quickly, arriving at the breakfast table before Lois.

"Dreadful morning," said Mrs. Silverman. "I just listened to the forecast, and it's not good. Rain set in for the whole day for our area. I hope you and Mrs. Meade brought your knitting!"

Dot managed a smile. Best to wait for Mrs. M to appear, and then she would make the decision. "Ah, well," she answered, and then Lois walked in, looking grim.

"So what shall we do?" Dot asked as soon as Mrs. Silverman had set their breakfasts on the table and disappeared.

"Well, one thing's certain," Lois replied. "We're not tramping about deserted moors in rain like this. And yes, I listened to the forecast, and there's no letup today. So here's what I'm going to do. First of all, I'll see if Mrs. Silverman can keep us for another day. Then I'll phone home and say we need to stay until Wednesday. It won't be easy convincing Derek, but he'll come round eventually. So we'll postpone our walking trip until tomorrow, when it should be fine, and do some shopping and visiting undercover things today. Is that all right with you, Dot?"

Dot sighed with relief. "Yeah, it's fine by me," she said. "And a very sensible decision, Mrs. M, if you don't mind my saying. Can you ask them to tell Floss to take on my Wednesday client? She's done it before, so it'll be okay."

Mrs. Silverman grudgingly allowed them another day, and

Derek, after some protesting, said he supposed that if that's what they wanted to do, he must put up with it. "Just remember you have responsibilities here at home," he had said, somewhat pompously, and Lois had laughed. "New Brooms won't fold up if I'm playing truant for one more day!" she said, and Derek relented. "Enjoy yourself, gel," he said. "And take care."

# Twenty-Nine

❧

Mrs. Tollervey-Jones was feeling bruised. Not physically bruised, although she had tramped over most of the estate with the agents. Her soul was bruised, she told herself. The thought of no longer owning Farnden Hall and all its farmland and park was like flying over the Atlantic. Although she had done it many times, she always felt as if the journey was too rapid for her soul, which didn't catch up for a couple of days. Her decision and action had been precipitate, some would say, and she felt that part of her was lagging behind, maybe looking for an escape route.

Now, though, with arrangements made, and a new day dawning, the reality of what it would be like, living somewhere else, was beginning to sink in. No more waking up and wandering to the window to see the sun rise over the park, or the first fall of snow in winter, with hoarfrost on the trees, transforming it into fairyland.

And what about her old mare, Victoria? Would she include

her in plans for a new property, either built on a piece of land reserved for the purpose, or buying a suitable house in the village, or another village nearby? In a way, she had too many alternatives.

When she had introduced John Thornbull, her tenant farmer, to the agents, she had been astonished to see that he and Hazel had tears in their eyes. Hazel had impulsively taken her hand, and said they couldn't imagine anyone else in the hall.

Every part of the house and the estate had memories for her. Was that what she meant by her soul? Memories make up a large proportion of your life when you grow old, she decided. Oh well, she'd have the photograph albums, and at least they didn't require constant maintenance and eat up all her reserves. The thought of money drew her out of what she now told herself was a sentimental attitude. Money had to be found. She was in debt, and the bank manager wanted his pound of flesh. Once the whole thing was finalised and she was established comfortably elsewhere, her soul would jolly well have to keep up.

She took her breakfast dishes to the sink, and began to wash up. Robert had bought her a dishwasher, but it was useless for one person. By the time she had enough crockery in there to make it worthwhile turning on, all the remains of scrambled egg and porage oats had hardened beyond recall. She never read the instructions to modern aids to a simpler life, and so it did not occur to her to rinse the dishes before stacking the machine. And anyway, she would consider that a stupid waste of time.

This morning, she had work to do. She was due in the magistrates court at nine thirty, and there was a full list of cases. "Just as well," she said aloud. "Fix your mind on somebody else's troubles. And who knows," she added, her spirits rising, "shaking off all the worries of the estate might be a lovely new start." She went to fetch her coat, and was confronted by the sight of a small herd of fallow deer crossing the park and disappearing into the woods. They were confident, knowing that nothing was likely to harm them.

So what would happen to the estate when she had left? Themed amusements? Family picnic sites? Racetrack for mini-vehicles? She shook her head, almost ran out of the house and in her four-by-four fled away down the drive.

THE MAGISTRATES COURT IN TRESHAM WAS IMPRESSIVE. THE courtroom itself was lined with mellow dark oak, and the windows placed high up, so that people involved in the proceedings of the court should not be distracted from the serious matters in hand. The magistrates bench was in the shape of an elongated pulpit, high up above the rest, indicating the authority of the law of the land. Today, as usual, there were three magistrates. First came a young woman with straight, well-cut hair and aristocratic features, then a middle-aged man with a kindly face and crinkled greying hair, and last but by no means least, the daunting figure of Mrs. Tollervey-Jones, smartly dressed in her good grey coat and skirt, her hair brushed neatly, and more than usual stern lines on her forehead.

"What's up with the old girl? She doesn't look too well today," whispered the young woman to the kindly-faced man as they stood waiting in the lobby.

He shook his head. "Don't know," he replied. "She's been off duty for a while. But I did see in the local paper that Farnden Hall is up for sale, so she's probably going through the

horrid business of moving house. Supposed to be the biggest
cause of nervous breakdown, along with retirement. Ah, off
we go." Then the usher said, "All rise," and the three walked
in and settled themselves, the man flanked by the two women.

The first case was a motoring offence. An elderly man of
eighty-two had parked his car in a side road, and had scraped
the side of a neighbouring vehicle. Then he had walked away
to keep an appointment with his optician. As he swore he had
not noticed the scrape, he had not reported it to the police.
His bad luck was that there was a well-known lace-curtain
busybody lurking by her window, and she had been only too
pleased to do so.

MEANWHILE, GLADYS MOWLEM SAT IN THE WITNESS ROOM,
which was freezing, and tried unsuccessfully to buy a beaker
of hot chocolate to warm herself up. She was to give evidence
in a case of vandalism in her street. A couple of girls done up
to look like zombies had deliberately thrown bricks through
the window of an old man living at the end of the road. She
had gone out after them, but they had disappeared. Now
they had been nabbed, and were up before the bench on a
charge.

When Gladys's teeth began to chatter with the cold, the
doorman took pity on her, and allowed her to move to another
room. He left the door open, and she was delighted to eaves-
drop on a conversation going on nearby. She recognised the
voices immediately. One was a friend of hers, Dolly, who was
a Victim Support volunteer, and the girl she was supporting,
the victim, was already familiar to Gladys as Trish, an ex-
girlfriend of her son Gerald.

Everbody knew everybody in certain quarters of Tresham,

and Gladys was very familiar with Dolly's voice, usually heard calling "Time, gentlemen, please!" in the bar of the Worcester Arms. She and Trish were just gossiping now, as far as Gladys could tell, and when she caught the name "Gerald" in their conversation, she decided to join them. She stood at their door and smiled. "Mornin', ladies," she said. "You was talking about my lads, an' I couldn't help hearing. Nice to see you again, Trish, though not in these surroundings! You heard from the boys lately?"

Trish said she hadn't, and it wasn't her choice to be here. "That silly old fool in his car, that's what. Anyway, where's Gerald and Clive gone then?" she asked, and firmly assured Gladys that she now had a really nice boyfriend and wasn't in the least interested in where Gerald was holed up. "In trouble again, is he?" she asked.

"Don't ask me," said Gladys. "They don't care about their ole mum," she continued. "But they'll turn up one night after dark, starvin' hungry and full of tales of what they bin up to. I reckon they're in Yorkshire, but I ain't sure. Their dad'll be out soon, and it'd be nice if they was home to welcome him. Mind you, I reckon some of them crooks are more comfortable in the nick than they are in their own homes these days! Not in the case of my ever-loving husband, o' course."

Dolly glanced out into the corridor, then returned and shut the door, putting her finger to her lips. "You ain't meant to be in here, Gladys Mowlem, but since you ask, I can tell you there's rumours flying round the pub that your boys have scarpered because they done a grievous bodily job over at Long Farnden. I reckon it'll be months before you see them again!"

The door opened, and the court usher looked in. The first case was under weigh, and she was here to escort Trish into the court. But before she could say a word, Gladys interrupted piteously, asking if the nice lady could tell her where she should be. "I know it's not in this room," she said. "I just got lost, and these ladies were tryin' to help me out."

After establishing that Gladys was a witness in the third case to come up, the doorman appeared and escorted her back to her rightful place, where she asked if she could have a nice hot cup of tea whilst she pondered what she had just been told by Dolly.

# THIRTY

꒰

ROBERT WAS WALKING BRISKLY ALONG FLEET STREET TO THE underground station, hoping to catch an early train home. His case had gone well, and he felt pleased in the way that he always felt pleased if he considered justice had been done.

"Robert Tollervey-Whatsit!" Robert stopped dead and looked around. An overly smart figure stood before him, grinning from ear to ear. He was a big man with a florid complexion, and Robert was quite sure he had never seen him before.

"I'm sorry?" he said stiffly. It was as well to be careful with strangers approaching unawares. Family members of convicted criminals had several times in his career followed him full of ire and bent on revenge.

"Norrington. Geoffrey Norrington. Don't you remember? Horrid little prep school near Tresham? Heard your name mentioned this morning, and was hoping to catch you. Fancy a drink?"

Now, the truth was that Geoffrey Norrington had never been in a prep school of any kind. Brick Road Primary, Middleton, was the nearest he came to it. But he had been doing some research, and was well primed.

"I'm afraid you have the advantage of me," replied Robert politely. "As far as I can remember, we have never met. Perhaps you have confused me with someone else?"

Geoff Norrington laughed. "I'd know you anywhere, Bob! And do call me Geoff," he said. "Always looked up to you from afar at school. And of course, we all change a bit, don't we. You probably don't know that we do have something in common. I believe your mother lives in Long Farnden, and we're in Fletching, not far away. Now, how about that drink?"

All Robert's hackles had arisen, and he knew he should make a polite excuse and walk away. But he was intrigued. Norrington? Geoff Norrington? He had heard the name somewhere, and quite recently. Ah well, one drink couldn't do any harm, and he had his hard-won case to celebrate.

When they were settled in a corner in the pub, Robert asked Norrington some questions about his house in Fletching. "I grew up in Farnden, of course," Robert said, "and knew the geography of every village around. We went everywhere on bikes in those days, and there's no doubt you see the countryside in more detail as you ride along."

Geoff Norrington nodded. "And now we all whizz along in our Jags, eyes glued to the road and music blaring in our ears. You're right, Bob, it's all changed, and not for the better. Mind you," he added, "me and the wife have got plans that should improve our lifestyle no end."

Robert thought that if this man called him "Bob" one more time, he might hit him. They were on their second drinks now, and Robert's reserve was beginning to fade.

"So what are your plans, Geoff?" he said.

"We're on the move," Norrington replied. "Looking for a nice big house, with plenty of land, to give ourselves privacy and space to expand our various ideas. I happen to have done a very good deal lately, and as they say, money's no object. At least," he added hastily, "no object within reason."

Robert began to see a glimmer of light. It had not been an accidental meeting. This man had accosted him for a reason. And he was even surer that all that stuff about prep school was rubbish. He had never met Geoffrey Norrington until today, and the reason for him lying in wait was about to emerge. Perhaps it would save time if he hurried things along.

"How interesting," he said. "Perhaps you are not aware that my mother's estate is up for sale? A big decision, and in some ways a very upsetting one for her to make. But she is a person of very strong reserves, and has come to the conclusion that if the right buyer comes along, she will leave the hall and the family estate, with all its memories and associations, and not look back. Of course, you may not know that there are two farms on the estate, and the house itself is very lovely and historic. Oliver Cromwell slept here, and all that!" He chuckled as he watched Norrington's face change. Robert doubted very much that this shiny person would be the kind of client Lord & Francis would be looking for.

"My goodness, what a coincidence that we should meet on the streets of London!" Norrington replied, shifting confidently in his seat. "Farnden Hall is on our list! I must tell the wife. I know she will want to see every inch of your boyhood home as soon as possible. You know these women, Bob! Impulsive creatures, aren't they. Just as well we men take our time and consider all aspects, don't you agree?"

Robert thought to himself that there was probably only

one aspect the Norringtons would want to consider, and this was how little they could spend on purchasing the estate. Farnden Hall was an extremely desirable property for the right client, and he would take some convincing that Geoffrey Norrington was the one.

WHEN NORRINGTON REACHED HOME LATER THAT EVENING, Melanie was deep in a pile of agents' particulars. "I just took a ride around and collected up all these from property shops in the area," she said. "Some very promising houses on the market. I think it is a good time to buy. Prices are at rock bottom, so the agents said. Very encouraging, they were. Perhaps we can have a look at some of them?"

"You've really got the bit between your teeth, Mel!" Geoff smiled. "Just wait 'til you hear who I met today."

"Who? Have they found the burglars yet?"

"No, no. Nothing to do with that. No, I was walking along Fleet Street and who should I see but a barrister called—guess what—Tollervey-Jones, son of Mrs. Tollervey-Jones, JP, of Farnden Hall."

Melanie stared at him. "How did you know it was him?"

"Ah ha! I know you've set your heart on Farnden Hall, so I've been doing some research. I have useful contacts, and from what I gather, the old duck who lives there on her own is flat broke. Now if we play our cards right, we might be able to make them an offer they can't refuse."

Melanie began to feel excited. She had told herself firmly that Farnden Hall would be well outside their means. But she knew from past experience that Geoff was by nature a cautious person, and if he had got this far, and was talking of ringing the agents for a viewing, then he must be taking their chances seriously.

"But," he now continued, "don't get your hopes up too high. There'll be a lot of haggling to be done. Still, you know your Geoff; he don't get beat too easily!" And he walked across the room and gave her a hug and kiss by way of encouragement.

In Shepherd Road, Robert arrived home somewhat later than he had intended, and feeling relatively expansive as a result of his session with Geoffrey Norrington in the pub.

"Hi, Dad," his youngest greeted him. "Mum's in the garden. Down the bottom by the muck heap. You okay, Dad?" she added as Robert attempted to throw his rolled umbrella across the hall and land it on its hook. He chuckled. "Fine, fine. Never better," he said, and walked reasonably steadily towards the garden and the muck heap. It was almost dark, and the fire sent a flickering light across the garden.

"You've been drinking," Felicity said with a smile as she saw him carefully picking his way down the narrow path. "I do hope we've got something to celebrate?"

"It is just possible we have a buyer for the hall. A character named Geoffrey Norrington intercepted me on my way to the station, and insisted on our having a conversation in the pub. Frankly, I wouldn't trust him an inch, and he'll doubtless drive a hard bargain. But he had that look in his eye. Quite confident that he could carry it through, and we can't afford to be picky. Beggars can't be choosers, as the saying goes. Claimed he knew me from prep school! I doubt very much that this was true, and merely a ruse to get me into conversation. Anyway, I gave him the benefit of the doubt, and listened to what he had to say. Seems he and his wife have the hall on a list of properties they intend to look at. They live over at Fletching, and already know the area."

Felicity leaned on her fork, and asked if this character looked like he had enough money.

"Careful to let me know he had, and he's the sort who doesn't tell you he's got money in his pocket unless he actually has," Robert replied, and added, "I say, darling, I hesitate to mention it, but you have what looks like a blob of muck on your cheek."

# THIRTY-ONE

~

"WHAT A DIFFERENCE THIS MORNING!" SAID MRS. SILVERMAN as Dot came down for breakfast. "You wouldn't think it could change so much overnight, would you?"

Dot agreed, but privately thought she would not have minded if today had been like yesterday. Then they would not have been able to prolong their stay, and the hearty walk promised by Mrs. M would not happen. But then, she told herself sternly, the money spent on her new walking boots would be completely wasted. She could think of no other possible occasion when she would need them again.

"Morning, Dot!" It was Lois, looking extremely cheerful and encouraging. "Look at that sun shining on the wet grass! Isn't it beautiful? We'll have breakfast and get going as soon as possible."

Yesterday had been a boring one for Lois. She was not a keen shopper, but had dutifully followed Dot from butcher to baker and all the other retail outlets Pickering had to offer.

"It's not that I want to buy too much, Mrs. M," Dot had explained. "I just like to see what they sell up here in the north."

"Much the same as they do in the south," Lois had muttered under her breath. She had suggested going to the museum, but Dot had said she was willing to follow Mrs. M to the ends of the earth, but not into a museum of musty old things nobody wanted. Lois gave up.

Now Dot agreed that it was a beautiful morning, and resigned herself to the long trek. They loaded the car with boots and waterproof jackets. Lois had filled a small backpack with energising food for their lunch, and also a map they had bought yesterday from the tourist office. Dot had remembered Gladys mentioning Harry's house, and was almost positive it was called Hilltop Farm. When they looked at the large-scale map, there it was. Hilltop Farm, not all that far from Grosmont, where they had seen Clive pretending to be a railwayman.

HARRY, TOO, HAD WOKEN EARLY AND LOOKED OUT OF THE WINdow with some relief. He had in the end decided to postpone his trek with Jess across the moor to his neighbour's farmhouse. The extra time had been filled by perfecting his plan to appeal for help in getting rid of his unwelcome guests forever. The young sons on the farm were big strapping lads, and he intended to ask them to cooperate in a scenario which would frighten the Mowlems into immediate flight. This involved anonymous telephone calls, a released bull at an appropriate moment and a chat with a friendly community policeman.

Now Harry dressed and tidied up his room. He gave Jess her breakfast, and was hoping to get on his way before Gerald or Clive appeared. Unfortunately, Gerald had also woken early and heard Harry moving about. What was the old fool up to? It wasn't as if he had cows to milk. No cows had been in the cowsheds for years. It was too much trouble, and each year Harry had made a loss on sales of the milk, so, like a lot of other dairy farmers, he had decided to give up milking. He kept the bull, which was past its prime, but a good old friend.

Gerald shook his brother's shoulder, and refused to let him go back to sleep. "Get up!" he hissed. "The old man is up to something. I'm going down to find out exactly what. I wouldn't trust him as far as I could throw 'im. Get dressed and come down."

Harry was just opening the door out to the farmyard when Gerald appeared. Jess growled, a low threatening sound, and Gerald aimed a kick at her. She was too quick for him and slid out of the door before he could have another try.

"Where d'ya think you're going so early in the morning?" Gerald said, walking towards Harry, meaning to shut the door and force him back into the room. Then he saw the gun.

"I'm going out on farm business," Harry replied coolly, hitching his gun onto his shoulder. Now that he was about to put his plan into action, he felt slightly light-headed with perhaps unwarranted confidence. "Shan't be back 'til late, so don't lock up, if you're going out."

Gerald stood staring at him, for the moment stuck for an answer. The gun altered things altogether. And there was something different about his reluctant host that made him hesitate.

In that pause, Harry stepped out of the door and shut it behind him. His newfound confidence was beginning to ebb, and he struck out at a fast pace, whistling for Jess to follow. He did not look back.

Meanwhile, back in the farmhouse, Clive had come down into the kitchen, rubbing the sleep from his eyes and pulling an old jersey over his pyjamas. "What's up?" he said. "It's too bleedin' early to get up. Not doing anything special today, are we?"

Gerald didn't answer, except to grunt that something special had come up, and he had to go out at once. Clive could stay back at the farm and keep a lookout for anything unusual, including strangers nosing about.

"Where're you goin', then?"

"For a long walk, I reckon. Our friend Harry is going somewhere, or seeing someone, an' it won't be good news for us. I got a feeling in me bones, Clivey boy, and I need to find out what he's got in mind. And if I'm not back by nightfall, come and look for me," he added, and disappeared out of the door after Harry and Jess.

Lois drove slowly out of Pickering and took a good road signed to Grosmont. "If we park somewhere near the farm, we can head for it on foot, as if we were long-distance hikers, and pretend to be lost. If that ex-lover of your friend Gladys is about, we can make conversation and soon find out the whereabouts of the Mowlem brothers. Then we can come back to the car, drive straight back to Pickering and make one or two phone calls."

"Including to Hunter Cowgill?" said Dot. Now that they were about to do some real ferretin', she began to feel nervous. She looked out of the car windows, and saw nothing for miles and miles. Few trees, and no life except for sheep dotted about the landscape like lumps of chalk. Runnels of water threaded their way through the moor, and everything looked boggy and dangerous.

"Yes, Cowgill, o' course. And Derek, too, just to keep in touch. Anyone you want to ring, Dot?"

"You make it sound like any last requests, Mrs. M! No, I don't need to ring anybody. Let's get this job done, and back to safety with Mrs. Silverman. That's all I want this minute."

They drove on in silence, until Lois said she had seen a sign to the left to Goatsherd, and she remembered from the railway trip that Grosmont was soon after that.

"I'll keep me eyes peeled, then," said Dot. "We have to turn off up a track to the right, just before we get to Grosmont, according to the map. That should be signed Hilltop Farm."

"And we need a likely place to park and leave the car. Just off the road would be best."

In due course, they turned up the lane, and Dot said suddenly that there was a widening out ahead. It was obviously a parking place next to a footpath sign, and they pulled off the road and got out. Lois said that the farm was not far ahead, and she intended to approach from across the moor, so they would take the footpath and then branch off when the house was in sight.

They set off, and Dot looked all around fearfully. "No human being for miles and miles," she said gloomily. "Let's just hope we don't sink in the bog."

"Cheer up!" Lois said. "We're close now. Hey, look, Dot!" she added suddenly. "Isn't that a dog over there? Can you hear it whining? D'you think it's in trouble?"

"What I think, Mrs. M, is that we should turn around and head straight back for the car, get in and return quick to civilisation! But as you won't never do that, let's go and look."

They walked carefully towards the dog, conscious that the ground was getting soggier. Dot stopped and grabbed Lois's arm. "Mrs. M," she said, quite calm now, "it's not just a dog. There's a man lying on the ground, and he looks very still. Have you got y'mobile? I think you should dial the emergency service."

Lois turned to look at her, and as she turned, she spotted a figure in the far distance, disappearing fast, and then it was gone. "Let's just see if we can help, an' if it looks serious, I'll call 999. He might be stuck in the mud, or something, and we could pull him out."

When they reached the spot where Jess stood, still whining and barking by turns, guarding Harry where he lay, Lois knelt in the wet turf and looked closely at Harry's face. "Oh my God, Dot," she said. "Look at that wound on the back of his head! I think he's dead. Here, you dial for help, and I'll give him the kiss of life."

She pulled the limp body onto its back, and tried first aid, but without much hope. Then all at once, Harry gave a great shudder, and choked.

"He's alive, Mrs. M!" yelled Dot. "Quick, let's get him sitting up! Here, take my jacket and wrap it round him. He looks really groggy to me. But still, it's worth a try."

When he was wrapped up and held half prone in Dot's arms, she and Lois looked anxiously over the moor for signs or sounds of an approaching ambulance. As they calmed down and speculated that it would take a while, Lois remembered the vanishing figure.

"Dot!" she said urgently. "There was another man. I saw him running off, over there."

"Could have been going for help," said Dot, ever practical. "Maybe found this chap before we did."

Lois was about to doubt this, when Harry choked again, and seemed to be trying to say something.

"Sit him up a bit, Dot," Lois said, and leaned forward to put her ear close to Harry's mouth. Nothing. "You try, Dot," she said.

"It's Dot here, Harry," she whispered, "Gladys's friend."

He moved his head, and groaned at the pain. Then his eyelids fluttered and Dot caught just one word. "Mo—Mo—lem," he stuttered. The effort was huge, and he sank back exhausted. Jess began whining again, and Dot sat like a stone, but still supporting Harry as best she could.

"Dot? What did he say?"

"Guess what," Dot answered. "Mowlem, that's what he said. Mowlem, as in Gerald and Clive, and my friend Gladys."

Lois nodded. "Makes sense, doesn't it. So we know who that bugger was, running back to the farm." She shivered. "Dot, I should ring home, and tell them we might be delayed."

"Now?" said Dot. "We might know a bit more later on."

Lois sighed. "To tell the truth," she said, "I could do with the sound of Derek's voice right now. Daft, I know."

Dot looked at her with compassion. "We got to wait for the ambulance," she said, "so do it now." She smiled. "Do it now, and I won't listen."

# THIRTY-TWO

❧

THE TELEPHONE RANG IN THE KITCHEN AT THE MEADES'
house, and Gran got there first, pushing past Derek,
who was still sitting at the lunch table, reading the paper.

Derek leapt to his feet, just as anxious as Gran to hear
from Lois. The extra day she had announced was odd. It was
unlike her to prolong a holiday because of the weather. And
she would not normally be so concerned that Dot should have
the benefit of another fine day. Lois was kindhearted, but
she was also a good businesswoman, and an extra day's absence from work would outweigh a small indulgence for Dot
Nimmo. No, Lois was concealing something from him, and
he knew, of course, what it was. She was ferretin' again, on
the trail of some villain, and he could guess which one, or
ones. It was all to do with the snatch and grab in Josie's shop,
and possibly the same ones who'd knocked him out cold up at
the hall. He knew Lois would not rest until she had those
thugs inside.

"Hello? Is that you, Lois?" Gran shouted. The north was a long way off.

Lois replied that it was her, and she didn't have much time. How was everything? Gran said all was going swimmingly, and they were looking forward to seeing her tomorrow. And were they having a good time? What had they done this morning? Lois answered briefly that they had had a lovely walk across the moors, and yes, Dot was fine.

"Me now, Gran," Derek said, taking the phone from her. "Hello, love. How's things?"

"Fine. Just thought I'd ring and see that everything was okay. Can't talk for long. Money's running out. Yes, we've been walking. This afternoon? Dot wants to find a small chapel that some man built himself, and there's carvings an' things. Yes, it *is* unlike Dot! But she read about it in a book, and wants to take me to have a look, Yes, it *is* quite a sacrifice on her part. So, yes, I am pleased. Anyway, must go now. See you tomorrow. Bye."

Derek signed off sadly, wishing Lois would occasionally say, as Josie did all the time to Matthew, "Bye, love you." But then, it wouldn't be his Lois. She sounded in a hurry anyway. He turned to Gran and said, "I shan't be really happy until those two are back safely in Farnden."

Gran was frowning. "Her voice sounded funny. Maybe not a good signal. Mind you, I could hear the sound of an ambulance siren quite clearly. Oh well, better get on. You should have been gone up to the hall hours ago. I suppose everything has to be working properly if the place is up for sale."

"Yeah, some more people coming to look over it tomorrow, and the yard light has broken again. It falls off the wall about three times a year, and it chose today to do it again. I'll see you later, then."

He drove slowly up to the hall, his mind still with Lois up north. A nice long walk on the moor, Gran had reported. Most unlike Lois, and Dot Nimmo, too, come to that. Ah well, all would be clear tomorrow when they got back. Or as clear as Lois decided to make it.

He parked in the stable yard at the rear of the hall, and got out. The kitchen door was open, and he could see Mrs. Tollervey-Jones at the sink. Washing up her lunch things, no doubt. There was that brand-new dishwasher installed, and she never used it. He had seen piles of beautiful china dinner services and teacups and saucers galore in the cupboards, so she wouldn't be able to say she'd run out of crocks before it was full. He supposed the new owner would take it on, unless he moved in and changed everything, like most people did. It was a puzzle to Derek why people bought a property because they liked it, and then proceeded to turn it into something quite different.

"Morning, Derek!" Mrs. Tollervey-Jones was standing at the door now, smiling and wiping her hands dry. "Have you heard from the travellers?"

Now how did she know about Lois and Dot? Because she had her sources of information, he supposed. Probably why she was such a good justice of the peace. What Mrs. Tollervey-Jones didn't know about this area was not worth knowing.

"Bad day yesterday," he replied, "but they're having a good time today. Walking on the moors and going to see a chapel in the woods."

"How lovely! I can't think of anything nicer. I only wish I was with them, instead of showing frightful people round the ancestral home."

The thought of Mrs. Tollervey-Jones marching along, with Lois and Dot trailing behind, was too much for Derek, and he laughed delightedly. "Now, Mrs. Tollervey-Jones," he said, "we have work to do. I was going to suggest moving the light fitting. There's so much loose stonework around it, it'd do better in a new place."

He was up a ladder when a big car cruised into the stable yard. A florid-faced man got out, and as he approached the door, he heard Mrs. Tollervey-Jones's voice. "I thought your appointment was tomorrow, Mr. Norrington," she said firmly.

Geoff Norrington was equally firm, not to be intimidated by old ladies, especially by one old lady trying to sell him a house. Well aware that times were hard, he knew that Farnden Hall could be regarded by some as a huge white elephant. He expected to strike a bargain that took this into account. "I just need to check a few things," he said confidently and walked swiftly past her and into the house.

AFTER HE HAD GONE, MRS. TOLLERVEY-JONES SANK DOWN ONTO her husband's chair in the study. "Oh dear," she muttered. "You would not be pleased with me, my dear," she addressed the stern face in the photograph on the desk. "Selling up is bad enough, but selling to a greasy oaf like that is a double sin."

She took out her handkerchief and wiped her eyes. It would be all right once the place was sold and she was safely ensconced in her new home. A suitable house in Farnden had become vacant, and she was negotiating the purchase. She felt quite excited at the prospect now. It was a lovely old house, reputed to have been a priory, and the gardens were manageable and full of old trees and shrubs, protecting it from the road. A high stone wall surrounded it, and she would have complete privacy, and at the same time be surrounded safely by the rest of the village.

That dreadful Norrington had unsettled her, but not for long. She would telephone Lord & Francis and see what exactly they had found out about the man. He was such an unlikely prospect as owner of an ancient, traditionally owned and run estate, that she was horribly afraid that he would do totally unacceptable things to it, and the village would blame her for betraying a long-held trust.

Lord & Francis were helpful. The nice young man who had come down to discuss the sale reassured her. "We make all the necessary financial enquiries," he said, "and would not dream of proceeding unless these are completely satisfactory. We have begun in the case of Mr. Norrington, and so far there seem to be no problems."

Mrs. Tollervey-Jones reminded him that there was some urgency in the matter, and again was reassured that they had not forgotten. "After all," he said with a light laugh, "it is just as much in our interest as yours to make sure the man is sound."


THE MAN IN QUESTION, GEOFF NORRINGTON, RETURNED HOME IN a good mood, and his wife once more began to hope that she would one day be lady of the manor. "So it looks as if it will go ahead?" she said, patting him on the shoulder as she leaned over to look at documents that he had in front of him on the table.

He shook her off rather abruptly, and put his hands over the paperwork. "I'm busy now," he said, "but I could do with a coffee."

The truth, which he had to conceal from Melanie, was that his newly acquired wealth was not nearly as secure as he was able to pretend. In a way, of course, he assured himself, it was safe as houses. His old friend, who had made millions from an invention to do with washing machines, had been keen to invest in Geoff's project. This was an ingenious idea, a real winner, in Geoff's view. He had come across a small outfit making baby food. Because of the recipes, which included a magic ingredient guaranteed to appeal to even the fussiest toddler, they had already hit the market running. The secret additive was rumoured by a few to be bad for a baby's emerging teeth, and as such might not be recommended, and could even be banned.

So far, so good. Geoff had been assured that the rumours were false, and there was no evidence to prove them right. He intended to buy the company and expand it to challenge existing brands. To him, it looked a doddle. All he needed was money, and his friend had promised to stump up. But many a slip twixt cup and lip, as his old mother used to say, and for the moment he intended to keep the details to himself.

"Darling, I'm not being nosy!" Melanie protested. "Just interested. After all, my share of sale of this house will be part of the purchase price, won't it? But anyway, you deal with it all, and I'll concentrate on making coffee."

A silence fell between them, and then, when the coffee was made and handed out, Melanie said that she had a request. Geoff looked up, irritated at being interrupted whilst making calculations. "Go on, then," he said.

"Can I tell young Andrew that we'll definitely be using him, if all goes through? Such a nice youngster, and I loved what he had in mind for this house. I won't commit. Just tell him he'll get the job, if all goes well?"

"If that's what you want," said Geoff, who had not really been listening. Whatever it was that Melanie had in mind, he could always revoke his permission if it proved unacceptable.

# THIRTY-THREE

ॐ

DOT WAS NOW CONVINCED THAT THIS WAS HARRY. EVEN covered with mud and in a decidedly poor way, he matched up to Gladys's jaundiced description. He was a funny colour now, and his breathing irregular. Dot held him close, smoothed his forehead and tried to warm his hands. The ambulance siren was very loud across the empty moorland, and Lois thought she had never heard a sweeter sound.

The paramedics were very kind, congratulating Lois and Dot on the efforts they had made. "Don't worry, girls," the older one said, "we'll have him in the hospital in no time. He'll have every chance there."

With every care taken, Harry was placed gently onto a stretcher and loaded into the ambulance. Jess stood by, held back by Lois from joining her master. Her whining and barking were such terrible expressions of despair that Dot asked the paramedics if the dog could come, too. On hearing the vestige of a moan from Harry, they said they would take the dog. She might help the old man to hold on.

After the ambulance had departed as fast as it could manage over the rough ground, Dot and Lois sat down on hillocks of grass and said nothing for a while. Then Dot sighed. "Well," she said. "What next, Mrs. M?"

"Back to the car, I reckon. I've got no stomach for going over there to tackle the Mowlems, I'm afraid. Anyway, I think we've got our answer, without going to the farm to confirm."

"What d'you mean?"

"The phantom runner, scarpering like a bat out of hell. Over there, look, you can see the chimneys of the farmhouse. Getting as far away as he could from the scene of the crime, no doubt."

"That'd be Gerald. Young Clive wouldn't hurt a fly. Always been led into mischief by his big brother. No, that'd be Gerald, an' I reckon you're right. The sooner we get away from here, the better. I always said he was not quite right in the head. Y'know, not always in control. Into rages, if he's crossed. That kind o' thing."

They walked quickly back to the car, locked themselves in and took out the picnic Lois had prepared. Dot accepted a sandwich, took one bite and turned a pale shade of green. "Sorry, Mrs. M, I don't seem to be up to eatin' anything just now."

Lois nodded. "Me neither," she said, and put the sandwiches back in the bag. She pulled out a bottle of Guinness, knowing that it was Dot's favourite. "We might manage this between us," she said. They sat drinking in complete silence.

Finally Dot spoke. "Let's do the chapel thing," she said. "Take our minds off it. But first, shouldn't we phone the police?"

Lois shook her head. "The medical lot will make contact

and do a report," she said. "We should stay out of it until they catch up with Gerald—or we do."

"But they might not know about Gerald," Dot objected.

"The old man will tell them. Remember what he said to you."

"It's poor old Gladys I'm sorry for," Dot said. "Nothing but trouble for her ever since she married that no-good and he fathered them boys. Bert were a friend of my husband, y'know. In the same line, in a manner of speaking. An' a very crooked line it was, too!"

Lois smiled, silently thanked God for giving her Dot Nimmo in times of trouble and started the engine. "Off we go, then," she said. "Back to Pickering. It'll be warmer down in the valley. Onwards and upwards!"

"Downwards, I sincerely hope, Mrs. M," said Dot, looking longingly at the way back into the valley of the River Esk.

THEY HAD MADE ENQUIRIES AT THE TOURIST OFFICE, AND WERE told to take the road towards Kilburn, stop there and ask for directions to the chapel. Kilburn was a small village which, as soon as they drove in, Lois could see must be somewhere special to attract visitors. "Is this the place?" she asked. There were cars parked nose to tail, a sign outside a building with the unmistakable air of a museum, and a pub obviously doing a roaring trade.

Dot shook her head. "No, the chapel is in the woods, it says here. We have to go up a track that goes off to the left, past a gliding club—that should be easy to spot!—and park where there's another track branching off to the right."

"Do you want to stop here first? Make sure we got the right directions, and maybe have a look round?"

Dot again shook her head. "Nope, nothing to keep us here," she said. "Maybe on the way back."

"Mowlem wouldn't come here anyway, with all these people," Lois replied. "And we're not looking for him at the moment. After we've found the chapel, I shall ring the hospital and enquire after the old man. If he's improved an' can talk, we might go hospital visiting."

They turned off into a narrow lane which wound its way uphill, past groups of walkers, some with dogs that reminded Lois about the sheepdog in the ambulance. "We must ask after the dog, too," she said, and Dot, not a dog lover, said nothing.

"There's the gliding club!" she said, glad to change the subject. "Look at all them gliders!"

"Ideal place for it," Lois said. "A good way of escape for Gerald, d'you think?"

Dot turned to look at Lois and frowned. "You're joking, of course, Mrs. M. Anyway, wherever Gerald goes, Clive goes, too. An' I reckon them gliders don't seat more than one."

They drove on, until they came to a bend in the road and a track going off, looking like the one they wanted. Lois parked the car on a grassy verge, and they got out. She locked up carefully and they set off down the track. Several times, Dot wondered aloud if this was the right way, and maybe they should give up and go back into town. She wanted one or two souvenirs, she said. But Lois wouldn't agree, and they marched on, coming to dense new woodland cut across by more sandy tracks.

"I think we're lost," Dot said, stopping short of Lois, who was striding ahead.

"Round this corner, then if we don't see it, we'll go back." Lois was beginning to think she was right, and now she remembered Dot had complained of a blister on her foot.

Perhaps Dot was in pain, and insisting on going on would be cruel?

They walked on a couple of hundred yards, and with huge relief saw a clearing of lush green grass, a stone wall and a small, neatly built chapel with outbuildings to one side. "There it is," said Lois, happily stating the obvious, and Dot said just as well, as she needed a rest.

"Let's go in now, and look around later," Lois suggested, still thinking of the blister. "We could sit in a pew and eat a sandwich. My appetite's come back, thank goodness." But when Dot tried the door, it was locked, and she saw no other way of getting in. She walked around the little building and rejoined Lois, who had retreated to a dry spot to sit down.

"There's a gypsy round the back there," Dot said, taking a sandwich and beginning to eat. "A gypsy woman with a baby."

"Really, Dot? Not just kidding?"

"Yes and no," Dot smirked. Her good humour was quite restored, now that they had found the chapel and could relax. "It's a carving, and large as life if not larger. Really good, it is. Painted in bright colours and you could swear she moved her head!"

"I'll take a look in a minute. Meanwhile, I just happen to have another bottle of Guinness in that bag. Shall we indulge?"

After a few minutes, Dot stopped eating and looked round into the trees behind her. "What was that!" she said, jumping to her feet.

"What? I didn't hear nothing," Lois said, taking another swig.

Dot said there had been the sound of footsteps crackling in the undergrowth. "Just like when we were in the Guides and had to learn tracking skills," she said.

"Could have been an animal," Lois said. "Sit down again and finish your drink, then we'll have a good look around."

Dot sat down reluctantly. "It's a lonely place, Mrs. M, ain't it. Nothing and nobody around. It's a war memorial, y'know," she added. "Built by this man who was difficult to live with. He got all this stone laid on and God knows what else, all to build this memorial. Makes you think, don't it? All in memory of them soldiers an' them that fought for our island."

"Have you still got the book? I wouldn't mind reading it." Lois could see that Dot was deeply impressed.

"'Fraid not. Didn't finish it. Bit too serious for me, Mrs. M. I gave it to the church jumble sale. A good cause. I thought the man would understand that."

Lois laughed. "Right, then," she said. "Let's have a walk round, and read the notices about the place, over there, where we came in. Then we'd better be getting back. I want to phone the hospital from the main road, where we'll get a signal."

As they drove back slowly down the steep, winding lane, Dot once more marvelled at the line-up of graceful gliders, and Lois stopped the car for a second or two so they could have a better look. When she began to round the next bend, they met a car coming up towards them. It was a tight squeeze as both drivers pulled over to pass. Lois turned to give the usual wave and smile of thanks, but saw only the profile of the driver. She drew in a sharp breath. "Dot! Look at that bloke!" she said quickly. But the car had passed on.

"Who was it? Somebody you know?"

"Not exactly," Lois said. "There were two of them, and one of them, the driver, looked something like the Mowlem we saw in church!"

"Oh, cripes," said Dot. "Then I suppose the other was Gerald, hiding from view. What do we do now?"

Lois pulled into a parking place in Kilburn, and dialled for the number of the nearest hospital. "Hello? Oh, can I speak to someone about an old man brought in earlier today. We found him in a bad way up on the moor, and the medics came and got him. I'm so worried. Would it be possible to tell me how he is?"

She put her hand over the phone, and mouthed to Dot that they had gone to find out. "Sounded very nice. Should tell us something," she added.

"Ah, yes, I'm still here," she continued. "What? Oh no! At exactly four o'clock? Oh, God, I'm so sorry. Right, well, thanks for telling me. Bye."

"He died," said Dot flatly.

"Yep. They tried everything."

"You know what that means, Mrs. M."

"I think so," Lois said. "It means murder."

# THIRTY-FOUR

❧

GERALD AND CLIVE HAD REACHED THE TOP OF THE HILL, AND came out into open countryside. Ahead of them lay two tracks branching off the lane, and Gerald said to pull off and park.

"Well, what are we doing here?" Clive asked, switching off the engine. "You've said nothing at all since we left the farm, except yell at me to turn left, right or straight on. What's goin' on, Gerald?"

Gerald grunted. His mind was in turmoil, ever since he'd caught up with Harry and the old fool had said he was on the way to shop them to his neighbour. He had told Harry he'd better give up on that idea. He was going nowhere, except back to the farm. Harry had started waving the gun about, and Gerald lost his temper. It had been easy enough to snatch the gun away from Harry and give him a crack around the head. Just enough to keep him quiet. Then he had seen those two women coming across the moor, and he had panicked.

What the hell had they been doing there anyway? He was certain it was no coincidence. Had they been heading for the farm? And were they onto him and Clive? Only one thing to do, he had thought in the heat of the moment. Get out, both of them, leaving no traces at the farm. Then sort out the two women.

That sodding dog would have led them to Harry, and they would hurry to get help. Then they'd be off somewhere else. He knew where most tourists went, and two women would very likely be going there, sooner or later. He had remembered that the favourite place was Kilburn, the village well known for its furniture works, all handmade and famous for the original woodworker's signature mouse carved onto each piece. The mouse man was dead now, but his family carried on. It was a long shot, he had reckoned, but worth it. If they didn't find them there, he and Clive could be on their way, over the moors, using the narrow lanes.

"Why did we need to take all our stuff so quickly?" Clive interrupted Gerald's calculations, and he answered abruptly that it was time they were moving on. He had given the women time to get back to their car, send for help and then be on the road to Kilburn. It was a wild guess; he had realised that when he calmed down. But it was better than waiting for the cops to arrive, and in a way he had been right.


"SO WHY DID WE HAVE TO STOP IN THAT MOUSE FURNITURE place?" Clive asked. "Traipsing round there wasted a lot of our time, I reckon. We could've been miles away. There's somethin' you're not telling me, ain't there." Clive sounded accusing, and Gerald snapped back that it had been interesting. "Shame you're too dim to appreciate it," he said.

Gerald had failed to see the women in Kilburn, and from the map he had worked out a shortcut to the Scarborough road, up a winding hill. Then he had seen them, coming towards them in their car! There was no way to turn around, and now, after he had lost track of them, Gerald was beginning to wonder if they were really as dangerous as he had thought. Sure, he had bashed the Meade woman's husband and Clive had lifted the takings from the village shop, but was that reason enough? They could have got the police onto them, without trekking up to Yorkshire. It could have been just coincidence.

And how did they know that they were at the farm? Not even Mum knew where they were. Or did she? Perhaps she had put two and two together, and remembered old Harry's place. That was it. She couldn't resist telling Dot Nimmo, and that's that.

But maybe they *had* told the police, and were leading the cops to where they thought him and Clive could be found? Perhaps following them had not been such a good idea.

"Gerald! Listen!" Clive's voice was urgent. "That's a bloody police car, coming this way!" Now the wail of a police car siren was getting louder. It seemed to Gerald to confirm all his suspicions.

"Get going!" he shouted. "Down that track there, towards the trees!"

"But—"

"Just do it!" yelled Gerald, and thumped his brother on the arm.

Clive obeyed. He drove the old car fast over bumps and ridges, shaking them both alarmingly. At last they reached the trees, and Clive slowed down. "How much further?" he asked.

"Keep going," Gerald said, trying desperately to think of a plan. "And watch out for rocks in the road. If we get a flat tyre, we've had it."

Eventually they rounded the corner and saw the chapel. It was beginning to rain, and Gerald said, "Blimey, just at the right time. Maybe the Almighty is watching over us, after all."

"I doubt it," muttered Clive, and parked the car by the gate. They cursed when they found the chapel door locked, but immediately went over to the outbuildings. With a hefty kick, Gerald managed to gain entry to a dark, damp-smelling interior. He slammed the door shut behind them, and took a box of matches from his pocket. The first two matches wouldn't light, and he swore. Finally, one flared into life, and they looked around. Nothing of interest, but that didn't matter. All they needed was shelter for an hour or two, time enough for Gerald to decide what they would do next.

Clive was exhausted with strain and fear. He knew from Gerald's mood that they were in trouble. Had a fight with Harry knocked him out cold? There was no sign of the old man when Gerald had returned, forcing his brother to drop everything and flee in the car. No sign of Jess either. He sat down on the cold floor and leaned his head back against the wall. It was no good worrying. Gerald had always got them out of trouble before. God, he was so tired. He closed his eyes, and in seconds was asleep.

Gerald looked across at him. Stupid idiot! But then, Clive had always been a millstone round his neck. Mum's favourite, of course, being the baby of the family. Spineless and brainless, that was Clive. Well, now it was time to leave him to his own devices. Somebody would rescue him. They always did.

Now that a plan had formed in Gerald's mind, he acted swiftly. He took off his jacket and covered the sleeping Clive, muttering that at least he'd be warm, and then he silently crept out of the building and into the rain. The keys were still in the car, and he started the engine, hoping that Clive would not wake. Turning the car around with difficulty, he went slowly back along the track until he reached the road. Once there he accelerated. He needed to get petrol, consult the map and then head south. He had decided what he would do. The best way to hide from the cops, his dad had once told him, was on your own, and where they would least expect to find you. Back home.

# THIRTY-FIVE

❧

Lois and Dot returned to Pickering, depressed and sad. They had tried to forget the tragedy they had witnessed, choosing to go out for supper to an Italian restaurant, where the staff were friendly and encouraging. But when the steaming plates of spaghetti Bolognese, lavishly sprinkled with Parmesan cheese, had been placed in front of them, they picked at it, having difficulty in clearing their plates.

"Pudding, Dot?" said Lois.

Dot looked at the menu. "There's that tiramisu Delia Smith went on about. We could try that. We could have one pudding and two spoons if you like. I don't think I could manage a whole one by myself."

"Good idea," said Lois. "Look, I'm sorry, Dot. This hasn't turned out to be much fun for you, has it?"

"On and off," said Dot honestly. "But then, I knew we weren't on a joyride, right from the time we left home. An' I reckon we're not done yet. Okay, so we're off home tomorrow, but we'll probably be wanted to give evidence about poor Harry. He didn't exactly trip over and hit his head on a rock, did he? No, it was squidgy grass all around. Like falling on a wet sponge. And then there's those two Mowlems. You reckon they were definitely at Harry's farm. If Harry died so soon in the hospital, he's probably not been able to tell the police what happened, has he? No, it'll be a long time before it's all wound up, if you ask me."

The tiramisu arrived, and they started to eat. The door of the restaurant opened, and Lois turned to see a familiar figure approaching.

"Evening, Lois, Mrs. Nimmo," said Chief Inspector Detective Hunter Cowgill. "All right if I join you?"

Lois was dumbfounded, but Dot was made of sterner stuff. "If you like," she said, "but we ain't coming apart, are we, Mrs. M?"

Cowgill chuckled. "Still the same old Dot," he said, and turned to the waitress. "Linguini, please," he ordered, and turned back to Lois. "Been busy, I hear," he said. "And now there's been a suspicious death. A poor old farmer murdered on the moor. It's the stuff of Sherlock Holmes," he added. "But I don't think we can blame a baying hound for this one, can we?"

"Oh, shut up!" said Lois, finding her voice. "We've had a rotten day, and can do without you turning up and being jokey! And why are you here anyway? Nationwide hunt for the murderer? Well, we're off to bed, so you can talk to us in the morning."

"I'm hoping you'll talk to me," said Cowgill mildly. "I believe you have a lot to tell, Lois dear. I'll see you at your lodgings at nine thirty. Meanwhile, won't you keep me company and have a coffee?"

"Yes, please," said Dot.

"No thanks," said Lois, and rose to her feet. "Come on, Dot. We'll get the third degree tomorrow." She reached the door and, as she left, looked back at Cowgill. He was smiling, and blew her a kiss.

NEXT MORNING, LOIS GOT UP EARLY. AROUND EIGHT O'CLOCK SHE rang Derek, and told him they hoped to be home around six o'clock that evening. "We're not hurrying," she said. "We'll make the journey part of our little break. Lots to tell you. All well at home?"

"Fine here," he said. "There was a bit of a rumpus up at the hall yesterday, after we spoke to you. That ex-client of yours, Norrington, turned up there quite late in the evening and demanded to look around the attics. Said he had a plan for them, and needed to take measurements."

"What a cheek!" said Lois. "What did Mrs. T-J say?"

"Tried to get rid of him, but he insisted. I got this from Floss, who rang last night to check when you'd be back. I think she was a bit worried about the old girl. She's been told to take it easy, so Norrington was the last person she needed to see. Anyway, it was all smoothed over, and Floss is going up early today to make sure she's all right."

"He's a fool," said Lois. "If he's not careful, she'll decide to refuse his offer, however high he puts it. She's a stubborn old bird, as we know. Anyway, love to Gran—and you—and we'll see you this evening. Bye."

Derek put down the phone and frowned. Lois sending love to Gran, and him? Perhaps she had read his thoughts. Anyway, he'd be glad to see her back home, and then, he hoped, she would concentrate on New Brooms, the family and nothing else.

*       *       *

WHEN DOT CAME IN FOR BREAKFAST, LOIS WAS GLAD TO SEE HER looking fresh and fully made up. "Sleep well?" she said.

"Slept the sleep of the just," Dot said, settling herself at the table. "Now, we've got himself coming to see us at half past nine. I'm going to nip out early, if that's all right. One or two souvenirs to get—presents for friends an' that. I'll be back in time for Cowgill. Okay, Mrs. M?"

Lois nodded. She was glad of the chance to do some quiet thinking. Dot was a great companion, but regarded silence as a challenge to fill it. So now she could put her mind to several points that needed resolving, not least the probable movements of the Mowlem brothers. After poor old Harry, and his confrontation with him on the hill, they would certainly have scarpered, and now could be anywhere.

Cowgill arrived ten minutes early, before Dot was back. Lois, annoyed, asked Mrs. Silverman if it would be all right to use her lounge to have a private talk with the gentleman. The landlady was not pleased. In fact, she felt the sooner those two women left for home, the better she would like it. They were up to something, she was sure, and did not approve of her guests entertaining strange gentlemen, even if it was nine twenty in the morning.

Five minutes later, Dot returned. She hesitated outside, and then walked defiantly into the lounge.

"What's that!?" said Lois.

"What does it look like? It's a dog. Its name is on its collar and it's called Jess. It belonged to that Harry, an' I've said I'll take it."

"And keep it?" said the astonished Lois.

"Yep," said Dot. "That's it. It's a sheepdog, o' course, an' there ain't many sheep in Tresham. But it'll be all right. I can take it on walks in the park. It's a she, and she's quite a nice old thing, don't y'think?"

After Mrs. Silverman had said dogs were not allowed, and insisted on Jess being put in Lois's car, they finally got around to answering Cowgill's questions. He knew better than to try and hurry Lois. She would take her time, and he relied on her loyalty to tell him what she knew. Well, most of what she knew.

Lois had told Dot to leave the talking to her, unless she had anything urgent to say. "I shall just tell him the facts," she had said. "But if you disagree, tell me later." Dot was not satisfied with this, and had said that if she had something to say, she had always thought the best thing was to come out with it at once. In the event, they both did a great deal of talking. Starting back at the time Josie's shop was burgled, Lois gave a clear and factual account of what had happened, all except the truth of why they were here in Pickering. She knew Cowgill would have realised the possibility of danger, and disapproved.

So Dot's presence came in very handy, and when she saw what Lois was up to, she invented a nasty attack of flu that had laid her very low, and said that Mrs. M had brought her to Pickering for the good Yorkshire air and a little break from work.

There was a short silence after this, as Lois resisted the temptation to laugh at Dot's barefaced lies, and Cowgill considered how to proceed without alienating the pair of them. Then he shifted in his chair, cleared his throat and spoke seriously, largely aiming his questions at Lois.

"What exactly did you know about these two men? They were acquitted of burgling the shop, and you discovered that

Dot knew their mother. Then Derek was attacked at Farnden Hall. What made you think his attackers were the same two men?"

"Their van," Lois said. "Derek saw it, of course, and he described it to Josie. She reckoned it was the same as the one outside the shop. Low-life thieves, the pair of them. And now murderers."

"Lois!" Cowgill raised his eyebrows and took a deep breath. "My dear, you cannot assume that at this stage."

"Oh yes I can," said Lois. "I can assume what I like. It's for you to abide by the rules. I'm just telling you the facts. Harry was murdered. One of them two murdered him."

"Quite right," said Dot loyally. "And we've told you all we know, so it's about time you went off and caught up with 'em, before they do any more damage."

Cowgill sighed. "Mrs. Nimmo," he said. "Do you think you could round up a cup of coffee for us? Tell the old dragon that I'm a member of the family, come here to break some bad news. Or whatever you like. Invention is clearly one of your many skills. Then you can leave us for a bit. I shan't be much longer."

Dot looked at Lois, who nodded. "See you in a minute," she said.

The coffee arrived with a disgruntled Mrs. Silverman. "I like my guests to leave by ten o'clock on the day of departure," she said huffily as she left the room.

"Now then," said Cowgill. "We won't waste time, Lois dear. I am not even questioning your motives for travelling miles to a charming tourist town in Yorkshire. I only want to know exactly who you think wounded the farmer and why, and where you think he might have gone to now. There are two of them. Which is the leader—there is usually one—and are they likely to split up? As for their past misdemeanours, we will catch up with them later. As of now, we have an old man viciously attacked. That must come first."

"And his dog," said Lois.

"I beg your pardon?" said Cowgill. "Did you say 'dog'?"

"That dog with Dot. She was Harry's. If you catch up with the two thugs, you'll know which one attacked him. Just let the dog go. She'll show you."

Cowgill nodded patiently. "Ask Mrs. Nimmo to leave the dog with me. And the rest?"

"They're brothers, as you know, and Gerald is the leader. He takes his young brother about with him. Protects him, Dot says. I doubt if they'd split up. Gladys would never forgive Gerald if he left Clive behind."

# THIRTY-SIX

❧

CLIVE WAS VERY TIRED. HE HAD WALKED AWAY FROM THE chapel and down the long, twisting hill to the main road. Uncertain which way to go, he headed towards Kilburn, walking on the verge, and sometimes turning into a gateway to rest. One car stopped, and offered him a lift, but he shook his head, saying nothing, and hurried on. He couldn't trust himself to get into conversation with a stranger. His tongue would run away with him, and if the driver was sympathetic, he might well blurt out the whole story.

Kilburn was crowded, and keeping his eyes down, he walked steadily straight through the village and out on the way back to Pickering. He had no clear idea of what he would do then, except a faint hope that if he could get back to the farm, then Gerald would return to collect him and take him home.

He reached a junction and was momentarily scared by the volume of traffic. He began to walk slowly, keeping close to hedges and fences, until he heard the sound of an engine slowing down, and a black car pulled up beside him.

"Do you want a lift?" said Cowgill. "It's very dangerous to be walking along here."

Clive thought the man looked respectable enough, even a bit familiar, and decided to accept the lift. He got in, heaved his bag onto his lap, and the car moved off. It was a great relief to sit down. His feet were sore, and his legs ached. But he must not say anything—just ask to be dropped in the centre of Pickering. Then he could make his way over the moors to the farm without being noticed. He did not expect to find Harry there, though it was still possible, if he'd made a quick recovery. But he knew that even if the house was empty, he could break in and hide until Gerald came for him.

"Where are you heading?" said Cowgill, glancing sideways at him. Looks a real down-and-out, he thought, probably sleeping rough. Ah well, at least I can save him from being run down by a juggernaut.

Clive hesitated, not knowing what to say. But then he had a bright idea. He would pretend to be dumb, and could even wave his hands about in a reasonable imitation of sign language. He brightened at the thought that Gerald would be proud of him! In answer, he shook his head, and moved his hands.

"Don't you speak?" said Cowgill.

Clive shook his head again, and smiled winningly. But then he thought of a snag. How would he tell the driver where to drop him?

Cowgill unwittingly rescued him. "Do you want to go to Pickering?" he asked, and Clive nodded vigorously.

"By the church, in the centre of town?" More nodding. Clive relaxed, feeling more confident. Maybe he could manage without Gerald, after all.

"Fine," said Cowgill. "Nearly there." He was planning to stay one more night, make another visit to the hospital, and ask questions around town. It was a relatively small place, and local gossip should be useful. He wished Lois had not gone home, partly because he loved to be with her, and partly because of her talent in worming information out of unlikely people.

Now they were in the outskirts of Pickering, and Cowgill slowed down. He pulled up in the centre of town and said, "Here we are then."

Clive got out of the car, then turned to grin at Cowgill. "Thanks for the lift," he said.

# Thirty-Seven

❧

"W HY DON'T WE PUT OUT FLAGS?" SAID DEREK SOURLY. HE had been shunted about by Gran all afternoon, and he was fed up. After all, it had been her idea that he should come home early, and now that he was here, he seemed to be permanently in her way.

"Don't be ridiculous," she answered. "Go and do something."

"Like polish the clothes prop, or paint the garden gate?"

"Derek!"

"I'm going," he said. "I shall be in the workshop, in the unlikely event that I'm wanted."

Gran watched him slope off into the garden, and wondered what on earth was the matter with him. He had not wanted Lois to go, she knew that. And then the idea of taking Dot Nimmo had met with stern opposition from him. Lois had, of course, done exactly what she wanted, but then that wasn't so terrible, was it?

She had so much to tell her daughter, but in view of Derek's mood, she decided to leave them alone together. She would greet Lois, offer Dot a cup of tea, hope that she would refuse and then shut the pair of them in the sitting room and let them get on with it. She might even go round to Blackberry Gardens and have a chat with her friend Joan.

LOIS CRUISED INTO THE VILLAGE, THINKING THAT SHE SEEMED TO have been away for weeks. All the familiar landmarks appeared strange, as if seen after a long absence. But that was fanciful. There were serious things to be done, now that she was back, and by far the most important was to sweeten her husband, who, she knew, would be grumpy.

"Are we there?" said Dot, surfacing and looking round.

"Yep. Home again," Lois said. "You've had a nice long sleep, and should be rarin' to go with a dustpan and brush tomorrow morning. Though seriously, Dot, I am grateful for your coming with me. Made all the difference. Now, all smiles, please," she added as she saw Gran standing by the gate. And yes, there was Derek.

As Gran had hoped, Dot refused a cup of tea, saying she had to get back and see what disasters had happened whilst she was away. "Bye, Mrs. M," she said, getting into the driving seat. "Give us a ring if you've forgotten anything."

"What exactly did that mean?" said Derek, who had come forward and given Lois a peck on the cheek.

"Exactly nothing," Lois replied. "Just one of the things people say. Anyway, Derek, aren't you pleased to see me back?"

"I'd have been twice as pleased if you'd come back yesterday, like you said in the beginning," he said. "Best come on in. Gran's got the place ready for a proposed visit from the Queen."

Gran's heart sank. It was worse than she had anticipated. "And I've made a super chocolate cake," she said bravely. "Plenty for everybody. I am very pleased to see you back, all in one piece, Lois dear," she added, with a scowl at Derek.

LOIS HEARD THE DOOR BANG SHUT, AND HER MOTHER'S FOOTSTEPS going down the path. They had consumed tea and cake in the kitchen, with only spasmodic conversation. Gran had asked Lois about Pickering, and said she'd like to go there someday. Silence. Lois had said the apples looked nice and ripe, and suggested picking some tomorrow. Silence. After one or two more exchanges of this sort, Gran had got to her feet.

"Joan's asked me to go round to see her new telly," she had said. "I should be back around six." And with that, she crammed a battered garden hat on her head and left.

Now Lois looked at Derek. "So, say it, and be done with it," she said.

Derek looked at her. "Right, I will," he said, and then his face relaxed into a broad smile. He put his arms around her and continued, "I love you, Lois Meade, and I have missed you and worried about you more than you might think. I am heartily relieved that you are back, and if you like, we could go upstairs and admire the new curtains."

"And I can tell you all about Pickering and what we did on our holidays." Lois grinned, and taking Derek's hand, she led him towards the stairs.

At that moment, there was single knock at the door, and Josie came in. "Welcome home, Mum!" she said, and then she saw her parents holding hands and looking rather foolish. "Oh," she said, "have I interrupted something?"

"Yes," said Derek firmly. "Your mother is tired, and needs a rest. And so do I."

"Right, yes, of course. I'll come back later. Far be it from me to—"

"Bye, Josie," said Derek, and gently directed Lois upstairs.

# THIRTY-EIGHT

❧

GERALD MOWLEM HAD THOUGHT HARD DURING HIS LONG journey back from Pickering. He had decided it would be madness to go straight home to Gladys. She was renowned for not being able to keep her mouth shut, and he intended to be hidden somewhere around Tresham where he could wait until things died down. Then he could let his mother know he was nearby, and use her to find out what had happened to Clive.

He had begun to regret leaving him. It would probably have been safer to bring him along, but then again, he thought of his dad's advice. You're safer on your own. As he got nearer to Tresham, he thought back over the last few weeks. They'd had a good time at Harry's, with successful forays into Pickering and around. Plenty of good food and drink, and the telly for entertainment. It could have gone on for years if Harry hadn't been such a bloody fool! Still, he'd sorted out the old man. He'd need a spell in hospital, probably. Old men didn't mend so quickly. But then he would be back home with that stupid dog, and he could carry on as before, like he'd never seen him and Clive.

As he neared Tresham, he saw a sign to Long Farnden and had an idea. He remembered the time he and Clive had gone to the hall to do a bit of thieving, and he'd thought then there must be plenty of places to hide, should the need arise. Well, it had arisen. He signalled turning right, and drove down a narrow lane. LONG FARNDEN 3 MILES, the sign had said. Perfect. He'd be near enough to home, and yet well out of sight. He was confident there would be a place to go to ground. Not even the cops would think he'd return to the scene of a crime! With luck, he could stay there as long as was necessary.

But what to do with the car? Enough people had seen him and Clive in it to make it a recognisable encumbrance. He would have to find a place to dump it temporarily, so that if he needed to get away again, he could use it. There was a back way into the hall estate, he knew, and so turned off down a grassy road that he was pretty sure led to the stables and the old dairy building. He drove very slowly, keeping his eyes open for a place to hide the car.

"Ah!" he said aloud. "That looks like it." In amongst the tall beech trees, he had spotted a wooden shed, half covered with brambles, and clearly not used. The brambles grew right over the doors, but if he pulled them all to one side, he could get the car in, and then replace the thorny runners so that it looked as if nothing had been disturbed.

"Great!" he said to a curious rabbit. "Safe as houses. Now for a place for me."

The rabbit disappeared through the bracken, and Gerald stood for a moment, considering his next move. Underground would be good, like the rabbit! He walked slowly on, keeping well away from any sign of the hall and its outbuildings. After a few minutes, he knew he was lost, and stopped to retrieve his bearings.

Then he saw it. In front of him, the ground rose into a mound. A burial mound? No, that was ridiculous. He had to crawl on hands and knees now, to get through near impenetrable undergrowth, until, to his amazement, he saw a wooden door. As with the shed, brambles covered the door, for all the world like something straight from *Alice in Wonderland*.

He moved closer, and felt himself tumbling forward, down three or four steps, until he was right up against the door. His clothes and bare skin were scratched and torn, but he persisted, tugging and pushing until the door moved. Exhausted, he sat back and rested, peering into complete darkness.

In his pocket, he still had the box of matches that they'd used up at the chapel, and he struck one. In the brief flare, he saw more steps going down into an empty, brick-lined interior, with a domed roof and what looked like a drain in the centre of the floor. An icehouse! He knew for sure that's what it was. Years ago, when he and Clive were boys, his mum and dad had taken them to Scotland for a week. They didn't have many proper holidays, and this one was special. They had gone to a stately home, where they trudged round the house, and then been let loose in the grounds. On the tourist leaflet, a little map showed places of interest, and one of these was the icehouse. Built in the sixteen hundreds, it had been used to store ice for the kitchens. Most of it was underground, with steps leading down, and the roof was dome-shaped, just like this one. The boys had shut themselves in to hide from their parents, and had got a roasting when they finally emerged. He could hear Gladys's voice now, yelling at them and saying they had frightened her half to death.

What better place to hole up? He would need a light and a camping gas stove. And a sleeping bag, and some food. A stream trickled by five yards away, so water would be no problem. All as easy as pie. When it was dark and the old girl had gone to bed, he could go up to the stables. She had a lifetime of junk stored in there, and he was sure he could find what he needed. As for food, well, Boy Scouts knew how to forage, and so did he. But now, he would shut himself in and have a couple of hours' sleep. His limbs ached with weariness, but he was happy. Everything had gone well so far. His luck was in, and like the rabbit, for the moment he was safe.

HIS BROTHER WAS NOT SO LUCKY. AFTER HE HAD LEFT COWGILL, and begun walking out of town towards the moors, he sat in the edge of a field for a snack and realised too late that what looked like a circle of dry earth was actually a juicy cow pat, and he had dropped down into it. He swore, dragging off his jeans and scraping as much as he could on the lush grass. "Ruddy cows!" he shouted, and then saw a distant figure waving a stick at him and shouting. Muttering more oaths, he pulled on his wet jeans and ran as quickly as he could out of the field. When he was a safe distance from the angry farmer, he stopped, sat on a tree stump and felt in his pocket for the sandwiches he had bought in Pickering. Gone. Must have fallen out in the field! He felt like crying, and found himself moaning for his mother.

After a while, he straightened up, realised that no one was going to help him and walked on in the direction of the farm. It seemed like hours later that he finally opened the yard gate and went towards the back door. It was locked, and there were no lights showing from the windows. Harry was either still in hospital, upstairs in bed or . . . dead? Depressed, hungry and cold, Clive felt all his optimism drain away. Gerald had gone after Harry, had one of his violent rages and done for him. It would be a matter of time before the cops caught up with him, and Clive did not intend to be there. He would vanish, change his appearance completely and start a new life. And this time, it would be on the right side of the law.

# THIRTY-NINE

~

M RS. TOLLERVEY-JONES SAT IN HER DRAWING ROOM, LOOK-
ing around and trying to decide which pieces of furniture she would take with her, and which would have to be
sold. She had decided to have a big, well-publicised sale of
whatever contents of the house remained after she had moved.
Now that she had made the big decision—to sell the estate—
the smaller ones were not so difficult.

The grand piano? No, there would not be room in the village
house. But she could not be without a piano, and considered
whether to buy a new one or pick up a good secondhand instru-
ment at one of the big piano sales in London. It was chilly in the
high-ceilinged room, and she decided to light the fire that was
already laid. Her thoughts took her back through pianos she
had known. The Bobart grand she had now was certainly not
her favourite. It had a jangly tone, and was difficult to bring up
to concert pitch. No, the one she had liked best had been a
heavy old Bluthner that was mellow and easy on the fingers.

What had happened to that? Her husband had disposed of it when he bought the grand for her birthday. Probably out into the stables, with all the rest of the unwanted junk. Perhaps she would find it, and have it restored. An upright would fit nicely into her new drawing room.

The telephone interrupted her thoughts. "Mrs. Tollervey-Jones? William Drew, from Lord & Francis. This is really just an update of where we have got to."

"Specifically," said Mrs. Tollervey-Jones, "where we have got to with the unlovely Norrington."

"Now, now!" said William jovially.

Mrs. Tollervey-Jones stiffened. "Just get to the point, Mr. er . . . er," she said coldly.

"Right, fine. Well, regarding Mr. Norrington, all seems to be going very well. He has cast-iron references, so far, and with your permission, we would like to go ahead."

"Are you saying there have been no other enquiries?" Mrs. Tollervey-Jones had been well schooled by her husband. Make sure you always have backup when taking big financial decisions.

William coughed. "Yes, indeed," he said. "We take every precaution. A very nice couple, again with all the right credentials, are keen to have a look at your estate. When would it be convenient to bring them along? There will be no need for you to be present, unless you would like to meet them. Thomas and I will do everything that is necessary."

"Except to see whether you would be happy seeing them take over your former life."

"Quite so. Shall we say tomorrow afternoon, around three o'clock?"

Mrs. T-J considered this. She had no appointments tomorrow and, except for hunting in the stable for a piano, nothing much to do. She approved the plan, and said she would see them tomorrow at three o'clock precisely. Meanwhile, she added, would they bring with them an interim report on their negotiations with Norrington.

"Phew!" said William to Thomas as he ended the call. "Marvellous woman! Don't make 'em like that anymore."

WHEN MRS. TOLLERVEY-JONES HAD FINISHED WITH WILLIAM, and the flames were leaping merrily in the fireplace, she reminded herself of her intention to contact Lois Meade. The woman should be back by now, she decided. She had been irritated to find that Lois was away, just at the time when she needed to plan her move to the village house.

Lois was deep in papers in her office when the phone rang. It was amazing how in such a short time, things had piled up for her to deal with.

"Good afternoon, Mrs. Tollervey-Jones," she said, forcing herself to be polite. In Lois's experience, a call from the old lady always spelled trouble. But in this case, it was good news. Mrs. Tollervey-Jones wished to have a discussion with her as soon as possible, in order to make a plan for moving to the village house. More work for New Brooms.

"And that reminds me," Mrs. Tollervey-Jones added, "my future home in the village is at the moment named 'Olde Timbers.' As you, with your impeccable taste, will be instantly aware, this is totally unacceptable. Perhaps you could give some thought to an alternative. I have asked my son, Robert, and his wife, Felicity, and they say that whatever they suggest will be turned down, so they are leaving it to me. Oddly enough, Mrs. Meade, I can think of no really suitable name."

"Olde Timbers has a number. You could always just have a number. A lot of people prefer that."

"Oh dear, no. Much too impersonal. I am sure the hall has a number, but can you imagine anyone using it?"

Lois sighed. This really did not come into the remit of New Brooms. Still, it would give them something to talk about this evening. She could ask Gran and Derek for help, and chuckled when she anticipated their likely suggestions.

"Do you want a cuppa?" Gran said, putting her head round the door. "You've been in there for hours. And if I'm not mistaken, you are about to have a visitor."

Lois looked across at the window. "Where?"

"Just parking outside. Not Josie's Matthew, but our other friendly neighbourhood policeman."

Lois groaned. "Oh no. Not Cowgill?"

"The very same," answered Gran. "Shall I show him in here?"

"If you can't get rid of him, yes."

"Have you ever tried to get rid of Cowgill? You don't argue with Cowgill, as you well know. I'll show him in."

Two minutes later, Gran tapped at Lois's door and opened it. "Inspector Cowgill is here to see you. Tea, Inspector?"

Why was Gran offering him tea? Lois glared at her, and she grinned back. "Sugar and milk?" she added, and disappeared fast.

"So I see you're back in harness, Lois dear," Cowgill said. "Did you have a good journey?"

"Let's cut the pleasantries, shall we," replied Lois. "I am extremely busy, as you guessed."

"Ah, yes. New Brooms business, I am sure. The trip to Pickering was all pleasure, I hope. Just so lucky that you were able to find poor old Harry, God rest his soul, and also give me useful information about the Mowlem brothers, who, by the way, seem to have vanished from the face of the earth. That is, Gerald is missing. It is really about the other one, Clive, that I am here."

Gran knocked once more. She brought in a small tray with an embroidered cloth, a cup and saucer of the best china and a plate of newly baked shortbread. She said nothing, but retreated rapidly, shutting the door with exaggerated care.

Lois held up her thick china mug, luridly decorated with dogs, and said, "What have you got that I haven't, Inspector Cowgill?"

"Absolutely nothing," Cowgill said seriously. "In fact, the thing I most want, I cannot have. As you must know by now. But let us return to the Mowlems. Before I left Pickering, I gave a lift to a man who looked every inch a tramp. I asked him one or two questions, and he indicated that he was dumb. Used his hands in sign language, which I could not understand. Now, I need to know from you or Josie anything you can remember about the thief who took cash from the shop."

"I can tell you what Josie told me," said Lois. "You'll have to ask her if you want more. She was very upset, I remember. Said this lorry with two men in it stopped outside the shop. The driver was a big man, and he stayed in the cab, whilst a little runt of a man came in and asked for cigarettes—"

"*Asked* for, did you say?" Cowgill interrupted.

"Yes, he asked for cigarettes. They were out of the brand he wanted, and when she went out to the stockroom, he emptied the till. Very quick and expert, he was."

Cowgill took a deep breath. "Lois," he said softly, "I have been fooled by a small-time, ignorant little thief."

"You mean Clive?"

Cowgill nodded. "It was Clive who accepted a lift. Mind you, he made a fatal mistake. After all that waving his hands about, when he got out of the car, he grinned proudly, and thanked me for the lift. Thanked me in the spoken voice, Lois. Obviously couldn't resist it. If he hadn't been such an idiot, I would probably never have given him a second thought."

"I know what Gran would say," Lois said, unable to suppress a smile. "Pride comes before a fall. Clivey boy will live to regret it, won't he?"

Cowgill drank his tea. "There is one more thing I need to know, and I'm afraid neither you nor Josie will be able to help. Did he recognise *me?* That is the question. If he did, he could be anywhere by now."

"He might still be the easiest to find. Gerald most likely took the car and abandoned his brother. What a berk! Thank goodness it's your baby now, Hunter. Let me know when you catch them, and I will come along and gloat."

Cowgill shook his head. Warmed by Lois's use of his Christian name, he was encouraged to go further. "Oh yes," he said sadly. "We're pretty sure to catch them sooner or later. Alive or dead. But that won't be much comfort to me. Perhaps I should consider early retirement?"

"Don't fish for compliments," Lois said brusquely. "You know you're admired and feared countrywide."

"All right, all right! But seriously, Lois, we shall wrap this up much quicker if you're still willing to help. The longer it takes, the more likely it is that something even nastier will occur. Together, the brothers Mowlem were nuisance enough, but singly, God knows what might happen."

# FORTY

꙳

Dot Nimmo walked purposefully through the back streets of Tresham, on her way to visit—"tackle" would be a better word—her erstwhile friend Gladys Mowlem. She had thought over her trip with Mrs. M, and after the drama of Harry's violent death, and sightings of the Mowlem brothers, it was her duty, she told herself, to let Gladys know what was going on.

This was only partly the truth. Dot found it impossible to believe that Gladys was totally without contact with her sons, or for that matter, with the amorous Harry. The criminal world had an efficient network of communication, and Dot intended to chat to Gladys, leak out one or two snippets of information and judge what she already knew.

Dot knocked loudly. She knew Gladys was deaf, though she hotly denied it. There were no signs of movement in the house, so she knocked again. The knocker was heavy, black iron, and even slightly deaf Gladys would have heard it.

After waiting patiently for a few minutes, Dot stooped, pushed open the letter box and shouted at the top of her voice: "Gladys! It's Dot Nimmo! Open up—I've got news for you!"

This did the trick, and Dot heard shuffling steps coming to the door.

"There's no need to shout, Dot," Gladys said. "I'm not deaf."

"What took you so long to answer, then?" Dot took in the uncombed hair, grubby dressing gown and down-at-heel slippers. "Can I come in? You don't look so good, Gladys. I'll make you a cup of tea." She pushed her way past Gladys and headed for the kitchen.

Unwashed dishes filled the sink, and the remains of a plate of cold, greasy chips stood on the table.

"Gladys Mowlem!" Dot said, turning to confront her. "What on earth is going on here?" Dot had always thought Gladys untrustworthy and sly, but she had also admired her housekeeping skills, especially as she coped so well in the face of a husband in jail and two sons who were more than likely to end up in the same place.

Money was short, Dot knew that, and poor old Gladys had to go out skivvying to keep the house going.

"I've not been well," Gladys said now. "And there's nobody to help me out, now that the boys have gone. I don't hear from them, you know, and I understand that. But, well, you know . . ."

"Sorry about that," said Dot, briskly clearing away dirty plates and filling the kettle. "It just so happens that I might have seen your Gerald and Clive in the last few days."

Gladys's face took on a wary look. "Oh yeah? Where was that, then?"

"Oh, up north. I was up there on business."

"What business?" Gladys thought she knew the only business Dot was into was the same as hers—cleaning other people's houses.

"Well, part business, part pleasure," answered Dot. "Went
on a wonderful steam train. My God, Gladys, that took me
back!"

"At Pickering, was it?" said Gladys. As soon as it slipped
out, she knew it was a mistake. Dot was onto it like a terrier
with a rabbit.

"You know Pickering, do you? Lovely place. Didn't your
Harry used to live up there somewhere?"

And then she knew instantly that Gladys had been told
the bad news. Dot watched as her friend's eyes filled with
tears, and she slumped down on a chair by the table, covering
her face with her hands.

"You knew, then? Who told you, Gladys? Was it your
boys? Poor old Harry didn't stand a chance, so I gather.
Bashed on the back of the head so hard that he never regained
consciousness." That was a bit of a lie, but only a necessary
white one. Dot was not about to make it worse for Gladys by
telling her that Harry's last word had been "Mowlem."

So Gladys must have heard from the boys. An edited version, no doubt, but she was not stupid. Useless as they were,
Gerald and Clive had never, to Dot's knowledge, been done
for grievous bodily. But now it looked as if the next charge
against them might be murder. Dot looked around at the
chaotic kitchen, and decided that Gladys had worked this out
for herself. No wonder the poor old thing had collapsed!

"Now then, Gladys, I don't think we have to spell it all
out. You need help, that's obvious, and we're old friends. You
and me, we go back a long way. So I am offering help. First

thing, clear up the house. That'll cheer you up for a start. Then we'll get out of here and go to the Chinese up the road for a bite to eat. And as for the rest, you got my telephone number and can give me a ring anytime. I reckon things might get worse, and you're goin' to need a friend."

DOT WAS PLEASED WITH HERSELF WHEN SHE CONSIDERED HER morning's work. As she got ready to go over to her client in Fletching, she wondered whether to tell Mrs. M immediately about Gladys, or to leave it until Gladys phoned her, as she was sure to, and then see what information she had to give.

As she took out her key to let herself into her house, she stopped suddenly. A well-honed instinct told her there was somebody behind her, someone who had been following her and now was up close. Do nothing. Wait for him to make the first move. It was all coming back to her. Soon after their marriage, Handy had told her the basics of self-preservation, and now here it was, the need to use them.

She waited. Then a voice hissed in her ear. "Open up, Dot. Don't turn around; just open up and go in. I'll be following." As he spoke, she felt a hand grip her arm.

She did as she was told. She turned the key and pushed open her front door, and when inside and the door had banged shut behind her, she turned around.

"Wotcha, Dot! Long time no see, eh? We go back a long way, you and me."

She stared at him, struggling to place him. Where had she seen him before? He answered her unspoken question.

"I bin away for a few years, an' a hard life in the nick changes a person. Don't you remember when we were Bert and Dot, a close twosome, sweethearts at school? That were before Handy muscled in on me. Still, Gladys were a good substitute, but I can't go home for a bit. So now then, Dot," he added, his tone changing to a harsh growl. "You bin a busy girl, ain't yer? Get goin', then, into the back kitchen. I got news for you, as they say on the telly."

# FORTY-ONE

❧

"Wow! What's all that about?" Derek blinked as he looked up from the remains of an early snack lunch. Lois had said she was going upstairs to change, and as she came into the kitchen, he blinked. She was quietly smart in a tailored black suit and crisp white shirt, and most unusually for Lois, high-heeled black shoes. She had secured her long, silky dark hair in a tortoiseshell clip, and was discreetly made up.

"Got an appointment," she said mysteriously.

"Not at the police station, I hope," muttered Derek, but not softly enough.

"I heard that, and no, not at the cop shop," Lois replied crossly. "I'm sure you haven't forgotten your daughter is getting wed in the New Year. No good leaving things to the last minute. Josie and me are going into that new wedding dress place in Tresham. And I don't intend to let her down by going in my floor-scrubbing gear. Satisfied?"

"Can I come?" said Gran, without much hope.

"No," said Lois flatly. "Did Grannie come when you and me went to get the material for my wedding dress? This is a mother and daughter togetherness day."

Derek raised his eyebrows and said nothing more. Lois teetered around the kitchen, and then suddenly collapsed into stifled laughter. "Oh my God, Derek, what am I saying? I sound like some awful women's mag! But I did think it would be nice to dress up a bit."

"And you look so good you'll be mistaken for the bride-to-be," said Derek gallantly. This was more like his Lois.

"And of course you can come, Mum, if you want to," continued Lois.

But Gran had taken the hint, and said thanks for the offer, but she had to go round to see Joan about WI teas.

LOIS HAD NO IDEA THAT CHOOSING A WEDDING DRESS COULD TAKE so long. Josie must have been through every single model in the shop, and was still undecided. She could not help remembering her own wedding. She and Gran had bought yards of white brocade and taken it proudly home. Then Gran had hoovered every single speck off the front room carpet and they had spread out the material, pinned on the pattern and cut it out, ready to sew up on Gran's old treadle sewing machine.

Dare she suggest this as an alternative? No, part of the whole expensive business these days was buying a wedding dress that would most likely be worn only once, but stay in the cupboard as a reminder of a magical day.

Lois knew that some people cut up their wedding dress for use as a christening gown for the first baby. And the top tier of the wedding cake for the christening! Lois had always thought

this a terrible idea. How did it taste? Still, nowadays the christening often followed so soon after the wedding that the cake
could be quite fresh.

"Mum? What do you think?" Josie broke into Lois's rev-
erie, and twirled around in a beautiful cream silk gown with
long sleeves that ended in a point over her hand, and a short
train trailing behind her. A long line of silk-covered buttons
emphasized Josie's slender shape, and Lois was near to tears as
she looked at her only daughter.

"Wonderful," she said, sniffing. "That's the one. And don't
tell me the price," she added to the assistant. "Just take my
card."

The assistant laughed, and said that in her opinion, Josie
had chosen the loveliest dress in the shop. "I bet you say that
to all the brides-to-be!" said Josie, having a last twirl in front
of the long looking glass.

"Actually, I don't," said the girl seriously. "I am sure you
agree with me, Mrs. Meade."

Lois looked at her more closely. "Sorry, but I think I
should recognise you?" she said. After all, the girl had known
her name was Meade.

The answer was a surprise. "I'm Mrs. Nimmo's niece, Barbara," she said. "One of the dreaded Nimmos, but I try to
keep that quiet. I shall be glad when it's my turn to take on a
different name at my own wedding!"

"Nimmo? Dot Nimmo's niece?"

The girl nodded, and laughed again. "There you are, you
see; you look horrified."

Lois denied this hotly, and said she was really pleased to
meet another Nimmo. "Dot is one of my best team members.
Mind you," she added, "they are all nice women. But Dot is a
great character, isn't she."

"The best," said Barbara. "She has been very kind to me over the years."

At this point, the manageress came in from the back room, and Barbara shifted back into shop assistant mode. "Ah, there you are. Just look at Josie in this gown," she said to her boss. "Isn't it beautiful?"

"Both the dress and the bride will outshine all others," said the manageress lavishly.

"You wait 'til you see Mum," said Josie, allowing Barbara to take the dress away.

Lois had already chosen a dove grey dress and jacket, with a grey straw hat to match. A small spray of white ostrich feathers tucked into the hatband was her only ornament. She had already decided that on no account would she compete with the bride, unlike some mothers she had seen. This would be Josie's day.

The manageress disappeared again to make notes on small alterations, and Lois asked Barbara if she saw much of her Aunt Dot.

"Quite often," Barbara answered. "We live at the other end of Sebastopol Street, almost opposite your office. My dad died some years ago, got killed in a car accident. Hit-and-run. Nimmos specialise in those. So there's just Mum and me, and we live very quietly."

"We'll tell Dot we met you, and how you helped Josie find the ideal wedding dress," said Lois as they turned to leave the shop. "Hope we see you again when we come to collect."

Dot had not felt her ears burning as her niece talked about her with the Meades. In fact, she was very cold, cold through and through. First, because the wind had turned as she walked home, and now came from the north, whistling through the gap in the ill-fitting back door, and causing a draught from front to back of the old house.

Second, she was not at all happy about being forced to sit in her own back kitchen, whilst an ugly brute of a man she had at first failed to recognise threatened her with a gun.

She had done as she was told, and sat only half listening whilst he talked a load of nonsense about what he would do to her. Make a plan as soon as possible, Handy would have said. Don't antagonise him, but make him feel he's got you where he wants you. And then, when you've made a plan, act on it.

"Are you listening to me, Dot Nimmo?" He put his ugly face close to hers, and stuck the gun into her ribs. "I always mean what I say, and you'd best attend to it."

"I ain't goin' nowhere. And I am listening to every word. You'll have no trouble from me. After all, I owe you something for old times' sake."

He frowned. This was not like the Dot Nimmo he remembered. Meek and mild? Huh! What was she up to?

"Right," he said. "Now this is what we're going to do. I need a place to stay for a bit, and I need a woman who knows how to keep her mouth shut. You came instantly to mind, Dot. Plenty of practice in the past! But I believe in belt and braces, so I'll just make sure you don't try a runner."

He pulled a length of narrow rope from his pocket and, putting down the gun for a moment, tied Dot's hands round the back of her chair. She aimed a kick at his leg, but he was onto her in a moment.

"No you don't!" he said, stepping sideways. He picked up the gun once more and levelled it at her.

"My foot slipped," she said, and managed a submissive smile.

"I'm not a fool, Dot Nimmo," he said. "And nor are you. As long as we remember that, we'll be fine. So here's the plan."

It was a simple plan. He would stay out of sight in Dot's house, and she would plead illness to her boss, arranging for food et cetera to be brought to her door.

"How long will that last?" said Dot. "People will begin to wonder."

"As long as I say so," he said fiercely. "I got people out there'd be very pleased to see me available, as you might say, an' I don't mean that in a nice way. I owe a few favours, Dot. I'm sure you know what I mean." Dot was no fool, and she nodded meekly.

# FORTY-TWO

ⅇ

ALTHOUGH THE WEDDING SHOP APPOINTMENT HAD BEEN SOON
after noon, and although Lois drove fast back to Long
Farnden to drop off Josie before going on to the hall, she was,
nevertheless, ten minutes late. A displeased Mrs. Tollervey-
Jones met her at the door.

"This is the first time, Mrs. Meade," she said, "that New
Brooms has let me down. I was expecting you at three."

Lois apologised, but explained the circumstances and said
that it would not happen again. "For one thing," she said,
"I've only got one daughter, and there'll be only one wedding
dress at the price they seem to be these days."

"That is neither here nor there," was the curt answer. "The
men from Lord & Francis have arrived, and I shall be glad if you
will bring in tea at four. They have another couple of prospective buyers with them, so there will be five of us. And by the
way, I appreciate your making an effort to be suitably dressed."

Suppressing an urge to tell Mrs. Tollervey-Jones the real reason why she was not wearing a pinafore and carrying a duster, she said instead that she hoped the meeting would go well, and if her help was wanted to show the couple round, she would be only too pleased to do so.

She busied herself in the kitchen, setting out the best Royal Worcester cups and saucers, plates and family teapot. The large, elegant butler's tray was just the thing for the job, and she added chocolate biscuits that she found in a tin. Taking a bite from one, she decided that they were not too stale.

Now wearing sensible flat shoes that she had hastily changed into, she looked at the clock. Five minutes to four o'clock. She picked up the tray and marched through the long passage, backed out carefully through the green baize door and stood outside the drawing room door, wondering how to knock with both hands occupied.

As she stood undecided, she heard a name mentioned in exclamation.

"Norrington!" said a strange voice. "Not Geoffrey Norrington! Good Lord, Mrs. Tollervey-Jones, you should steer clear of that one!"

Lois was surprised that someone had revealed the name of the first prospective buyer, but when she finally negotiated her way into the room, she saw that it had clearly been Mrs. Tollervey-Jones who had let it slip. The agent was looking thunderous, and for possibly the only time in her life, she was blushing guiltily.

"Ah, Mrs. Meade, there you are. Please put the tray over there, and perhaps you would like to pour out tea for us?" Mrs. Tollervey-Jones quickly regained her composure, and silence fell as Lois expertly poured out tea. Thanks to Gran, she thought, for insisting on small household skills!

"Now, Mrs. Meade," said Mrs. Tollervey-Jones when all were served, "I should be grateful if you would accompany Mr. and Mrs. er . . . er . . ."

"Blenkinsop," said William helpfully.

". . . round the house, and then, if it is fine, on a short tour of the grounds. I am sure . . . er . . . er . . ."

"Thomas," said William.

". . . yes, Thomas, will want to go with you." She turned to the rest, and said that Mrs. Meade was an extremely knowledgeable person on local matters, and could answer any questions that Mr. and Mrs. Blenkinsop might have.

Lois said she would be pleased to be of help in any way possible, and left them to their tea. She returned to the kitchen, and sat down at the table. She had a list of things she needed to confirm with Dot, largely times and places they had been whilst they were in Pickering. She took out her mobile, checked that the kitchen door was shut so that she would not be heard and dialled Dot's number.

There was no reply, and she left a message asking Dot to call her as soon as possible. It was odd that there was no answer. Dot's mobile was virtually part of her right arm. "Never without it," she said often. "What did we do without our mobiles?" Well, whatever it was Dot was doing, she had not answered.

After half an hour or so, the kitchen door opened and Mrs. Tollervey-Jones came in. "Have you kept busy?" she said. "Good. Now, if you would take the Blenkinsops—ridiculous name!—for a tour with the Thomas person, I shall tackle the thorny question of the Norringtons' financial status with the other one . . . er, William, was it?"

"Perhaps it would have been a good idea to have Mr. Robert here?"

Mrs. Tollervey-Jones bridled. "Good heavens, no. I am perfectly capable of dealing with this lot."

Lois nodded dutifully, and went out to gather her tour party together.

Unfortunately, the Blenkinsops were not prepared to skip any part of the estate, except the farms, which they said they would come back to another day. So Lois efficiently led the way in and out of bedrooms, utility rooms, stable yard and stables, the cold, damp chapel and muddy kitchen garden.

Mrs. Blenkinsop clapped her hands together like a delighted child at every new discovery, and Lois began to wonder if they would get back to the house before dark.

"That's about it," she said, turning up her collar against the cold wind. "This way," she added, and led them firmly towards the house.

Mrs. Blenkinsop lagged behind, and Lois stopped, waiting for her to catch up. "Oh, Mrs. Meade," she said, "I knew there was one other thing. We are great ones for visiting National Trust properties, and in one or two we have seen these lovely old icehouses. Very old, of course, prefridge! But they are charming relics of a different way of life. Is there one here? I would love to see it."

Lois felt like saying they didn't need an icehouse. Her feet were frozen already. But she said politely that she had never heard anyone speak of an icehouse, but if there was one, she suggested that as the light was fading, she would make sure Mrs. Blenkinsop was taken to see it on their next visit.

DEEP IN THE WOODS, GERALD, BUSY CLEARING OUT THE INTE-rior of his new home, heard far-off voices. He stopped work and listened. Were they coming this way? But no, there was no easy way through to where he was, and in any case, the voices were fainter now, going away from him. He relaxed and carried on with his housework.

# FORTY-THREE

CLIVE WAS HUNGRY. HE HAD BEEN THROUGH WHAT WAS LEFT in Harry's fridge, and that was not much, and when raiding the garden for vegetables, he had found nothing left. They had eaten it all, the three of them. No wonder he had wanted Mum to come and look after him!

After a scary time, soon after he got back to the farm, when uniformed policemen had come looking for him, and had turned the place over in their hunt, Clive had slowly begun to feel more or less safe. Whilst they were there, he had hidden in a place that he and Gerald had earmarked for just such an eventuality. At the far end of the bull's stall there was a cupboard where they had hidden their loot. It was more of a room without windows, and it was so dark, and the door covered with cobwebs, that it was scarcely visible.

What's more, thought Clive, grinning as he remembered the searching policemen, you had to get past the great snorting bull, and only he and Gerald knew that the animal was all huff and puff and wouldn't hurt a fly. Or so they hoped! Anyway, the old fellow had only stared at Clive as he had pushed past to reach the cupboard and shut himself in.

It occurred to him now, as he stood in the kitchen thinking about food, that maybe he should feed the bull. He had given it water this morning, but the great beast must need a lot of grub to keep him happy. But as his stomach rumbled, Clive decided his own hunger was a priority. He looked at his situation squarely and saw that, first, he had no transport, except Harry's tractor, and he had no idea how to drive it. And second, third and fourth, it would be madness for him to show his face in Pickering. They probably had "Wanted" posters out by now, and someone would be bound to recognise him.

He thought back to all the round trips he and Gerald had made, looking for likely items to steal under cover of darkness. They had mainly stuck to villages, and never looted the same place twice. As he thought about thumbing a lift and going wherever it took him, he ruled out villages. A town, where strangers were coming and going all the time, would be more sensible. Nobody was likely to notice him amongst the rest.

So, he would get down to the main road and thumb a lift. After all, he'd done it before with that man who'd taken him into Pickering, and nothing bad had come of that. He would go now, and get back by the same means. He must do enough shopping to last until Gerald came for him—*if* he came for him. If Gerald didn't, then he would have to think again. The prospect did not terrify him as much as before, and he began to feel again that perhaps he would be able to cope on his own from now on.

The next thing was money. He had a few pounds left, but it would not be enough for a big shop. If he went to a supermarket where they asked if he wanted cash back on his card, he could take enough to keep him going for a good while.

Feeling pleased with himself, he found an old tweed cap of Harry's, and pulled it down over his eyes. He looked at himself in a cracked mirror in the kitchen, and decided he looked like a man on the run, so he changed the cap to a jaunty angle, smiled approval at himself and set out across the fields to reach the main road, intending to thumb a lift.

It was not until he was sitting comfortably in a lorry driver's cab that he remembered the bull. He must remember to feed it when he got back.

"Where d'you want to go, mate?" asked the driver.

"Helmsley, if you're going through there," Clive said. "I've got a car to pick up. Passed its annual checkup by a whisker!"

The driver laughed, and Clive joined in. This life on your own was a doddle, he thought, once you got used to it.

His brother, on the other hand, was missing company. He had made the interior of the icehouse habitable, just about, and realised he had not spoken to anybody for several days. He opened the door and listened to the sounds of the wood for several minutes. His sudden appearance had caused a pigeon to fly off with a clatter of wings and an alarmed squawk. Then silence fell, and he imagined all the animals of the forest—it had become a forest in his imagination— motionless, and listening for his next move. He was not a countryman, and had always been glad to return to the busy back streets of Tresham. Silence frightened him.

He turned to go back to the safety of the icehouse, when a more domestic sound came from behind the mound. A tiny mewing sound. He pushed his way through the brambles and heard it again, coming from a hollow stump of a felled tree. He bent down and looked inside. Two almond-shaped, pale blue eyes looked out at him. "A kitten, for God's sake!" he said aloud, forgetting where he was for one shocked moment. What on earth was a kitten doing in the middle of the forest? Probably picked up by a foraging owl and rejected, dropped in the underbrush, Gerald guessed.

Tentatively, he put his hand out towards it, and it backed away. He peered more closely, but could see no other animals, just one kitten. Ginger, as far as he could make out. A ginger tom kitten, then. He grabbed it firmly and held it against his chest. It mewed pathetically and tried to burrow into his coat. He put his hand over it protectively. "Come on, then, young fella," he whispered. "A cat's better than nothing."

Back inside the icehouse, Gerald shut the door behind him and released the kitten. It shook itself so vigorously that its fragile legs almost collapsed under it. Then it mewed again, and looked straight at him.

Milk, that's what kittens liked. He reached out to his make-shift larder, and found the half-pint bottle he had brought with him and had not yet opened. "It should be fresh," he said, smiling at the kitten. "We are in an icehouse, after all." He poured the milk carefully into the lid of a jar of pickles he'd packed to brighten up a hunk of cheddar, and put it in front of the kitten.

It approached the lid warily, and then began to lap with a tiny pink tongue. Gerald sat back on his heels and watched, and then he heard an unbelievably loud rhythmic sound and realised it was coming from the kitten. It was washing its whiskers with small paws, and purring.

Gerald covered his face with his hands, and tears sprang out from between his fingers. "Clive," he sobbed, "where the hell are you?"

# FORTY-FOUR

❧

HUNTER COWGILL SAT IN HIS OFFICE, STARING AT THE FRONT page of the *Daily Telegraph*. He was not reading. His thoughts were miles away, up in North Yorkshire, where he had sent his nephew Matthew to pursue the hunt for the Mowlems. Ever since Matthew had become engaged to Josie Meade, Cowgill had felt close to the Meade family, and he had shared with Lois and Gran their anger and concern at the attack on Derek in the stable yard up at the hall.

The family had wanted to take no action, no official action, but he knew that Lois's prime motive for helping him out—and more important, for her trip to Pickering with Dot Nimmo—was to track down the brothers and make sure they paid for the attack.

So far, searches had failed to track down either of them, but he had no doubt it was only a matter of time. He had sent Matthew to join the hunt because he, too, would be feeling an extra compulsion to see that justice was done for his future father-in-law.

His thoughts switched to Tresham, and to Gladys Mowlem. From what he already knew about the brothers, the one person they would be likely to contact was their mother, although she was a woman renowned for her inability to keep secrets. A number of felons had been rounded up as a result of her loose tongue. She was not exactly a police informant, but because of her contacts amongst the criminal fraternity, members of his force often dropped in for a cup of tea with Gladys.

He stood up, folded up his newspaper and moved to the window. It was raining, and umbrellas jostled for position on the pavement below. It was time, he decided, for Gladys to have a visit from the chief detective inspector.

GLADYS, UNAWARE OF THE IMMINENCE OF AN IMPORTANT VISITOR, sat in her back kitchen, her feet up on an old milking stool, drinking a cup of instant coffee well sweetened with two heaped teaspoonfuls of sugar, and reading with relish the latest scandal to emerge about her favourite television personality.

"Well I never," she said aloud. "He'll not get away with it this time! And her an Honourable!"

Cowgill's firm knock at her door startled her, and she got to her feet. "Now, who's that?" she said. The sudden thought that it might be one or both of her sons sent her scuttling along the passage to the front door. She drew back the bolts and opened it a crack. Peering out, she saw an unfamiliar man in a raincoat and broad-brimmed hat.

"Wotcha want?" she said truculently, then saw the man was holding out an identity card. She recognised it from regrettably long familiarity with the local police. So this was a plainclothes one. She sighed, opened the door wider and beckoned him in.

Cowgill introduced himself, and he could see she was suitably impressed.

"May I sit down for a moment?" he said. "Perhaps we could have a little chat about the boys. I haven't seen them lately," he added in a friendly voice that suggested they all inhabited the same social gatherings in town.

Gladys was not fooled. The appearance of this important cop meant that whatever the boys had done, it was serious. She was immediately on the defensive, and said they had gone off without telling her where they were going. "They're grown men now, Inspector," she reminded him. "Their old mother is the last to know where they're working. But they are good boys, always sending money for housekeeping an' that."

This was such an unlikely piece of fantasizing that Cowgill knew he could not expect the truth from now on. But never mind, he could always sift the wheat from the chaff, and gain something useful.

"What work are they doing at the moment, Mrs. Mowlem?" he asked pleasantly.

"Oh, this and that," Gladys said. "Whatever comes up, really. It's not easy these days to earn an honest living."

"Let alone a dishonest one," said Cowgill in the same bland tones.

"Wotcha mean!" replied Gladys. "My boys are good boys."

"Come now," said Cowgill, his voice sharpening. "You must remember the rather frequent occasions when they have been up before the bench, accused of theft or trespass?"

"And maybe *you* remember that they've never been sen-

tenced to more than a small fine, Inspector Cowgill." Gladys
frowned. She had been going to offer him a cup of tea, but
now decided against it. But she did intend to find out just
what he knew about the boys. More than she did, she guessed.

"I agree they've never been done for grievous bodily harm,
or anything approaching that." Cowgill paused, and then
added, "So far, Mrs. Mowlem, so far."

"Wotcha mean by that?" And him sitting there like a
nodding Chinaman ornament. Still, there was no point in
antagonising him.

Cowgill knew they were now engaged in a battle of wits,
and changed the subject. "Terrible morning out there," he
said casually. "Did you have a holiday this year? Get away to
the coast? I know people who are taking holidays in this
country instead of abroad this year. The budget cuts are hit-
ting us all."

"You can say that again!" said Gladys hotly. "There's me
with me poor old legs, still going out charring. And the boys
finding it more and more diffy to get casual work. They went
off in search of it, and God knows where." There, that should
fix him.

"And yourself? Did you manage a break? Maybe with relations up north? Yorkshire, was it?"

It's like shutters coming down, thought Cowgill, as he
watched Gladys's face close up. "Didn't go nowhere," she said.
"Is that all you come for, to ask me about me hols? If so, I'm
busy, and I'll show you out."

He had his answer. They were still up there. He returned
to his car, and dialled Matthew's number. He was on his way
back to the station when he considered that they might have
split up, and when he gave Clive a lift, the young fool was on
his own for good.

\*   \*   \*

THE RAIN HAD BECOME HEAVIER AS THE MORNING WORE ON, AND in the main street of Long Farnden, the usual river had formed, ending up in a lake by the blocked drain. In the past, men in orange jackets had turned up occasionally and had a go at freeing it, but seemed always to fail. The next storm would see the lake rising as deep as ever.

"We need milk," said Gran, coming into Lois's office and standing, hands on hips, waiting for instructions. She would never normally need these, but had looked out of the kitchen window and decided she was not going out, even the short distance down to the shop.

"I'll go at lunchtime," said Lois.

"You've got a team meeting, and there's none for coffee."

"Oh, all right then," Lois answered, smiling at her mother's transparency. "I'll run down. What else do we need?"

With a short list of items, Lois pulled on her raincoat and set off. Her umbrella was worse than useless in the gusty wind that blew sharp flurries of hail into her face. She lowered it, and ran the last few yards to the shop steps.

"Morning, Mum!" said Josie, looking perky on the other side of the counter. "Terrible weather! Here, sit on the stool, and I'll get us a coffee. There's not likely to be many customers this morning."

"I'll hold the fort anyway," said Lois. "I'm going into Tresham after the meeting, to see if I can find Dot. She hasn't turned up at her job this morning, and I can't get any answer on her phone. I need to go to the tax office anyway."

"Matthew can help you with tax matters," Josie said. "He's a wizard at it. But then," she said dreamily, "he's a wizard at most things."

"Except finding out who coshed your dad," said Lois without thinking.

Josie drew herself up. "Then why has he gone chasing off to Yorkshire, do you suppose? They're hot on the trail."

"Mm," said Lois.

Josie flounced off to the kitchen to make coffee, and Lois glanced idly at the newspapers on the counter. She turned to the property pages and saw that the hall was still advertised for sale. So the agents were not necessarily happy about Norrington's offer. She hoped it would be settled soon, both for the sake of New Brooms and Andrew's interior décor.

Josie returned, and said cheerfully that the gutter outside the back door was blocked again. "What we want is a good plumber," she said, and then noticed the page her mother was reading.

"How did you get on at the hall with the new prospective buyers?" she asked.

"The Norringtons?"

"No, the ones who came last week. Blenkinsop was the name, so I heard."

Lois marvelled at the ability of the village shopkeeper to know everything. "I liked them," she said. "The wife was so excited about everything. I thought I'd never get home. But it would be nice if they got it. Much better than slimy old Norrington."

The rain had stopped by the time Lois returned home, and she planned to tell Gran that the watery sunshine had turned the village into a fairyland of twinkling raindrops. But not in those words! Gran would never let her forget it.

"I think I'll skip lunch," she said to her disapproving mother. "I stayed too long talking to Josie, and I need to go into town after the meeting. See if I can catch Dot."

"She rang," said Gran.

"Why didn't you tell me?"

"You didn't give me a chance. She said she was poorly, and would let you know when she was well enough to come back to work. We didn't have a chat like usual. She seemed in a hurry to end the call."

Lois frowned. Such a bald message was unlike Dot. She would normally have organised her own replacement and added that she'd be back tomorrow, come hell or high water. "I think I'll pop in and see if she needs anything," she said.

When the team had gathered, they wanted to know all about Pickering, and Lois gave them an abbreviated account. She explained Dot's absence, and asked if any of them had heard from her. No one had, but they confirmed that flu was everywhere. "People going down like flies," said Sheila, adding that her Sam had been very middlin' with it.

Lois asked them all to let her know at once if they saw or heard anything about Dot, noted their surprised faces and brought the meeting to an early close.

THE TAX MAN HAD BEEN HELPFUL, AND LOIS FELT REASONABLY cheered as she drove round to Sebastopol Street and parked outside New Brooms' office. She opened the door and said to Hazel that she would be back in two minutes, after she had checked on Dot.

"Dot? I thought she'd sent a message?" Hazel said. She frequently saw her teammate walking from her house up and down the street. "I have been thinking, and I definitely haven't seen her for a day or two."

Lois walked along to the end of the street, and knocked at Dot's door. No answer. She peered through the window, but there was nobody to be seen. She knocked again, and put her ear to the door. Sounds coming from the back of the house encouraged her to knock once more. Perhaps Dot was in the garden. But no, she was poorly. Perhaps she shouldn't get the poor thing out of bed? She might have the flu that was rampant in town.

The sounds ceased, and still no one came to the door. Lois gave up, but thought she would ring Dot's sister, Evelyn, later, to see if she had any news. She walked back down the street to the office and went in.

"No luck," she said to Hazel. "I'll try again tomorrow."

"Don't come in specially," Hazel said. "I'll go up after work and see how she is."

Lois thanked her, and cautioned not to go into the house for fear of catching the bug. "Just make sure she is all right," she said, and added, "and let me know how you get on."

Hazel thought to herself that the boss was making a mountain out of a molehill, but she would do as Lois said. Anything to keep her happy.

# FORTY-FIVE

꙰

Lois had been trying to talk to Evelyn Nimmo on and off all day, and now it was half past seven and they were settling down for an evening of television.

"What's eating you, duckie?" said Derek, patting the sofa for Lois to sit down next to him. "You've been like a cat on hot bricks all day."

"Oh, it's nothing, really. Just that I am a bit worried about Dot. She told Mum she was poorly, so I went to see if she needed help, but nobody answered the door. So I tried ringing Evelyn, but all I get is the answer phone. It seems odd, that's all. Not like Dot."

She sank onto the sofa and closed her eyes. She felt weary with anxiety, and decided she would have one more go at Evelyn before they went to bed. Dot lived all alone, and apart from her sister, she had no one keeping an eye on her in case she needed help. She had quarrelled with her neighbours—not surprising, this, since both sides had tried all ways to get rid of the Nimmos when her husband and son were alive. And although the Nimmo family members were numerous, most of the others regarded Dot with suspicion on account of her working for Lois Meade. They stayed well away.

At ten o'clock, Lois said she would go and make a cup of tea, and disappeared off to the kitchen.

"She's going to ring Evelyn," said Gran. "Won't leave it alone until tomorrow. The woman might be away on holiday. There's sure to be a simple explanation."

Derek shook his head sadly. "I'm afraid not," he said. "When Lois gets one of her feelings that things are wrong, she's always right. So now she'll be off on her white charger to rescue Dot Nimmo. Just see if I'm not right."

Sure enough, Lois came back with a tray of tea and said she had just got through to Evelyn. "She says Dot had rung her with the same message. She's got flu, didn't need anything and would ring when she was better. Said on no account to try to see her, as it was a really nasty bug and she didn't want Evelyn to catch it."

"There you are, then, that's plain enough. I expect it'll be a week or so before she's back. Flu can be a devil to get rid of." Gran finished her tea, leaned her head against a cushion, closed her eyes and said to wake her when the news came on. Derek waited until Gran was whiffling gently in her sleep, and then put his arm around Lois. "Are you happy now, me duck?" he said, pulling her close.

"Not sure," said Lois.

"But whatever, it'll wait until tomorrow. Shall we creep away upstairs and leave Gran to switch off the telly?"

Lois smiled. She looked at her mother, and whispered that they could try. They got as far as the door when, without opening her eyes, Gran said coldly, "Don't worry about me.

I'll do it all. Switch off the telly, put the dog in the garden for a pee, lock all the doors and turn off the lights. Just bugger off, the pair of you."

NEXT MORNING, LOIS WAS UP EARLY. SHE HAD DECIDED TO HAVE another try at Dot's front door, and if there was still no reply, she would talk to Cowgill and ask his advice. This was not something she did often, if ever, but now she was really worried. The more she thought about Dot's calls, the more suspicious she felt.

After breakfast, she announced that she would be in for lunch, as she planned half a day in the office in Sebastopol Street.

"Don't you go chasing after Dot Nimmo," said Gran. "We don't want flu running round the family. It's dangerous for old people like me."

"You've had the jab," said Lois. But she knew Gran was right. It was foolish to persist, when Dot had left perfectly sensible messages explaining why she was away from work. Still . . .

DOT SAT IN HER KITCHEN, STARING OUT THE WINDOW. HER unwanted companion had insisted on sitting in her bedroom all night, saying he would never trust a Nimmo and knew she would be trying every way of escaping. She had hardly slept, and felt fuzzy and confused.

"But you'd better not try to get away," he said again when they had had a far from companionable breakfast together. "I've got a lot of contacts now, useful ones, an' we all stick together. You could run wherever you like, Dottie, but we'd always find you. An' then, God help ya!"

From a lifetime's experience of lies and half-truths, Dot knew that he was telling the whole truth. She wished her head would clear so that she could think her way out of all this. The person she wanted to tell more than anyone was Mrs. M. Just her luck that it had been Gran who answered the phone. She only had to say one or two code words to Mrs. M, and she would know something was wrong. But this big idiot wouldn't let her make any more calls.

He had taken her mobile, so she couldn't even try from the lavatory. Every time her house phone rang, he forced her into a chair so that she couldn't touch it. Then she heard her own voice on the answer phone and a message from Mrs. M, and was nearly reduced to tears of frustration.

Now he sat on the other side of the kitchen table, leafing through piles of old magazines he had found in the box room upstairs.

"Rotten selection," he said, throwing a couple of knitting patterns on the floor. "Ain't you got no decent mags? I like them top-shelf ones meself, but I don't suppose they'd be much in your line." He chuckled, and Dot felt sick. How much longer could she take this?

"There's no food left in the fridge," she said. "What you going to do about that? I can go for days, y'know, without anything, but you look to me like a greedy guts."

He clenched his fist, but Dot dodged. "Wouldn't you like me to go to the shop on the corner? If I promise to come straight back?" she said without much hope.

"You must be jokin'," he replied. "No, Dottie dear, you'll do what you're told, and ask your sister to leave some shoppin' on the doorstep. I'll give you a list, and you can phone 'er. An' you'll not say more than I tell you, or else!"

He found a stub of pencil in his pocket, tore off the edge

of the newspaper and laboriously wrote a shopping list for Evelyn. He gave it to Dot, and handed over her mobile phone. "Just the list, and yes and no to any questions she asks. Got it?"

"Why don't you do it?" Dot asked slyly.

"Hah! You must think I was born yesterday! That would get her round here with a posse of the law, wouldn't it? Just what you want? Don't underestimate me, Dot Nimmo. I've learned a thing or two in the last few years, and I'm not about to be outsmarted by the likes of a silly woman. Here, do it."

"Evelyn's been a nurse," Dot lied in a moment of inspiration. "She'll want to come in and check me over. Don't forget I'm supposed to be very poorly with flu."

He paused in thought, and then brightened. "I've shot all the bolts and locked up, an' the keys are in my pocket. So your nurse, if she really is one, can knock and call all she likes. She'll not be let in."

Dot thought of dialling Evelyn and shouting for help, regardless of this fool in front of her. But she looked at his piggy little eyes, and knew he wouldn't hesitate to put her out of action if necessary. Then she looked down the list, and her spirits lifted. She took the mobile phone from him and dialled her sister's number.

# FORTY-SIX

୬

"Four tins of SARDINES, DID YOU SAY, DOT?"

"Yes," answered Dot dutifully.

"But you hate sardines! They make you sick, even the smell!"

"Yes."

Evelyn frowned. "Are you sure you're managing?" she said.

"No."

"Then why—" The line cut out, and Evelyn did not finish her sentence. Oh my goodness, she said to herself, there really is something wrong. Without hesitating, she disconnected from Dot's call and dialled Lois Meade. It never occurred to her to get the police. Nimmos never called the police.


Hazel Thornbull remembered as soon as she turned into Sebastopol Street. She had completely forgotten to check on Dot yesterday after work. Mrs. M would kill her! Best to go at once, she decided, even if it meant opening up the office a few minutes late.

She parked her car and half ran up the street to Dot's house. She knocked and called, but heard nothing. Stepping back, she looked up at the bedroom windows. They were drawn across, but as she peered hard, she could swear she had seen a face for a split second, looking out through a crack in the curtains, and then gone. Dot? Even in that fraction of a second, she knew it was not Dot. It had been a man's face. Oh Lord, so Mrs. M was not making a fuss about nothing.

Sprinting back down the street to New Brooms' office, she opened up and at once picked up the phone. Lois's number was engaged, so Hazel set about opening the post. Best to keep busy until she could speak to Mrs. M, she thought, but her hands were clumsy, shaking as she opened the envelopes.

IN HIS BURROW IN THE WOODS, GERALD SAT HAPPILY FEEDING THE kitten tiny pieces of chicken. He had made a successful trip to the hall kitchen, checking first that Mrs. Tollervey-Jones was out. The locked door was child's play, and he had rapidly raided the fridge, taking only milk and half the carcass of a cooked chicken, then from the freezer a couple of packets of fish fingers and two burgers. He calculated that it would do for the moment. Enough for him and the kitten, and he could always come again to replenish stocks.

He had locked the door and run back to the wood, where he checked that his car was still there. It was, untouched, with the brambles still drawn over the door, so no one had found it. Then home to the icehouse, similarly safe and undiscovered. He had pulled open the door and the kitten jumped to its feet and ran to greet him, purring loudly.

Now he had eaten, and so had the kitten. "I must give you a name," he said. "What do you fancy? Marmaduke? Orlando the marmalade cat? Yes, that's it. We had a book, Clive and me, when we were kids. *Orlando the Marmalade Cat*, it was called. He was ginger, like you. I think I'll call you Orly for short."

The kitten miaowed in answer, washed its paws and curled up in Gerald's lap, where it went instantly to sleep.

Gerald sniffed. Oh God, cat mess. He had forgotten that the kitten would need to go outside. Now he couldn't move in case he disturbed him. He closed his eyes. A nap for a few minutes would be a good idea. Then he would clean up the floor and take Orly outside.

His sleep was roughly interrupted by his mobile ringing insistently. He fumbled in his pocket and saw it was his mother calling.

"Wotcha want, Mum?" he said sleepily.

"Where are you and Clive? That's what I want to know. I've had the fuzz here, a top fuzz, asking for your whereabouts. You'd better tell me, in case I send them where you are by accident. An' what you bin up to, the two of you?"

The signal was breaking up, and she just made out Gerald's answer before it cut out altogether. "Not far away now, Mum! Don't you worry about us. Home soon, after everything's—"

"Damn!" Gladys tried dialling again, but could get no signal. Still, at least he'd answered at last, and had said he was not far away. Home soon, he had said. She wished she had spoken to Clive, too. He was always more forthcoming than Gerald. Maybe next time. She was sure now that things would turn out all right. Luck of the devil, these Mowlems, she thought, and began to plan a welcome home meal for the pair of them.

\*     \*     \*

CLIVE, HOLED UP IN HARRY'S FARMHOUSE, THOUGHT OF CALLING HIS mother, but remembering Gerald's strictures never to tell her anything confidential, he decided to leave it for the moment. Best to get home first, and then follow Gerald's lead. He had no doubt at all that Gerald had gone home. Like pigeons, we are, he thought. Homing pigeons that always fly back to the loft. His dad had kept pigeons for a while, but after he'd been put away, Gladys had got rid of them to a breeder who lived up the road.

Now Clive faced his situation squarely. He was safe here for the moment, but the police were bound to come and have a second look. He could hide again, but—

"Oh, sod it!" he said aloud. The bull. By the time he had returned from Helmsley, he had completely forgotten, and not remembered since. He looked out of all the windows in the kitchen and living room, and could see no signs of visitors, so he unlocked the back door and went out across the yard. He knew where the feed for the animal was kept, and taking a wheelbarrow, he headed for the bull barn.

"Sorry, old fella," he said as he opened the door, "here's food, an' I'll top up y'water."

He turned to push in the barrow, and the bull was on him. It had broken its tether, and now tossed him up in the air, out of its way. It tore across the yard, through a gate and out onto the open moor. In no time, it was out of sight.

Clive lay unmoving where he landed. One leg stuck out at an unnatural angle, and a sticky dribble of blood came from the side of his head. It began to rain, and Clive, lying on the concrete yard, still did not move. Soon the wail of police sirens drifted up from the valley below. But Clive did not hear them, not even when they arrived at the gates of the farm.

# FORTY-SEVEN

❧

"HELLO? IS THAT YOU, LOIS?"

"No, Inspector, it's Lois's mother. Can I help you?"

"Yes, you can get her to come to the phone as soon as possible. Thank you, Mrs. Weedon." Cowgill remembered just in time to be polite. Lois's mother was about as tricky as her daughter, and quite likely to tell him to ring at a more convenient time. But this was urgent, and he tapped his pen on the desk impatiently.

"Morning," said Lois. "What now?"

"Yes, good morning, Lois. I need some information urgently."

"What's happened?"

"Clive Mowlem's been found. Seems he was tossed by a bull on that farm on the moors. Nobody else there. He's in a bad way, and it's touch and go. I'm arranging for his mother to go to the hospital, but I need to get in touch with his brother *urgently*."

"I bet she knows where Gerald is. Have you asked her?"

"She's spoken to him, she says, but swears she has no idea where he is. Not far away, so he told her. But those two are congenital liars, so he could be anywhere. Apparently the young one keeps muttering his name, so the medics are anxious to get hold of him."

"I'll get back to you as soon as possible," said Lois. "But before you go, there's something else." She gave him a succinct account of her fears for Dot, born out by the latest message she had had from Dot's sister, Evelyn. "Time to do something," she said.

"Leave it with me," Cowgill said. "As you say, it looks suspicious. *Sardines*, did Evelyn say?"

"Don't leave it too long," Lois said. "And don't go storming in. She may be in danger."

"Anyone else there?"

"No idea," said Lois. "But I'll find out."

GERALD SAT INSIDE THE ICEHOUSE, MASSAGING HIS LEG WHERE HE had a painful spasm of cramp. There was not much room to stretch out, and he felt depressed. How long should he stay here? Sooner or later someone would come stamping through the undergrowth and find him and Orly. Or else they'd set a trap for him, once Mrs. Tollervey-Jones had noticed the missing food. She had an eagle eye, the old girl, in spite of her age.

His mobile vibrated in his pocket, and he saw it was his mother again. "Mum? I don't want you ringing like this. It could lead to me being traced, and I'm not ready yet. What? I can't hear you very well? Did you say Clive? Oh God, no! The sodding bull! Clive must still have been at the farm. What hospital did you say?"

Gladys was crying now, and said through her tears that it was touch and go with Clive, and she was going up to Yorkshire straightaway. "He keeps asking for you, Gerald," she snuffled. And then she was gone, leaving Gerald to make the most difficult decision of his life.

DOT'S KITCHEN STANK OF SARDINES, AND SHE SAID SHE FELT SICK. "You'd better go and have a lie down," her captor said. "I'll be up in a minute. D'you want a cup of tea?"

Dot nodded, and went slowly up the narrow stairs. She desperately wanted to hurry, but knew that would arouse suspicion. Once in her bedroom, she relaxed. Alone!—but for how long? She went to the window and looked out, up and down the street. Then she saw a car approaching, definitely slowing down outside her house. Mrs. M! She pulled up the sash window as quietly as she could, and when Lois got out of the car, she waved madly with one hand, and with the other put a finger to her lips to signal not to shout.

She could hear him starting up the stairs, and knew it was too late to get a message out. Then, just as she was about to leap onto the bed and pretend to be asleep, she heard the sound of slipping feet, then a crash of broken crockery, and loud cursing and swearing as he tumbled back to the floor.

"Mrs. M!" yelled Dot, returning to the window. "I'm coming down."

She pelted down the stairs, risking life and limb on the broken crockery and the prone figure, and rushed to the front door. But then she realised she had no key. He had taken all the keys and put them in his pocket. Tough little Dot, one of the bravest, looked round and saw him coming unsteadily towards her, his fist raised. "Can't get out!" she yelled. "Go for help!" And then she burst into tears, and sank into a heap on the floor.

BERT MOWLEM STEPPED OVER DOT, SHOUTING AT HER THAT IF she breathed a word about him, he would make sure she regretted it. "For always!" he shouted as he unlocked the door and ran off down the street.

"Who's that?" said Hazel, going to the office window. Lois had just rushed in and was on the phone, trying in vain to talk to Cowgill. She put down the phone, and joined Hazel. "Where? Can't see anybody," she said.

"Probably running for a bus," Hazel said. "D'you want a cup of coffee whilst you're waiting for Cowgill?"

"Might as well," she replied. "Looks like he's busy for once. I think I'll go back up to Dot's house. Something bad is going on there."

"There's not much you can do on your own," Hazel said. "Best wait for reinforcements."

In the end, Lois did not need to leave the office. After ten minutes or so, a wild-looking figure arrived, looked furtively behind her and sat down heavily on Hazel's chair behind the desk.

"Dot! For God's sake, what's happened?"

"He's gone," Dot said. "Done a runner."

"Who has?"

"Bert. Bert Mowlem. Gladys's husband. I know, you thought he was in prison. Well, he was, and he ain't now. I dunno whether he's escaped or been released. All I know is he's got to keep his head down for a bit. He says there's one or two so-called friends who'll be after him, once they know he's out. Needs to make a plan, he says. So he landed on me. He thought I'd keep him safe, for the sake of old times in our schooldays. God knows where he's gone now. Is that coffee?" she added, and helped herself to three large sugars.

BERT SLOWED TO A STEADY WALKING PACE, LIMPING A LITTLE from his crash down the stairs. It would be stupid, he thought, to attract attention by running through the market day crowds. No, he'd keep an even pace, and maybe stop to look in the occasional shop window. He was relying on Gladys being at home, but in case she'd come to market, he kept his eyes peeled for her.

Only yards away from his house, he saw a taxi draw up. He bent down to fiddle with his shoelace, and watched. Gladys came out, all dressed up, and got into the taxi. It drove off, and Bert straightened up. He still had his house key in his pocket, and he walked casually up to the door and let himself in.

# FORTY-EIGHT

❧

"D<sup>AD?</sup>"

"Yeah, it's yer father. Where is everybody, Gerald? Yer mum's gone off in a taxi, and there's no sign of you and Clive. Where are you, boy?"

"Never you mind where I am. Where are *you*, Dad? I suppose you're out—on parole? Skipped, 'ave you?"

"All legal an' aboveboard. If you'd kept in touch, the lot o' you, instead of leaving your poor ole dad to fester in prison by himself, you'd know I am out for good. There's nothin' wrong with trying to find out where yer family is, is there?"

"I can't——" Once more the signal went. Gerald supposed it was lucky there was any signal at all here, practically underground.

So Dad was out. Probably lying low for a bit. There were plenty of former cronies of his that might want to sniff him out. Debts to be paid, matters to be settled.

His phone rang again. "Dad? Look, I'm out of circulation

just now. I'll be in touch. But there's something you ought to know. Clive's had a nasty accident. Up north, in Pickering. Yeah, Yorkshire. That's where Mum's gone. It's serious. You could go. Me? Dunno yet. Bye."

The kitten jumped up on Gerald's lap, and rubbed its head against his hand. "Orly boy," he said, and sniffed hard. "What the hell am I goin' to do? Clive's nigh unto, and askin' for me. Dad's just outa prison, and if I get caught, I shall be in his cell by t'morrer."

He sat for a long time, stroking the kitten until it stopped purring and fell asleep. Then he heaved a deep sigh. That's it, then, he said, putting Orly down carefully on his cap, requisitioned to make a soft bed. He dialled his home number and waited until his father answered.

"It's me again. I've decided to visit Clive. With you. This is what we're goin' to do. You come here where I am, bring me some different clothes an' a pair of sharp scissors. Are you listenin'? Yeah, I said scissors. Now, here's how to get here."


MRS. TOLLERVEY-JONES HAD BEEN BUSY. SHE HAD WALKED AROUND the house all morning, from room to room, making lists. Furniture to be moved to the new house, stuff to go up to Christie's auction rooms in London, a small amount to Robert and Felicity. It was a huge task, but she was not daunted. In fact, she considered it was quite cathartic. A new start, ditching all the clutter of her past life.

Time for something to eat. The list making was going to take all day, and she should have a rest and sustenance. The doctor had told her that her "funny turns" had been a timely warning of the need to slow down. She had heard somewhere that one of the things most likely to cause ill health or a breakdown was moving house. Well, she did not intend to follow that route. She would tackle things in a measured way. After all, she had only herself to think about.

She opened the fridge to take out milk for coffee, and looked in surprise at the bottle. Surely there should be more than that left? She shook her head. She had no recollection of leaving only half an inch in the bottom of the bottle. Perhaps she should go into town and borrow a library book on memory training!

A sandwich, then. There should be cold chicken left over from yesterday, and she could use some of that creamy horseradish sauce the children had given her for her birthday. At the time, she had thought it a very peculiar present. But now it would be useful.

Not much chicken! She must have eaten more than she thought. Ah well, enough for a quick snack. Then she would take the old dog out for a short walk before getting back to her lists.

With the newspaper propped up on the now empty milk bottle, she ate her sandwich and munched an apple. She smiled to herself. No carefully laid tray with dainty cloth and glass of wine. No, in the new life she would pare down all the ridiculous frills. She fetched a piece of cheese from the fridge, remarked on the smallness of the piece left and ate it with her fingers, together with two cherry tomatoes ripening on the windowsill.

Must go shopping tomorrow, she reminded herself and wrote a note to that effect. At the foot of the page, she wrote, "PS. Gone for a walk. Baxoon." Mrs. Meade was coming over sometime today to help her sort things out. She had a key, and would be able to let herself in.

The sun was out now, and the sky washed a clear blue.

Calling her dog, Mrs. Tollervey-Jones set out for a brisk walk. She went through the kitchen garden, out through a gate at the end of a grassy path and into the wood.

"Come on, dog!" The poor old thing was finding it hard to keep up, Mrs. Tollervey-Jones noticed. Never mind, she would have a lovely warm kitchen in the new house, with a new bed to sleep in. She waited patiently, and then slowed down her pace. After they had been walking for fifteen minutes, she was about to turn around and retrace her steps to the house, when out of the corner of her eye she saw something move. Too big to be a fox. She stopped, and called the dog to a halt.

"Who's there!" she called in an authoritative voice. It was a man. She could see that now. A big man, and he was fast disappearing into the trees.

"Fetch!" she said, taking a ball from her pocket and throwing it expertly in the right direction.

The old dog started off obediently, and Mrs. Tollervey-Jones followed. They came to a narrow path, the undergrowth newly flattened down, and she knew at once where they were heading. The old icehouse, buried under brambles and neglected for years. At one time, when Robert was small, he and his friends used it as a den, and nobody was allowed near it. She had respected this, and when Robert went off to university, the den had been forgotten.

With no thought for her own safety, Mrs. T-J pushed her way through the brambles and finally came to the icehouse. The door was not quite shut, and she put her stick into the opening and prised it open. At first, she saw nothing but darkness, but then, as her eyes adjusted, she could see two shapes huddled into the back of the interior.

The kitten slipped out of Gerald's hand and jumped to the

floor. It trotted over to Mrs. Tollervey-Jones, purring loudly. Then it saw the dog, and fled back to safety.

"That's my kitten," Mrs. Tollervey-Jones said. "Got taken off by an owl. Saw it go. What do you think you are doing here? I suppose you know you're trespassing?"

In a swift move, Bert went to one side of her and Gerald the other. In a firm grip, they pulled her in and shut the door behind her. The dog was left outside. Well trained, it sat down to wait.

"WHAT A DAY!" DEREK SAID AS HE SAT AT THE LUNCH TABLE with Lois and Gran. "After all that rain, and now you'd never believe it. Warm as toast out there, out of the wind."

"Pity we can't all drop everything and take a drive out," Gran said.

"You can do that in the rain. A nice long walk would be better," Lois said. "But unfortunately I have to go to the hall to help the old lady sort out her treasures, and I presume Derek has to get back to work? So that leaves you, Mum. And Jeems, of course."

Gran stiffened. "I suppose you've not noticed that great pile of washing waiting to be ironed?"

"You'll just have to make do with opening the kitchen window," said Derek soothingly. "And anyway, Lois, why are you wasting time following her majesty around with a clipboard at the ready? I thought you had admin to catch up on?"

Lois stood up. "Blast," she said. "Look at that ladder, and these were new tights on this morning."

"Mrs. T-J is shortsighted," said Derek. "They'll do, surely?"

"Can't let standards slip," said Lois loftily. "I shall go and change, and then be gone to the hall. I'm not shortsighted, thankfully, and I can see that the more I can help the dear old thing now, the more work she'll put our way when she moves."

Derek sighed. "You win," he said. "As usual. Just be careful, that's all I'm saying. Some of them attic floors are downright dangerous. Every kind of beetle's been gnawing away up there for years."

# FORTY-NINE

⁓

JOSIE SAW HER MOTHER GO BY IN THE NEW BROOMS VAN, AND wondered idly where she was going. Not to Tresham, so no summons from the wedding shop. She was probably off to visit a new client, or rescue Dot Nimmo from the clutches of a dissatisfied customer. Gran had said this morning that she'd been proved right. Lois had been mad to have anything to do with that Nimmo lot. Nothing but trouble.

She went out to the stockroom and came swiftly back when she heard the shop door open. Since the Mowlems had made their snatch and grab attempt, she had been much more careful. But this time it was a welcome customer.

"Matthew! You're back!" She rushed around the counter and straight into his policeman's arms. "Wow! I wouldn't like to be escaping from you," she said, eventually trying to free herself.

"Yep, I'm back. Left one very sick Clive Mowlem in a hospital bed, and now the hunt is on for his brother. I just wanted to drop in and warn you that we think he's now around these parts, and what's more, his father is out of prison and also back in town."

"Ye gods!" said Josie. "Should be a shoot-out anytime now, then?"

"Hope not," said Matthew seriously. "There's been enough damage done. One old man killed, and a young one at death's door. That's enough to be going on with, Josie love."

"What happened to Clive?"

"Seems he was up at that farm by himself, and must have released the bull. It tossed him, and then escaped. Left him lying unconscious."

"Who found him?"

"A neighbouring farmer. He saw the bull, and him and his son caught it. Knew it belonged to old Harry, apparently, and took it back. That's when they found Clive. He hasn't come round properly since. Just keeps saying his brother's name, over and over. That's why we have to track down the lovely Gerald. So just be extra vigilant. If he does show up here, don't let on you know him. Just phone at once."

"Right," said Josie. "But how will I know him?"

"Good question," said Matthew. "Here, here's a photo, but it's an old one. Your mum had a good look at him up in Pickering, so she could help. He's been living rough, probably, so won't look too smart. In a hurry to get away, that kind of thing. But don't worry, he's not likely to come here. Now, must go. Love you," he added with a quick peck on the cheek.

"Love you, too," Josie answered nervously, and returned to stand behind the safety of the counter.


LOIS DROVE SLOWLY UP TO THE HALL, TAKING IN THE BEAUTY OF the autumn colours and the artful way the landscape enclosed the house. She reflected how wonderful it must have been for the aristocratic owners in the days when every part of the estate worked as if by clockwork, like a small, self-sufficient state, and all directed to the health, wealth and preservation of one family.

And now Mrs. Tollervey-Jones was being turned out by circumstance. The world had changed and, Lois sometimes thought, not for the better. Her great-aunt, who had lived in the country on just such an estate, had once said to her that you felt safe with someone over you. As a child, Lois had easily seen the sense of this, but in adult life her views had changed. Equality for all. Opportunity for all. All very well, but . . .

She parked the car in the stable yard and walked across to the kitchen door. It was locked. Ah well, Mrs. Tollervey-Jones had told her she might be out with the dog. She felt in her bag for the key, and let herself into the kitchen. At once, she looked around and saw the note on the table. As she thought, Mrs. T-J and her dog were out for a walk. She knew where they had got to in sorting out, and so went through to the study to make a start.

The third time Lois looked at her watch, she saw that a whole hour had gone by. Mrs. Tollervey-Jones had said a short walk, hadn't she? With the huge volume of work they had to get through, Lois was sure she would not have gone for a long ramble. She returned to the kitchen and read the note again, then went out into the stable yard and looked around. No sign of the dog, but then a short burst of barking came from the direction of the wood. It sounded as if it was well into the trees, and Lois looked down at her shoes. Not at all suitable for trudging through the undergrowth.

She returned to the house and went into the boot room.

Rows of Wellington boots stood neatly against the wall, relics of time past, when house parties had spent happy outdoor weekends at the hall. She changed into a pair roughly her size, and locking the back door behind her, she set off for the wood, calling the dog as she went.

Perhaps it had walked into a trap, and Mrs. Tollervey-Jones was trying to free it. Heaven help the poachers if this was the case!

IN THE CROWDED INTERIOR OF THE ICEHOUSE, THE ATMOSPHERE was stuffy and unpleasant. Gerald had lit a candle, and it guttered and flamed up, sending shadows round the three occupants who sat on the damp floor—Gerald, Bert and Mrs. Tollervey-Jones, with her skirt pulled well down over her knees. When the dog barked, Gerald struggled to his feet, but Bert pulled him down again. "She'll go for yer legs, boy," he said. "Best like this, until we decide what to do with 'er."

They had tried unsuccessfully to persuade Mrs. Tollervey-Jones to agree to say nothing, and then she would be released unharmed. She had refused indignantly, asking them if they were aware that she was a justice of the peace, and one with a reputation for dealing fairly with any accused who came up before the bench.

"Oh yeah?" Bert had said, "I remember you, all right. You may not remember me, but I wouldn't've called it fair dealing what you handed out to me!"

Now Gerald cleared his throat and said he had a suggestion to make. "What say we tie her up so's she can't move, and then get outa here as fast as we can run? It'll be some time before she's found, and we can be well away."

"Good idea," said Bert, and moved towards her. With surprising agility, Mrs. Tollervey-Jones got to her feet. "Oh no you don't!" she said, and to Bert's horror, she picked up her stick and drew from the handle a shining blade, which she held out in front of her, inches away from Bert's face.

"Where the hell did you get that sodding thing from?" said Gerald.

"Been in my family for generations," she said, and added conversationally that the stick was made from very strong blackthorn, and the blade kept sharp and lethal by her husband. "He always said I should keep it by me when alone in the house."

"It's illegal," said Gerald. "A concealed weapon. You could get done for that."

"Wrong," said Mrs. Tollervey-Jones. "It's illegal to take it out on the streets, but perfectly legal to keep at home. A curious antique most of the time but, as you see, occasionally useful."

"You're enjoying this, ain't you, Mrs. Tollervey-Jones," said Bert bitterly. "Why don't you just back out of that door and bugger off! Leave us to get away best we can, an' then you can set the dogs on us."

"Dog, singular," she replied. "Old dog, very slow on her pins now. No, I think we'll wait here a little longer," she added. "I think we may find a solution very soon."

As if on cue, the old dog outside the door barked again, a sharp anxious sound, full of alarm. Lois, following the sound, was very near the icehouse now, but because of the surrounding undergrowth, did not immediately see it. She called the dog again, and the answering bark led her through the tangled brambles to the icehouse door.

"There you are, you silly old thing!" Lois said. "Why don't you come on home? Your mistress is probably looking everywhere for you? There's nothing in that old hovel, not even a rabbit. Come on, let's go."

The dog did not move, but looked at her pleadingly, as if begging her to understand.

Then Lois heard another voice, instantly recognisable. "Mrs. Meade! Open this door, please. And be careful."

Her warning was well meant, but in the end, when Lois pulled open the door, she was pushed violently aside by Gerald, quickly followed by Bert, both of them disappearing very fast through the wood, and so was confronted by Mrs. Tollervey-Jones, still holding what to Lois looked like a very sharp sword.

Lois struggled to her feet, gasping with amazement. "What . . . What on earth is that? Oh, blimey, Mrs. T-J, whatever has been happening here?"

"I have been protecting my honour, my dear," said Mrs. Tollervey-Jones. "If you will give me a minute or two, I will make this thing safe, and then we can return to the house and start work."

"But the Mowlems?"

"They won't get far. I am sure you are keeping the police up to date with developments? Your reputation goes before you, you see. Come, shut the door tightly. I must get it seen to. Off we go, dog. Well done," she added, and patted it approvingly on the head. "Life in the old dog yet, Mrs. Meade," she said, and chuckled. "Dog and me, both of us," she added cheerily.

# FIFTY

꙰

GERALD AND BERT COULD NOT BELIEVE THEIR LUCK. GERALD had led the way to his car without much hope of escape. "And now the bloody thing won't start!" his father had said. But after a couple of turns, the engine fired.

"Any sign of them?" Gerald asked.

"Nope. No sign. 'Ere, watch out for yer tyres!"

The car bumped along as fast as Gerald dared on the rough track. But eventually they reached the tarmac lane and he put his foot down.

"Where are we going?" Bert said.

"Where d'you think? Part two of our plan. Go and see Clive. No point in trying to do anything else now. If they catch us, they catch us. But we stand a chance. I'm not quite sure what that Jones woman was on about, but when we told her we had to go and see my brother what was near to death, she seemed to take that in. Changed some'ow."

"Huh! The likes of her don't make allowances for the likes

of us. Anyhow, we'll just keep going and see what happens."
Gerald neatly avoided a cat that ran across the road in front of
him, and then suddenly stood on the brake. "Oh no! I forgot
Orly! We'll have to go back!"

"No we won't, you soft fool," Bert said, and put his hand
in his jacket pocket. "Here it is, though why you should care
about a ginger tomcat is beyond me. Now for God's sake, let's
get going, and no more holdups." He pulled out the protesting kitten, and stroked it until it settled on his lap.

They continued in silence for more than an hour, and then
Bert said they should stop for something to eat. "You'll fall
asleep soon," he said, "an' that won't be much use to anybody.
Pull in at a garage an' we'll get a sandwich."

"We got enough petrol to get there," objected Gerald.
"Why risk being spotted?"

"You ain't got no alternative. I'm as tired as you are. Food,
that's what we need. Then we can carry on and get there
tonight."

BY THE TIME LOIS ARRIVED HOME, SHE WAS DESPERATE WITH
worry. Mrs. Tollervey-Jones had seemed to shake off her experiences in the icehouse with no ill effects. But she had
sworn Lois to secrecy, saying she had no wish to appear more
of a fool than she was already. Lois had challenged this, saying she had a duty to report the Mowlems' movements to the
police. To her surprise, this had been approved, Mrs.
Tollervey-Jones pointing out that the police already knew
where Clive Mowlem was.

"You'll see, my dear," she had assured Lois, "Inspector
Cowgill will know exactly what to do."

Lois doubted this, but agreed reluctantly to telephone and

tell him to expect Mowlem father and son at the hospital within the next twenty-four hours. "You're taking a big risk," she said. "They are much more likely to vanish into the woodwork again."

Mrs. Tollervey-Jones had ignored her, and went back to packing up her husband's books, ready to be conveyed to London and her son, Robert.

Now Lois sat at the supper table with Derek and Gran, pushing her food around the plate, not eating much and saying little.

"All right, Lois," Derek said finally. "What's all this about? You look worried sick. Is it one of the children, an' you're not telling me?"

Lois shook her head. "No, it's something Mrs. T-J has done, and I think it was stupid and even dangerous."

"You'd better tell us, love," Derek said. "Sounds serious."

"Could be," said Lois, and gave them an edited version of what had happened, from the discovery of Mrs. T-J and the Mowlems in the icehouse, to the old lady's strange attitude to giving the police all the details so that they could pick up the thugs as soon as possible. "I reckon it'll be a miracle if them two walk straight into the arms of the police in Pickering."

"None s'queer as folk," said Gran. "I always did think the old tab had a screw loose. Comes of living on your own in a great big echoing house. Nobody to talk to but yourself, Lois. That's what does it."

"So have you phoned Cowgill?" asked Derek. The inspector was not his favourite person, but in this case he agreed with Lois. He should be told the whole story.

Lois nodded. "Yep."

"And what did he say?"

"Just thanked me. Said the information was very useful,

and he would be investigating. That's all. I must say he didn't sound as if the entire local police force would be rising in a body to catch the Mowlems."

"Well, there you are, then," said Gran. "Nothing more you can do. Now eat up and have some of my blackberry and apple pie. Freshly made this afternoon."

Lois did her best, but still felt that until she had news tomorrow that both those crooks had been caught, she would not relax. She could still see Derek lying unconscious on the stable yard cobbles, with a big cosh mark on the back of his head.

# FIFTY-ONE

⤮

GERALD SLOWED DOWN AS A PETROL STATION CAME IN SIGHT. "You sure about this, Dad?" he said.

"Yes. Just trust me, boy."

Gerald had every reason to distrust his father, but on this occasion he could see no reason for him to be up to anything but getting them safely to see Clive. He drew in, and filled up the car with petrol. It was already half full, so it did not take long. He went quickly into the paying booth and, keeping his head down, paid with a credit card which his father had handed him. He had had a bizarre haircut in the car as they drove along, Bert giving him a close and brutal trim, and instead of feeling disguised, he felt chilly and exposed.

Back in the car and driving away from the garage, he looked in his driving mirror.

"Dad, do you reckon we're being followed? There's a dark-coloured car behind us, difficult to see with the light going, but I could swear it was behind us before we stopped."

Bert twisted round and stared out of the back window. "Can't really see, but it's possible, if the old woman got on to the police. D'you want to do a detour, and then we'll know?"

Gerald said nothing for a moment or two, then shook his head. "Nope," he said. "We'll just keep going. They'll be there waiting for us anyway. That Meade woman is a snout. Her and Cowgill are close as a couple o' turtledoves, so they say. No, our aim now is to get to Clive before, well, before . . ." He choked, and said nothing more.

Bert looked across at him and gave him time to recover. "All right now, boy?"

Gerald nodded. "Here's yer sandwich," he said.

The ate in silence for a while, then Bert cleared his throat. "What happened between you and our Clive, then? Why was he up there in a deserted farmhouse, all by himself? I thought your mum told you to look after him?"

Gerald had been expecting and dreading these questions from his father. The truth was that he had panicked after he'd knocked old Harry for six, and then, when he had thought some more at that old chapel shed, he knew that the two of them would be a much easier target that one on his own. So yes, he had deserted his younger brother in a determined effort to look after number one. But he couldn't tell Bert that.

Instead, he told him that he had meant to go back for Clive after he had sorted out things back at home, but it hadn't worked out. "Don't think I don't feel guilty!" he said honestly. "If I'd been with him, we'd never have let that ruddy bull loose. Funny, really. It were a lazy old sod of a bull, never turned a hair if you went close. Something must've upset it."

"Did you feed it?" asked Bert, who in the dim distant past had had a holiday with a group of wayward boys on a farm, where being in close contact with Mother Nature was supposed to have turned them away from a life of crime. All he remembered was that he had been assigned the job of feeding the animals. Horses, cows, the old bull, chickens, ducks and geese. Every morning, rain or shine, he had trudged round with buckets of this and that. And all of 'em desperate for their food, as if they hadn't been fed for weeks.

"I never did. Harry wouldn't let anyone else do it. So probably Clive didn't either."

"There you are then," said Bert. "There's one answer. And here's another question. What happened to Farmer Harry? And by the way, was he the one who was after your mother while I was banged up? If it was, he had it coming to him."

For Gerald, this was like a ray of sunshine on a dark day. Of course! Here was his way out. He had always been good at making up stories. Used to invent them to amuse Clive when he was little. Now he set his imagination to work. Harry had been after his mother, and was taunting him with having a father in jail, so much so that he had lost his temper.

"Yeah, it was him," he repeated. "Used to go on about getting Mum to divorce you whilst you were inside, and then he'd marry her and carry her off to Yorkshire. We happened on his farm when we were driving round doing a bit o' business in Pickering, and stayed a few days there. I thought I could sort him out, stop him bothering Mum. But he was an awkward old sod, and wouldn't give up. Taunted me and Clive rotten, he did."

"So what snuffed him out? I presume that's what happened to him. The reason why Clive was alone with a hungry bull in the farmyard?"

"It was an accident, really," said Gerald, managing to sound humble. "Harry went out with his gun after we'd had a row, an' he'd forgot to take his old waterproof coat. It started to pour down, an' I ran after him. When he saw me coming, he lifted the gun and pointed it straight at me. I told him to put it down, but he just went on walking towards me. He was really close, an' I knew I had to do something. I just shoved him round so's I could get the gun, and he tripped and fell back. Hit his head on a bit o' rock. There's loads of it out on the moor. I ran back to phone for an ambulance, but those women got to him first and called for help on their mobile.

"I 'ope you're telling me the truth," Bert said doubtfully. "If you are, mind, it don't sound like you'll be in too much trouble. Provocation, most likely. Anyway, what happened next?"

"Is there another sandwich?"

"Here, it's the last. So what next?"

"I reckoned Clive and me had better scarper. We got all our stuff together so there was no trace of us being there. Then we left."

"That bloke's still on our tail," Bert said as they stopped at traffic lights.

"Yeah, he will be," said Gerald. "I'll tell you the rest later. I got to concentrate now. This is the tricky bit."


"MATTHEW'S HAD TO GO BACK UP TO YORKSHIRE," JOSIE SAID, appearing at the Meades' kitchen door. "Can I come to supper, Mum?"

"Course you can," said Gran. "You'll have to get used to him going off like that when you're married. Not an easy job, you know, and sometimes very dangerous."

"Well, thanks a lot, Gran. That fills me with confidence!"

"Sit down, Josie, and take no notice," Lois said. "We'll have a nice quiet evening watching telly. Your dad should be home any minute."

Lois brought Josie up to date with what she knew about the Mowlems, and they all had a good laugh at the thought of Mrs. Tollervey-Jones holding up two ruffians at the end of her sword stick. "You should have seen her!" Lois said. "I wouldn't like to get the wrong side of her in court."

"She'll be retiring soon," Gran said. "And moving to the village. She'll have time on her hands after all what she's been used to."

"Plenty of time to put us all in our places, then," said Josie. "She'll be dangerously near the shop. In and out every spare minute, I shouldn't wonder!"

"It should be very interesting," Lois said, "and here's your dad. We can have supper as soon as he's ready."

"Steak and kidney pie," said Gran. "Just what the policeman ordered."

"Gran!"

# FIFTY-TWO

༈

By the time Gerald and Bert were in the outskirts of Pickering, it was completely dark, and Bert looked at his watch.

"They won't let us in, coming so late," he said. "Perhaps we'd better find somewhere to stay. And don't say Harry's farm . . ."

"Mum didn't say where the hospital was. She was too upset, and then the signal kept breaking up. There must be signs."

"Or we can ask a policeman," said Bert.

Gerald was too anxious to see the joke, and stopped by the kerb. "We could kip down in the car," he said. "Then go good and early to the hospital. It'll be easier to find it in daylight. There's some old rugs in the back there. I'll drive into a side turning somewhere, and we'll do the best we can."

"How's the petrol? I ain't got much more money."

"Doesn't matter," said Gerald. "Now we're here, we won't be going back in this car," he added gloomily.

"Our tail is still behind us. Perhaps we should offer him a rug?" said Bert.

SAFE AT HOME, WARM AND SECURE, LOIS NEVERTHELESS FELT restless and ill at ease. She looked at her watch. Eleven o'clock. The Mowlems should be under lock and key by now, if Mrs. T-J's hunch that they would go to the hospital was correct. But if not, they could be driving through the night to a hideaway anywhere in the country. And then all the time she and Dot had spent in Pickering would be wasted. "Derek," she said as he got up to prepare for bed, "I'm going to ring Cowgill. And no, before you start, I shan't sleep if I don't."

"I forbid it!" said Derek. "You're being absolutely ridiculous."

Lois frowned and stared at him. "Forbid! *Forbid?* Since when did you forbid me to do anything? I'm going into my office, an' I'll be up to bed when I've found out what I need to know." And she stalked out of the room, leaving Derek scratching his head.

She dialled Cowgill's number, and waited. Just when she was about to give up, he answered. "Lois! Is something wrong?"

"Yes," she said. "I can't sleep."

Cowgill was fully dressed, wide awake, and had been working on some papers before he would allow himself to go to bed. "Sorry to hear that, my dear. I can suggest several lovely ways to help, but I won't."

"No, don't, for God's sake. My husband has just forbidden me to ring you at this hour, so I don't need any more muckin' about. The thing is," she began, now beginning to feel a little foolish, "I can't stop thinking about the Mowlems. What's the latest? And don't tell me you are pursuing enquiries, because that won't do. Please, Hunter."

Cowgill paused. He could not remember when Lois had ever said "please" to him in that pleading voice, so he answered her truthfully. "Mrs. Tollervey-Jones was right," he said, "so far. We picked up the trail very quickly, thanks to your call, almost as soon as they left. They've been followed to just outside Pickering, and it looks like they've bedded down for the night in the car. Our chap is out of sight but near enough to monitor their movements."

"So what are you going to do?"

"There is a complication, but not serious. They obviously think young Mowlem is in hospital in Pickering. But, in fact, he's in York. Much too serious for the facilities in Pickering. No doubt they'll find that out in the morning, and we'll trail them back to York."

"Why don't you just pick them up now, and take them to the hospital? You could let them see Clive and then do whatever it is you need to do. I suppose you'll hold them in custody, an' all that?"

"Ah, well, that does sound the most sensible thing, but we are trying to do what Mrs. Tollervey-Jones instructed. And I say 'instructed' advisably, Lois. She telephoned me after your call and said we should, in her words, 'Pick them up *after* they have seen the brother. Give father and son time to catch up on their ill-spent past. Could be very useful,' she said. Wrongly or rightly, I have decided to do it her way. Call it a parting gift on the occasion of her retirement from public service, that kind of thing."

"That's stupid!" Lois said, irritated that Mrs. Tollervey-

Jones had thought it necessary to speak to Cowgill personally. "They might get away, if they decide after all to abandon Clive. Gerald has done it before and could easily do it again."

"But Bert is with him this time. That could make all the difference. Anyway, my dear Lois, they won't get away. Trust us. We know what we're doing."

"Mm. Well, let me know first thing how things work out. And if Gerald and Bert vanish into thin air, I'll never speak to you again."

"Trust me," said Cowgill seriously. "Good night, Lois my love, sleep well."

# FIFTY-THREE

❧

DAWN BROKE OVER PICKERING, AND A HEAVY MIST DAMPENED down sounds of human activity in the small lane where Bert and Gerald had parked. Bert woke first, and looked across at Gerald. His head was resting against the door frame, and he appeared to be peacefully asleep. Bert wondered whether to wake him, and looked at his watch. Seven thirty. Gerald stirred, and Bert remembered when he used to sit with the boys when they were children and couldn't get to sleep. They always shared a room, and it seemed as if when one was awake, the other couldn't sleep. Like twins, they were, except for the difference in ages.

"Gerald, wake up," he said, gently shaking his shoulder.

"What? Where? Oh, blimey Dad, what time is it?"

"Time we was on the move. We need a bite of something an' a hot drink, and then we can find out where the hospital is. 'Ere, put this cat out to do his business. He's just farted. Best get some milk for 'im, too." He looked behind him and saw the car that had shadowed them all the way from Tresham. "Hey! Look back at the tail," he said. "That car is empty, ain't it?"

Gerald hauled himself upright, still half asleep. He looked back, and said, "It *was* empty. He's just coming back with paper bags in his hand. Took a chance there. Now he's got breakfast, and we haven't."

Bert thought for a moment. "Look, Gerald," he said. "If they'd wanted to pick us up, they could've done it several times over. They're not going to. But they mean to keep tabs on us, just the same. We got to carry on with what we came for. You stay here an' I'll get us some grub. The money'll just about take care of that. And as you said yesterday, we'll no doubt be getting a lift home."

Gerald blinked the sleep from his eyes and agreed. "Be quick as you can, then," he said. "They start the day early in hospitals, and they're bound to let us in, especially with our police escort . . ." He locked the car and watched Bert disappear up the road.

It seemed to Gerald that only five minutes had passed before Bert was back, signalling to be let in.

"Sodding hospital!" he said. "I asked the man in the bread shop, and he said any serious accidents got taken to York Hospital. Or somewhere else. Can't remember the name. I mentioned a man tossed by a bull, and he said right away that he read about that in the local paper, an' he'd definitely been taken to York."

"Damn and blast! Why didn't I ring Mum and check?"

"Well, why didn't you?"

"Because you know perfectly well what she is. It'd be all round the hospital that we were on our way. As it happens, we don't need to worry, what with Sherlock behind us. But I never thought."

"Right," said Bert. "It ain't that far, maybe twenty-odd

miles, back to York. We can eat as we go. Start the engine an' we'll check the petrol."

There was more left in the tank than Gerald had thought, and they moved off. As they passed the plainclothes cop, Bert gave the man inside a cheery wave. It was not acknowledged, but at the next junction, they saw their shadow three cars behind them.

"Ah," said Bert, "glad he's caught up. It'd be lonely without him, wouldn't it."

The lights changed to green, and Gerald started to move forward with a jerk. "Steady on, boy!" said Bert.

"Oh, give it a rest, Dad!" said Gerald loudly. "You're beginning to get on my nerves!"

"Sorry, I'm sure!" said Bert. "Never mind, we'll soon be there an' it'll be mission accomplished."

"If he's still . . . well . . . you know . . ."

"Alive?"

"Yeah. I can't help thinking we're goin' to be too late. Mum said it was a very serious accident. She sounded desperate."

"Don't give up hope, boy. We Mowlems are a strong lot. Clive may look a bit of a weakling, but he's got a good constitution. Remember how sick he was with measles when he was a kid? Blowing on their fingertips, they were. But he came through. Now, slow down so's I can read this sign."

After what seemed like an eternity, they finally drove into the hospital car park. "Hey, look at this!" said Bert, getting out and reading a charges notice. "They make you pay to visit the sick here. It's a disgrace."

It took some time to explain who they were, where they had come from and who they wished to visit. At last it was sorted out, and they turned to follow the red line that led to Clive's ward.

"Well, this is a surprise!" said a voice behind them, and there stood Gladys, staring at Bert in astonishment.

"Hi, Mum," said Gerald. "How is he?"

Bert stood back, whilst Gerald gave his mother an awkward peck on the cheek.

"Much the same, but stable. That's what they say. He sleeps most of the time, but now an' then he surfaces. Doesn't seem to know me, but they say I should be by his side in case he regains consciousness properly."

"You mean he will?" said Gerald anxiously.

"They don't say. You'd better go on up where they told you, an' I'll have a word with my ever-loving husband here. We'll join you in a few minutes."

Gerald walked quickly through long echoing corridors, until he came to the right ward, and then explained to a nurse who he was.

"Come this way, please," she said, and opened the door of a side ward. In a forest of wires and tubes, Clive lay motionless, his eyes closed. The nurse brought a chair close to the bed and indicated that Gerald should sit down. Then she left, saying he had only to call if he wanted help.

Gerald stared at his brother. Several minutes passed, and nothing seemed to change. Then he thought he saw Clive's eyelids flicker. "Clivey boy? You awake? It's Gerald, come to see you." Nothing. More minutes passed, and then he heard his mother's voice. The nurse came in and said that Gerald must come out now and let his father take his place.

"Clive?" said Bert as he sat down beside the bed. "Wake up, boy. It's yer dad here. Long time no see, eh?"

Clive's eyelids flickered again, and his eyes opened. He looked straight at Bert, and said clearly, "Dad? You out, then?"

# FIFTY-FOUR

❧

AT NINE THIRTY, LOIS DIALLED COWGILL'S NUMBER.
"I thought you were going to ring me first thing?" she
said.

"This is first thing!" Cowgill said. "I had my hand on the
phone ready to talk to you."

"Huh! I'll believe you. Thousands wouldn't. Anyway, you
sound cheerful. What's new?"

"Ah, let me see. A fish and chip shop in the back streets of
Tresham was vandalised. Wet fish all over the pavement. Cul-
prits caught red-handed. And here's a good one: Two school-
boys pinched ladies' knickers from a lingerie shop in the High
Street. Claimed they wanted them for their mothers, who
denied—"

"Cowgill! I swear I'll swing for you if you don't cooperate!"

"I couldn't let that happen," he said, his voice serious now.
"Oh, the thought of it! No, sorry, Lois dear. It's just that we
have had one piece of good news, and I feel quite light-headed."

"Could you bear to share it with me?" asked Lois, restraining herself with difficulty.

"Of course. Now, first of all, young Mowlem has regained consciousness and is doing remarkably well. It seems the gratifying turn in his condition was triggered by a visit from his father. Not, by the way, that Bert is known for his sympathetic handling of the sick, but he seems to have done the trick. He and his other son, Gerald, and the redoubtable Gladys, are all at a hospital in York, discreetly held in custody by the local police. Oh yes, and Matthew is up there, ready to bring Gerald back to Tresham.

"But Gladys and her husband haven't done anything. Can't they go free? It's just that foul thug Gerald that needs to be kept safe until justice can be done. As you know, Derek won't press charges, but he'd not be at all pleased if Gerald sodding Mowlem went free."

"Lois, Lois. How many times have I let you down? Of course Gerald Mowlem will be charged and brought to court. There will be much work to be done before it is all cleared up, but Gerald will be in our care until that time. You can be sure I shall keep you up to date with progress. Meanwhile, Clive will continue to improve, we understand, and will be able to be of help to us. His father and mother, too, whilst reestablishing their relationship, will be on hand to answer our questions."

"Wow, so all's right with the world and everything ticketyboo? Nothing more for me and Dot to do, then?"

To her great surprise and amusement, she heard the extraordinary sound of Chief Detective Inspector Hunter Cowgill singing into the phone. She was speechless as she listened to the words of one of her late father's favourite songs: "'Stay as sweet as you are, don't let a thing ever change you . . .'"

"You can sing!" she said when he had stopped.

"Best tenor voice in Tresham Choral Society, though I say so myself," he answered. "Must go, Lois. Work to do. Bye, love." And he was gone.

LOIS FOUND IT VERY DIFFICULT TO SETTLE DOWN TO NEW BROOMS' cleaning schedules. There were a number of messages on her phone, three of them from potential new clients. She had been worried that the gloomy financial situation in the country would mean a loss of customers in her business. But so far, this had not happened. Women were still hiring cleaners. Lois did not judge. She was sometimes tempted to tell an overweight client that it would do her a power of good to get down on her hands and knees and give the floors a good scrub. But as far as her team was concerned, they were all trained to treat clients as needy people whose lives could be made sweeter by the ministrations of New Brooms.

"Lois?" It was Derek, dressed for work. "What are you doing, staring into space? I'm off now. Everything sorted out for you? I can see from your face that all is well. Anyway, I'm late, so you can tell me all the news at lunchtime. Bye, duckie."

Lois watched from her window as Derek's van drove away. Perhaps she would not attempt work this morning. She felt completely drained, and decided to fetch Jeems's lead and take her for a walk through the woods. The trees were turning now, a riot of red, orange and yellow, and the sun had cleared the mist from the village. On the way back, she would call in and tell Josie that her wedding dress was ready for the first fitting.

She turned away from the window, and as she went towards the door, her phone rang. "Mrs. Meade? Felicity Tollervey-Jones here. I thought I would come down and help my mother-in-law with her sorting out and packing. Would you be able to give us a hand? I should be with her soon after lunch. Such a lot to do! And apparently the Norrington man, in spite of being so slimy, has actually got cast-iron finance to buy the hall. Wants to be moving in as soon as possible. His wife is spending a lot of time measuring up and so on, much to Ma's disgust! Any chance of you being free? Ma is full of praise for your efficiency."

"So sorry," said Lois. "Very important engagement with my daughter this afternoon. Tomorrow morning perhaps?"

WHILE COWGILL WAS LIFTING LOIS'S SPIRITS WITH HIS NEWS, THE chief protagonist in the drama was not feeling so good. Things had not gone as Gerald had imagined. He had had genuine anxiety about his young brother, but he had also seen himself as the hero of the hour, bringing Clive back to life. But instead, it had been his feckless old father who had stolen the limelight. Now he sat in silence, locked in a room by himself, waiting for the next thing to happen. Questions, questions, he thought. Well, I got my story right for Dad. He was convinced. So that should be all right. Serious provocation. But then he remembered the sophisticated methods now used by the police to find out exactly who and what had hit Harry on the back of his head. Not just fingerprints, but all the other malarkey they could use.

He sat in a fog of self-pity until the door was unlocked and Matthew came in.

"Morning, Mr. Mowlem," he said. "We shall be taking you back to Tresham shortly, but before we go, I'd like to establish one or two details whilst our memories are fresh."

Gerald was not deceived by Matthew's courteous tone. He had had too much experience of being handled by the police to be fooled by that. No, he must be on his guard from now on. His story must be watertight.

"We shall be talking to you in detail later, but for now could you cast your mind back to an evening when you and Clive were found by a citizen of Long Farnden, attempting to take objects illegally from Farnden Hall. This citizen was subsequently found unconscious by his wife, with injuries to the back of his head, on the cobbled yard at the rear of the hall. What can you tell me about that?"

"Two things," said Gerald confidently. "One, we weren't nowhere near Farnden Hall, and two, if we had been, which we weren't, we would never have done nobody no harm."

Matthew sighed. This case was obviously going to run and run.

# FIFTY-FIVE

ᔓ

Lois arrived at the hall promptly at ten o'clock, as instructed by Mrs. Tollervey-Jones. She and Felicity had already started work in the library, cataloguing books and carefully packing them into tea chests. Each one was labelled, ready for the new house or book dealers in London.

"Ah, there you are, Mrs. Meade." Felicity pushed her long blonde hair behind her ears and said with relief that they could take a break whilst her mother-in-law gave them fresh instructions.

"Coffee, I think. Perhaps you could do that, Felicity, while I catch up with Mrs. Meade on local matters?" Mrs. Tollervey-Jones sat down in a comfortable-looking library chair, and waited.

When Felicity had gone off willingly to the kitchen, Mrs. T-J looked enquiringly at Lois. "Well, and where have the police got to in their hunt for the missing Mowlems? There is no need to protest that you don't know. I, along with half the criminal fraternity in Tresham, know that you have a hotline to our Detective Chief Inspector."

Lois felt her colour rising. "I sincerely hope that is not true, Mrs. Tollervey-Jones," she said. "My family and my business are my chief concerns, and the less I have to do with the police and criminals, the better."

"Apologies, my dear," said Mrs. T-J soothingly. "Now what has been happening?"

"Well, apparently Mowlem father and son were tailed all the way to Pickering, as a result of our report to Cowgill. They didn't even try to shake off the tail, and obviously knew they were being followed. So I suppose they were determined to see Clive, and to hell with the rest. Says something for them, doesn't it?"

"Nobody is all bad, Mrs. Meade. Thirty years on the bench has taught me that. And the young one in hospital?"

"Woke up from a coma when he heard his father's voice, apparently. Doing well now."

"And Gerald—that was his name, wasn't it?"

"Under arrest, I should hope. They'll all be coming back to Tresham today—except Clive, of course. Bert and Gladys should be going home, and Gerald taken into custody ready for questioning."

"That should please your husband, Mrs. Meade," Mrs. T-J said as Felicity came back into the room. "I trust he sustained no permanent damage to his head."

"How did you know—"

"It is my business to know everything, Mrs. Meade. And by the way, may I call you Lois? Seems I shall be seeing a great deal of you in the future. I am relying on you and your team to see me safely into the new house. Oh yes, and while we're drinking our coffee, let us have a brainstorming session on house names."

Felicity looked at her mother-in-law with respect. The old thing was back on form.

"I'm no good at this sort of thing," she said. "How about 'The Grange'? That's a favourite."

"We've got one of those already," Lois said, and then added with a perfectly straight face, "What about 'Dunromin'? That would be apt. Or you might like 'Tollervey Rest'?"

Mrs. Tollervey-Jones gave a hoot of laughter. "All right, all right. It's not fair to ask, I know. But nothing seems to be quite right."

"Shall I tell you what Derek suggested? I'm not sure, but I think he meant it seriously." Mrs. Tollervey-Jones nodded. "He said 'Stone House' was what he'd choose. Simple and correct. It is built in our lovely local stone, with its beautiful thatched roof. Nothing more needed. That's what Derek said anyway."

There was a short silence, during which Lois wondered if Mrs. T-J was offended. But then her face softened into a big smile, and she said, "Perfect! Exactly right! There, that's settled. Stone House. You know, Lois, I always thought your husband was a man of good sense. Please thank him."

Coffee finished, they began work again. Towards the end of the morning, Mrs. Tollervey-Jones called a halt. "Before you go, Lois," she said, "I have remembered my own short stay in custody. The icehouse. I intend to do something about it, before Norrington brings in a bulldozer and razes it to the ground. I would like us to take a walk now and get some idea of what can be done. Will you come, Felicity? Plenty of suitable footwear in the boot room."

Felicity was glad of the suggestion to take some fresh air, and all three set off, with the faithful dog trailing along. As they went, Mrs. Tollervey-Jones fell behind, and Lois slowed down to walk with her.

"You know, Lois, I am not at all sure I can allow that dreadful Norrington man, and his equally dreadful wife, to take over the estate. And certainly not if I am to stay living in the vicinity."

"But what if you don't get a better offer?" Lois said practically.

"He's not offered the asking price. I am very tempted to let it go to auction. Those Blenkinsop people seem very keen, and it is quite possible they might be able to top Norrington's highest bid."

Lois smiled. "It'd be worth seeing Norrington's face," she said, and then added hastily that the plan should be discussed with the estate agents. They would give expert advice.

"Expert advice?" said Mrs. T-J, and seemed to be struggling for words. But all she said was that Lois was quite right. She would do it as soon as they returned to the house.


"SHE LIKED YOUR SUGGESTION," LOIS SAID TO DEREK AS THEY SAT at lunch.

"What suggestion?" said Gran.

"The name of her new house," Lois answered, winking at Derek. "She said she thought 'Dunromin' was the perfect name. Said she had done roaming for good. All she was after, she said, was a peaceful retirement."

"But—" Gran frowned. "You're pulling my leg, aren't you, Lois Meade," she said.

"True," said Derek. "I actually suggested 'Stone House.' Plain and simple. Never thought she'd go for it, though, Lois. It's a bit humble for the Tollervey-Joneses."

"Speak of the devil," said Lois, who was sitting opposite the kitchen window. "Large as life, here she is."

"Why didn't she come to the front door?" said Gran, hurriedly taking off her apron. She hastened to admit Mrs. Tollervey-Jones, and asked her to come through to the drawing room. Derek's eyebrows went up, and he said he was sure Mrs. T-J would be happier in the warm kitchen.

"Now, now, I don't want any fuss," their visitor said. "I just want a quiet word with Lois."

Gran and Derek dutifully left the kitchen. "How can I help?" said Lois.

"I have been thinking about my future."

Now what? thought Lois. More work for New Brooms, she hoped.

"I am retiring from the bench, and since I shall be moving to a much smaller establishment, I shall have very little to do."

Lois began to protest, but Mrs. Tollervey-Jones held up a restraining hand.

"Please don't suggest I take up knitting! My body may be failing, but my brain is as active as ever. So this is what I suggest. I know that you, and sometimes members of your team, work with the police in their enquiries into local crime. I am offering my services as a noncleaning member of New Brooms. You may be sure that I have useful contacts and a considerable amount of knowledge of the criminal classes. This will, of course, be completely confidential, and everything I discover or suggest will be siphoned through you to your police connection."

Lois was astonished, and could think of nothing to say for

a few moments. Then she began to see a way out. The old girl was right. Her knowledge of local people and places could be invaluable. If she wanted a bit of excitement, no doubt Lois's continued ferretin' would provide that.

"Good idea," she said firmly, making a mental note not *ever* to pass on this new development to Gran or Derek. "Nothing doing at the moment, but I'm sure something will come up. Now, can we offer you a cup of coffee? And a slice of cake, of course," she added, seeing Mrs. T-J stare longingly at Gran's chocolate sponge. "My mother would be so pleased."

# EPILOGUE

❧

*Three months later*

W INTER HAD ARRIVED WITH A VENGEANCE, AND LONG
Farnden on frosty mornings was a sight to behold.
The great trees in the hall park were covered with sparkling
hoarfrost, and the procession of cars drove slowly up the long
drive in covetous admiration as the auction day approached.
Mrs. Tollervey-Jones had, as she had threatened, decided to
put the entire estate up for auction in one lot.

Lord & Francis had done their best to give her good advice,
in spite of her frequent reluctance to take it, and now the biggest room in the local pub was booked, brochures showing the
estate in glowing terms had gone round to a satisfactory number of enquirers and all parties to the auction were ready.

The village had been disappointed in Mrs. Tollervey-
Jones's decision and grudging with their support at first, hat-

ing to have the status quo interrupted. Although their working lives were no longer affected by the family at the hall, they all agreed that the village would never be the same after the sale. Now, however, as the date drew very near, excitement had risen, and many residents decided to go to the auction, though they had absolutely no intention of bidding.

Thomas and William from Lord & Francis had been endlessly patient and efficient, and a kind of friendship had developed between them and their client. "Never seen anything like this one," Thomas said as they drove back to London one afternoon when Mrs. Tollervey-Jones had been at her most demanding.

"I feel like she's my grandmother," William said sadly. "I hope she'll be okay on the day."

"I'll take whatever you like on the old thing being on top form. It'll be the weeks after she's moved out and the lucky man has moved in. I don't give much for the peace of mind of young Robert then! He seems a decent kind of fellow."

"Splendid wife, too," said William. "Shame, really. I could just see her as the lady of the manor, taking hot soup to the sick."


Lois and Josie, meanwhile, had been hard at work finalising the details of the wedding, fixed for only a few weeks hence. At the same time, the New Brooms team had put in many extra hours helping Mrs. Tollervey-Jones with the huge task of clearing the hall of everything she did not want to take to the Stone House, and doing their best to keep her from descending into a pit of despair. At least, this last was what Lois had instructed the team to concentrate on, but one and all had reported that there was no sign of depression. On the contrary, Mrs. Tollervey-Jones seemed more and more excited as the auction day drew near.

The date fixed was for a Friday evening, when, according to auctioneer lore, they could expect a good crowd. "As many as possible," was the hope. That way a good auction fever would build up, and many an indecisive buyer would leap to the winning bid at the last minute.

On Friday morning, Lois, Gran and Derek sat at the breakfast table in total silence. After about five minutes, Derek said, "So, are we expecting that the end of the world is nigh?"

"Mm," said Lois, staring out the window.

"Fancy," said Gran.

Derek shouted with laughter. "Come on, girls! It's certainly not the end of the world. We'll still have the old girl living in the village, and the hall might be bought by a really nice family with young kids and plenty of lolly to spend on doing up the place. Good business for New Brooms, and for the best electrician in the area."

"Who's that, then?" Lois said, concentrating now on what he was saying.

Derek stood up. He puffed out his chest, and said he had heard that Derek Meade Incorporated had installed electrical heating systems for royalty. "And now," he said, "I must get on. Big night tonight, and I mean to be there."

"Give my love to Her Maj," said Gran, and began to collect up plates and bowls.

Lois retired to her study and started work on next week's schedules. She knew already that once the sale had been completed, and her last assignment for Cowgill cleared up, life would fall flat on its face.

She remembered Mrs. Tollervey-Jones's avowed intention of becoming one of New Brooms' detection team. At the moment there was nothing to detect, and she told herself at intervals that it was just as well. Derek, when aware of Mrs. T-J's plan, made sure she heard him say to Lois that with all the extra work in the future, there would be no more ferretin' for New Brooms. But he'd said that many times before.

"Mum! Mum, are you there?" It was Josie, and the interruption was welcome.

"What's up?" Lois looked up in surprise. Josie was smiling broadly. "Guess what? Matthew's got promotion, and it's all round the station that Cowgill is retiring forthwith."

"No!" said Lois involuntarily. She saw Josie frown, and hastily said wonderful news about Matthew. "Best wedding present you could have," she said, and kissed Josie's hot cheek.

"Who's in the shop?" Gran asked. "Do you want me to go down there?"

"No, no. Floss came in and offered to hold the fort whilst I dashed up here to give you the news. No, I'm going straight back, thanks."

THE AUCTION WAS DUE TO START AT SIX THIRTY, AND BY FIVE o'clock there were cars parked down both sides of the village street. It was already dark, and children ran about excitedly, jumping out on passersby with whoops and yells and vanishing off into the darkness of the playing field.

In the bar of the pub, loud voices competed to order drinks, and though the publican had hired extra help, there were still queues waiting to be served. But it was all good-humoured, and bets were being placed on everything from the size of the successful bid to the colour of the auctioneer's socks. This last bet was a usual one with the particular auctioneer sent from Lord & Francis. He was a jovial, well-rounded figure with rosy cheeks and a penchant for brightly coloured socks and scarlet ties. Robin "Redbreast" Forsyth was a favourite in the district and well known for his entertaining patter and skill in extracting large amounts of money from people who had certainly got it, but had been hoping to have some left over.

It was fortunate that the pub had a large function room, built in more prosperous times for wedding receptions, birthday celebrations, games of carpet bowls and table tennis. There was some competition with the village hall, but on the whole there were enough functions for both.

Conversation had now reached a climax as the door of the function room opened, and taking the steps to the stage in one bound, in came Robin Forsyth. He sat at a table with his assistant at the ready, and beamed at the very large audience.

"Friends, Farndeners and countrymen, lend me your ears," he began, and was cheered by faithful followers who knew his signature opening. "But if you'd rather keep them, please feel warmly welcome, nevertheless, to this important auction here tonight. I have been instructed by the Honorable Mrs. Tollervey-Jones to introduce the very desireable Farnden Hall estate, comprising . . ." He referred bidders to the glossy brochure, which he hoped gave all a good idea of the particular beauties of mansion, park and farms.

Lois and Derek sat halfway down one side of the room, and Gran had joined her cronies in the front row.

"Just don't raise your hand and wave," Derek had said earlier to Gran. "You might find yourself the proud owner of the Farnden Hall estate."

Robin Forsyth proceeded with great efficiency and pleasantness to remind potential bidders of terms and conditions. He also stated his autonomous standing whilst the auction was taking place.

"In other words, ladies and gentlemen," he said, "I am the boss."

A ripple of laughter went round the audience, and the auction began in earnest. Lois had looked in vain for signs of the Norringtons, but had seen Mr. and Mrs. Blenkinsop, both of whom smiled sweetly at her. Mrs. Blenkinsop was wearing a beautiful pale blonde mink coat, which Lois thought a good sign of affluence, though perhaps not a good augury for her popularity with animal lovers in the village.

By the time the bidding had reached an unbelievable number of millions of pounds, Lois was beginning to feel confident that the Blenkinsops were going to succeed. But then the auctioneer declared that the reserve had not yet been reached, though they were close, and invited sensible bidding to continue. "This property will be selling tonight," he announced, and his statement was followed by a dramatic pause. Then a man's loud voice from the rear of the hall offered a figure of a quarter of a million pounds more, and the bidding began again with extra feverishness.

The Blenkinsops were looking worried, and Lois turned around to identify the new bidder. As she had dreaded and half expected, it was Geoffrey Norrington, who had appeared seemingly out of nowhere, his face alight with determination. At his side, his wife, Melanie, stood like a statue, afraid to move for what might happen.

The bidding continued, and Norrington's voice swelled confidently. In the end, the next bid was to be with the Blenkinsops, and Robin Forsyth looked kindly at them. After what seemed like an age, Mr. Blenkinsop put his arm around his wife's shoulders and sadly shook his head.

The gavel came down with a hearty thump on the trestle table, and the deal was done, a legally binding contract with Mr. Geoffrey Norrington.

An instant hubbub of excited conversation broke out, and Lois and Derek stood up in an attempt to signal to Gran. But she was in an urgent huddle with her friends, and Lois said they should sit down again and wait until the room had cleared.

"Well, what do you think of that?" said Gran, coming up finally to join them.

"Not a lot," said Lois, and Derek shook his head. "No good can come of that, I reckon," he said.

"Ah, well," said Gran. "The others seem to think it was a good result. He's been talking about introducing stock car racing and clay pigeon shooting, and lots of other things for the village."

"One's thing's certain," replied Lois, "there's going be big changes." Her eye was caught by the figure of Mrs. Tollervey-Jones, standing by herself behind a group of officials. Lois thought she looked lost and lonely and, without thinking, went across to where she stood.

"Good evening, Lois," Mrs. Tollervey-Jones said. "Not the outcome I had hoped for, but we shall see. And did you see the Blenkinsop woman's fur? Never any part of a real live mink, I'm afraid. Not quite the thing for tonight's little event. No, Lois, Norrington's money is as good as anybody else's. As for the rest, who knows? We may all be pleasantly surprised. Now, I have to go and find Robert and see to tiresome things. So, thank you and your girls for, well, for everything."

"Glad to have been of help," answered Lois, turning to rejoin her family. But Mrs. Tollervey-Jones had not quite finished.

"And what is more, Lois," she said, with what could only be described as a cheeky grin, "I am very much looking forward to being the new ferret on your team."